With *Love's Abundant Harvest* we're reminded again how God's love and care can set broken spirits free and heal the deepest wounds. This is an emotional and riveting book I read in one sitting.

—ADINA SENFT
AUTHOR OF THE HEALING GRACE SERIES

Love's Abundant Harvest

The
SPIRIT
of the
AMISH
BOOK TWO

Love's Abundant Harvest

BETH SHRIVER

REALMS

Most products are available at special quantity discounts for bulk purchase for sales promotions, premiums, fund-raising, and educational needs. For details, write Charisma House Book Group, 600 Rinehart Road, Lake Mary, Florida 32746, or telephone (407) 333-0600.

Love's Abundant Harvest by Beth Shriver
Published by Realms
Charisma Media/Charisma House Book Group
600 Rinehart Road
Lake Mary, Florida 32746
www.charismahouse.com

Although this story is depicted from the town of Lititz, Pennsylvania, and the surrounding area, the characters created are fictitious. The traditions are similar to the Amish ways, but because all groups are different with dialogue, rules, and culture, they may vary from what your conception may be.

Cover design by Bill Johnson
Design Director: Justin Evans

Visit the author's website at www.BethShriverWriter.com.

Library of Congress Cataloging-in-Publication Data:
An application to register this book for cataloging has been submitted to the Library of Congress.
International Standard Book Number: 978-1-62998-008-9
E-book ISBN: 978-1-62998-009-6

First edition

15 16 17 18 19 — 987654321
Printed in the United States of America

Wherever we go, God is there.

Whenever we call, God is listening.

Whatever we need, God is enough.

ᕍᓚᕘ Chapter One ᕘᕥᕗ

The horses stamped their impatience as Lucy Wagner scooped a pail full of oats. The dust lifted into the early morning sunlight as she dumped the feed into the bin. Lucy filled a large container with cane for the cows, gentle creatures waiting for their due.

"You're slow today." Her husband, Sam, didn't stop walking even though he favored his right hip, a sure sign the cool April breeze was causing an ache in his bones.

"The babe's kicking." She put a protective hand on her belly as he glanced down at the bulge in her stomach. The familiar silence swelled with each step. "It's getting hot." She wished she had a handkerchief to wipe off her sweaty brow and envied the one Sam had around his neck.

"You're always complaining about the weather. It's been nice this spring." He checked her work to make sure the teat cups were clean.

"*Nee*, you're just cold-blooded," she mumbled, and dropped her shoulders as if to hide from the knowledge that his was the coldest of hearts she'd ever known. The sweat trickled down her face, seeping over the scar on her right cheek that had been there since she was a child and made her self-conscious about her appearance.

She brushed the thoughts to a faraway place.

He grunted and looked up over her head. Although he was a good five inches taller than she, it was customary for him to look around but not at her.

Lucy couldn't get used to the Pennsylvania weather. It was plenty cold for about three months every winter, and she was always glad when it started to warm up again. But since the baby, it seemed she was always too warm.

"You'll wish for days like this come summer." Sam handed her a bottle of milk from the cooler and turned toward the *haus*.

Her mind wandered to musing over what her sisters were doing about now down in Tennessee. Being the youngest of six girls had left her lonely and discontented when two of them moved to Colorado to join the new community there. Her heart wrenched to see her sisters go, so much so that her *mammi*, Frieda, had come for a visit and ended up staying in the area when she found out Lucy was in a family way. Now that she was pregnant, visiting Tennessee was out of the question, which meant family would have to come to her, namely her *mamm*, Verna.

She worried about her *daed*'s health, but her *mamm* was quite well. Lucy shook her head when reading the letters her sisters sent, subtly mentioning a hurtful word or action. Her *mamm* Hochstetler was an uncompromising woman who expected strong daughters. Lucy would honor her *mamm* as God commanded, but she found it necessary to hold fast to Christ's commandment to love Him with all her heart, soul, and mind in order to gain strength for the challenge.

"Lucy, pay attention." Sam's stern voice broke into her thoughts as she looked up in time to keep from running into him from behind.

"Sorry, Sam." Lucy looked past him and walked to the barn door. As she cracked open the heavy door, the wind slapped her cheeks. She paused, waiting for it to die down and scanning Sam's farm. A tall silo filled with grain, corn, and other harvested crops, the largest in the community, was a beacon on the plains.

Sam shut the gate to the back pasture then walked through the barn. "What are ya waiting for? The wind's not gonna stop blowing today."

Lucy was still standing at the entrance to the barn. "I wanted to go through the barn instead of going around to let the dogs out."

She waited. He didn't respond, a rarity for him; he usually wanted the last word.

He frowned. "You go ahead. I'll let 'em out and catch up with you at the *haus*."

When the swirl of dirt and leaves slowly disappeared, she opened the barn door just wide enough to fit through and shut it tight behind her. Pulling her shawl over her *kapp* and keeping her head down, she walked quickly to the *haus*. It was much larger than she felt they needed, but Sam wanted to have room to grow a family.

Their border collie ran to her and bounded straight up in the air with excitement. "Skip, stay down." She looked around to see what had him stirred up. A buggy rumbled down the lane, a surprise considering how rare it was to have unexpected visitors here in contrast to Lucy's Tennessee experience. There, she had enjoyed the large community where she spent time with her sisters and made new friends. At Sam's place, she was forced to make herself invisible.

Abner Umble pulled the horse to a stop. His place was just behind them to the south, behind the Ecks'. He was a bit crotchety but always kind enough to bring them the mail. "Boy, it feels more like spring."

His gravelly voice made Lucy want to clear her throat. "Would you like to come in for coffee?" She kept walking, feeling a bit rude, but it was too hot to stand still.

When he didn't answer right away, Lucy wasn't offended; Abner knew she was not the best cook. Uncommon for an Amish wife, but with six older sisters, she'd spent her time helping her father while her *mamm* taught her sisters to do the domestic work. Some had done the cooking; others had taken care of the mending and laundry while she and her sister Fannie, the next youngest, learned how to best help *Daed* work the land and tend the livestock.

"I might need a little coffee this morning." Abner climbed the steps carefully and took out a hanky to wipe his stubbly nose. "Got a letter for ya. Looks like somebody back home." He flipped the letter over and read the return address again. "One of your sisters."

If he were anyone else, Lucy could have taken offense at his prying, but the fussy old man had grown on her after his wife became ill. "Thanks for saving us the trip to the mailbox, Abner. I know we should check it more often, but sometimes that community mailbox seems so far away." The community mailbox was located next to the store by the frontage road. Considering she and Sam were at the other end of the community, they didn't check all that often.

Abner shut the door behind him and sat at one of the eight chairs in the kitchen. The table was large, but the room was big enough to hold it, with plenty of space to work around. Lucy had tried to add some color with the rugs she'd hooked, and she had made the quilt that was draped over the rocking chair.

She started the coffee and stirred up some eggs, sausage,

and grits with gravy. Her *mammi* had taught her how to make a few more dishes, but she mainly cooked breakfast food. It was easier, and she always had the ingredients needed.

She handed Abner a cup of coffee and poured one for herself. "How are you and Grace with this weather, Abner?" Even though they were neighbors, they both had big farms, so they didn't see one another often, and she knew how the weather made his knees ache.

"Me and the missus are getting along. She complains of ailments, but I figure it's just old age." He slurped the coffee and winced. So did Lucy. "She's finally catching up with her old husband." He grinned with affection, something Lucy wished and prayed for from Sam.

"Would you like some cream?" Her hands were still sweaty from doing the morning chores, so she handed the creamer cup to him to pour.

"And sugar, if you'd be so kind." He handed her the mail. "Just so I don't forget."

She'd walked back to the kitchen cabinet to get another mug when she heard Sam enter the mudroom. The gravel under his boots crunched against the floor, annoying her that he didn't take a moment to wipe his feet.

The three-page letter was written in fine penmanship. Abner talked about the weather as if she wasn't preoccupied, but she couldn't pull away. The more she read, the faster her heart beat and her breathing sped up. By the end of the last sentence she felt her face flush with anxiety.

"Abner." Sam glanced at him, but his eyes stopped on Lucy. "What's wrong with you?" He grabbed the letter and glanced at it just long enough to understand.

Abner looked at one and then the other, thoroughly confused. "Did someone die?"

Lucy's shoulders slumped, and she closed her green eyes. "*Nee*, *Mamm* is coming home. My sister Hanna had her baby not long ago, so she must be ready to send our *mamm* on up here."

Lucy had hoped she wouldn't be with her *mamm* alone, without her sisters by her side.

The one time Sam had met Lucy's family, he'd said he'd never forget it. They were independent women, and so many. And then there was *Mamm*, a beautiful woman with sharp eyes and sleek build who ran her house like a business more than a place to call home.

Abner studied her as he set his cup on the table. "Who's her *mamm*?"

"My *mamm*..." A sigh lifted from her chest as she said the word. In view of Verna's strict parenting, the title *Mamm* never quite fit in Lucy's mind. The name *Verna* automatically came in her thoughts when she considered her mother, but she was respectful enough to refer to her as her *mamm* out loud.

"Maybe she doesn't need to come just yet," Abner counseled.

"*Nee*, it'll be fine." Lucy looked at Sam.

"*Jah*, sure"

Nee, it wouldn't. But Lucy knew he wouldn't tell her that with company in the room, and there wasn't any way to tell her *mamm* no. Lucy was nearing her third trimester, which was probably the reason for her visit.

"How many of them?" Sam sat and waited for Lucy to bring his coffee.

"Just *Mamm*, as far as I know." That kicked the wheels

turning. If she could get Fannie to come stay for a while, it might be manageable. The second youngest, with some fire in her, was just what Lucy would need to get through the visit. Sam was not a hospitable man; he barely spent time with his own family, let alone hers.

"Though maybe a sister or two, as well." Saying two were coming might make him agree to just one. Guilt sank through her chest. She disliked manipulating Sam, but she'd learned it was a matter of survival living with him. She was sure if she didn't find a reprieve in some small way, she would lose her mind. Her loveless marriage and difficulty conceiving, along with a miscarriage, had given her little hope she could please her husband.

The thought made her stop and pray for her unborn child's strength and growth.

Sam's lips turned white as he pressed them together. "Your *mamm* might want some time alone with you."

When his nose lifted after taking a sip of his coffee, she quickly handed him some milk, but bumped the table and spilled the contents of the pitcher. A trail of the cream crawled off the table onto Sam's lap. He slapped the wooden table and stood, wiping his pants with a cloth napkin.

Lucy couldn't get there fast enough. She stopped the trail of milk and righted the creamer cup, avoiding his eyes. "I'm sorry." She took the napkin to the sink, listening to his work boots hitting the wood floor as he left the room.

Awkward silence radiated in the room in which Lucy was never comfortable and couldn't do anything right— not even make a cup of coffee or clean up a simple mess without making it worse.

"I'm sorry, Abner." Not wanting to face him, she continued squeezing the napkin, watching the white turn clear. She could hear his lopsided gait as he walked closer to her.

"A *mamm*-to-be shouldn't be so upset about such things." Abner tapped Lucy's arm. "Whether you're with child or not, for that matter."

All she could do was nod, unable to turn and look at him with the tears threatening to spring.

"Maybe I should go. You let me know if you need me, ya hear?" He slipped out the door and was gone, leaving her alone to receive her husband's wrath.

~ Chapter Two ~

*M*anny Keim clucked to his bay mare, Sweet Pea, in the pasture beyond the fence. She was stubborn and old, but she still reminded him if he hadn't taken her out for a while.

The stud hitched to the wagon held his head high as his dark mane bounced against his neck. Puffs of air floated from his nostrils into the humid air. Summer couldn't come soon enough for him, but fortunately it was right around the corner.

Manny ran his fingers through his hair and put his felt hat back on. He needed a trim. Minister Eben wouldn't appreciate his blond hair hanging down past his collar, but he hadn't had the time to cut it, nor did his cousin, Emma, who was more like a sister to him. Since his wife, Glenda, had died, Emma had shown more care for him than any of his other relatives had. He thought she had a special place in her heart for Glenda and missed her now that she was gone, almost as much as he did.

A piercing whistle pulled him away from the memories as his eyes focused down the dirt road to Caleb Lapp. The two men couldn't look any different, especially with Manny's eyes being two different colors. He was used to the stares and double takes from the *Englischers* in town. Their eyes would dart back and forth as if not believing what they were seeing. Glenda had told him he was unique. There was no mistaking that he was, she'd say.

Caleb set his rifle in the wagon bed. Then he pulled himself up and into Manny's wagon, giving him a stare. "You deaf today? I had to whistle twice to get your attention." He brushed away the curls from his eyes as he waited for a response.

"Just thinking." Manny knew how much his mind had wandered toward his deceased wife over the last year. He wondered what a normal time of mourning was and whether her fair face and bright blue eyes would ever fade from his mind. He was grateful not to have woken in the night expecting to see her there for some time, but now that he'd had the thought, she would most likely appear next to him in a dream.

This time, Caleb's yodeling stopped his thoughts. It was something he'd started doing since he came back from the city with Emma just two years ago. He looked over at him with pinched brows and tight jaw. "Can you warn me when you're gonna do that?"

"You just wish you could do it as well as I can." Caleb nodded for emphasis and started in again, louder.

Manny tapped the horse with the reins. He obliged with a quicker step that jolted Caleb back into his seat. "He must smell summer in the air."

"Long before we did, I'm sure." Manny smiled as he thought of Sweet Pea and Glenda being the same age; Sweet Pea should be put to pasture, but Manny needed her company now more than ever. Just a year older, at the ripe old age of thirty-one, he felt robbed of the best years he and Glenda could have had together.

"Look over there!" Caleb pointed out to the north pasture.

Manny slowed the horse to a walk and studied the dry grasses and brown dirt covering nearly fifty acres.

"Well, I'll be darned. We found him already." A stray coyote had been picking off farm animals at both of their places. Manny wasn't a big hunter as some of the Amish men were, but in cases like this, he knew they had to defend their livelihood.

"He's heading back toward your place."

"I suppose I should turn around before he gets any closer to the chicken coop; that's the first thing he goes for."

Caleb leaned with the wagon as Manny turned around. "Him being alone makes ya wonder if there's something wrong with him. Maybe hurt or too young and inexperienced to bring down bigger prey."

"He left the pack for some good reason or they got rid of him. Might be sick."

Manny had lost the resilience for death and wondered whether he would be able to pull the trigger. He'd done it whenever it was necessary before, but not since Glenda's death. He sighed. Even dealing with a coyote involved her. There was a time he would have taken care of this coyote without another thought, but this time he knew better than to even try.

"You all right?" Caleb stared at him more than at the coyote. Knowing he'd never get away with a lie, Manny just didn't answer.

Caleb jumped out of the barely moving wagon, and Manny hopped down onto the moist dirt road after him. A drizzle of icy rain had covered the land overnight, but the morning sun was melting it away.

"I'm right behind ya, Caleb." As soon as he had his rifle

in his hand, he heard a gunshot and jolted back as the sound traveled down the field, followed by a scream.

"Caleb!" Manny ran to the edge of the road where Caleb stood with rifle in hand, his eyes staring farther down the road. Manny followed his gaze to an Amish woman, but he couldn't make out her face. She held on tightly to a rope with a horse by her side—his horse, Sweet Pea.

Manny took off running and didn't stop until he got to her. He slid on the gravel road, coming to a stop, and instinctually reached for the woman's hand. "Are you all right?"

She flinched and pulled away, but then nodded quickly and brought her hand up over her cheek. "The shot, it surprised me."

"I'm sorry, we didn't see you there." Manny had met the woman before, but he didn't see her around much. Their community was large enough that a number of different groups met for church, so he thought he should introduce himself. "I'm Manny Keim."

"I know who you are." Her eyes lifted, but she kept her head down. Dark strands of hair whipped around her thin neck, and her soiled black dress was wrinkled, probably testimony to a busy day working on the farm.

He took the lead rope from her and rubbed Sweet Pea's side to calm her down. "How did you end up with my horse?"

"Found her running wild around our place." She almost smiled when she glanced at Sweet Pea. The horse seemed to have that effect on people.

"We've lost some livestock due to that coyote." Manny looked away and to the field where Caleb was walking.

"Have you had any trouble with the coyotes around your place? Sam's farm, right?"

"*Nee*, maybe you should make stronger coverage for the animal enclosures." She glanced over toward Manny, revealing her left-side cheekbone and skinny frame—too skinny for his liking. He wondered whether she'd been ill. It couldn't be that they didn't have enough food on the table; Sam's place was always thriving. Then he thought back to what she'd said and chuckled.

"I happen to have solid coops for the chickens and adequate fence lines for the larger stock..." He held a grin as he explained, but she stepped back and slowly shook her head. His voice tapered off and drizzled away like the water on the frosty ground when the sun beat down on it.

She turned to her right side and then looked down at her worn boots. "I'm sorry. I didn't mean anything by it. I just hate to see anything get hurt."

He turned back to see that she had looked at Caleb and then turned away. "*Jah*, me too." An awkward moment passed, and he was pleased to think of something to say. "Do you need a ride?" The more he looked at her, the longer she stared at the ground. "It's no bother."

She glanced over just long enough to see him walking back to the wagon. "*Danke*, but *nee*."

"*Hallo* there, Lucy. Haven't seen you for some time. How's Sam?" Caleb rested his hand on his hip, huffing out small breaths.

Manny felt bad for not helping him, but not only did he not want to have anything to do with what just happened, he had also become intrigued with this woman standing in front of him practically swallowed whole by the big dress she was wearing. She seemed timid, but firm in what she thought. He suspected she just didn't express it often, which was why it captured his attention that she'd spoken out to him concerning his animal enclosures and the coyote.

"Fine, *danke* for asking, Caleb." When she glanced up at Caleb, Manny saw the darkness in her eyes—something darker than the deep brown of her pupils.

When she noticed him staring at her, she shifted her weight, keeping her hand on her cheek.

"How are ya feeling?" Caleb's brows lifted.

"We're both well, *danke*."

"*Gut* to hear! It's nice seeing you out and about. Where are you headed?" Caleb seemed to want the conversation to continue, which didn't make sense to Manny. This young woman had shown very clearly she wasn't comfortable, yet he kept going on.

Manny tied Sweet Pea to the back of the wagon, listening to them.

"Going to the *haus*, but I can walk."

"*Nee*, come on, I'll sit in the back." Caleb made his way on to the flatbed before she could say no. "Help her up, Manny."

Manny shook himself into action, not thinking of his manners. "*Ach*, sure." He went around to his side of the wagon and offered her his hand. When she reached out with her left hand and held his grasp, a shock of electricity sparked. She yanked her hand away from his.

Caleb chuckled. "Whoa. If we had electricity around here, I'd say you two just shut down a converter."

Manny chuckled, and Lucy actually gave him a small smile, adjusting herself on the seat.

"Are you comfortable?" Manny didn't know what ailed

her, but he wanted to make her as comfortable as possible. He noticed she held the hand that touched his turned up on her lap. "Does your hand hurt?"

She pulled the sleeves on the dress over her arms and tucked her free hand on the bench. "*Nee*, I'm *gut*." The smile hadn't left her lips. "Where is your farm?"

He was both surprised and glad that she was talking to him. "Two farms back, with the blue porch swing."

"That's your *haus*?" She actually turned to him and smiled wider. "I like that color of blue." She finally dropped her hand far enough for Manny to see a patch of dark skin from a lingering bruise.

Manny saw Caleb smile out of the corner of his eye. He knew more about Lucy than Manny did, and Manny was determined to find out about this mysterious woman by his side. "I wondered if anyone would complain, but even Minister Eben sat down on it and had himself a leisurely swing."

"That sounds nice." She kept her eyes on the road, but she said it in a way that he was sure she meant it. Her shoulders eased down against the back of the seat, as if she would melt into the wooden slats on which she was seated.

"I think summer might come early this year." Caleb filled the gap once again as he looked to the sky as if it had told him the weather.

"It's this place here." She pointed to a tall silo towering above the trees.

Manny drove down the long dirt path that led to Lucy's home. There were acres of land spread in all directions. "This here's a lot of land to care for."

Lucy let out a sigh. "*Jah*, it is."

"Let me help you down." Manny ran around to her side

and gave her a hand, then realized when she teetered to one side that he'd need two. Looking at her petite size, he was surprised helping her down was so awkward.

The sound of a door and then a squeaky screen door caused them to turn toward the *haus*. Sam stood tall, his eyes squinting, taking them all in. "Caleb, what's going on here?" He yanked a chunk of hard bread in two and starting chewing a piece like he was eating beef jerky. His eyes rested on Lucy as he waited for a reply.

Manny felt the need to stand up for her. "We were out after that coyote that's been causing trouble." He nodded toward Lucy, who was twisting the front of her dress, revealing why her dress looked the way it did. "Ran into Lucy, so we brought her home."

Judging by the look on Sam's face, there wouldn't be any thanks for that, so Manny tipped his hat to Lucy and nodded to Sam. He walked around to the other side of the wagon and climbed in.

Caleb stayed in the back. "What a pitiful thing. She didn't look well."

Manny was glad he wasn't the only one to see it and wondered what was going on. As they waved and turned around to head down the path, Manny had half a mind to go back, pick her up, and take her to his home, but from the way Sam stared after them, he decided that wouldn't be a smart thing to do.

He glanced back at Caleb. "Is she sick?"

"Could be—with morning sickness."

～ *Chapter Three* ～

The scent of cinnamon lingered in the air as Lucy walked through her *mammi*'s family room and in to the kitchen. "Sticky buns?"

Three sets of eyes turned her way as she stepped into the large room with too many chairs in disarray around an oak table. Steam sputtered up through a boiling pot, warming Lucy's cheeks.

Frieda, her *mamm's* mother, nodded her head, fuzzy gray strands popping out of her *kapp*. She hiked up her black dress and walked over with a bowl of chopped walnuts. "Just in time to spread the nuts."

"Come over and give us a hug." Nellie, the oldest of the three widows, wiggled her white eyebrows as she strolled over with a smile stretched across her face. Her embrace warmed the broken places in Lucy's heart. When they released their hug, the feeling of security lingered.

Rosanna, or Rosy for short, seemed like a youngster compared to the other two women, with rosy cheeks to match her name. She took Lucy's hand and guided her to the counter where the dough to make homemade noodles was ready to cut. "You have to make them with just the right thickness. Too thick, and they're doughy; too thin, and they look like shriveled-up worms." She lifted her nose.

"I'll need more flour." Lucy jumped right in with the others and was soon in rhythm with the hum and glow of the room. Here she found peace, acceptance, and unconditional love with these beautiful women. It wasn't physical beauty but a certain way of living and thinking that kept their eyes lifted up to the Lord and their hands never idle.

"These are going to be great." Nellie came closer with her hooked cane, which she wagged toward the noodle dough.

"You all know how to talk me into something." Lucy grinned, knowing they were glad for her presence and appreciated her help just as much. Cooking was their life, always keeping them busy, and the tourists appreciated their mouthwatering meals, pastries, and preserves. This was what they did, along with a good bit of chatting. The exception was Nellie, whose quilting took up a good part of her days.

"How are you feeling, Luce?" Frieda asked without taking her eyes off the knife she was using to chop more walnuts.

"Oh, yes, the baby." Nellie's memory wasn't what it used to be, and Lucy, like the rest of them, gave her pardon for forgetting even the most important events.

Lucy looked into Frieda's soft, wrinkled face and smiled. "He's just fine. Kicking up a storm, though." She knew what was next and relished the coming conversation. She felt sure that no one cared more about this babe than these three ladies. Not even her own husband.

"You stand firm that it's a boy, yet you told us when you first found out you were pregnant that you wanted a girl." Frieda stopped chopping long enough to glance at Lucy.

Lucy shrugged. "As long as the baby is in good health, I don't care which." But she did care very deeply, as she knew Sam wanted a boy. Pleasing him was most important, and Sam wanted a son to help with the farm and carry on his legacy. There were times Lucy wished she weren't pregnant…at least not now…not with Sam.

Rosy set a glass of milk on the counter where Lucy was cutting the dough. "I'd like to be auntie to a cute little girl with a button nose just like yours, Lucy." She tapped Lucy's nose and smiled.

"And if she had Lucy's pretty red hair…" Nellie looked at the strands of auburn curls that had escaped her *kapp*. "You just don't see that color very often."

Frieda waved a hand. "What's that matter when it'll be stuffed up in her *kapp*?" Then she grinned. "But what a cute little *kapp* that would be."

The three of them stopped and glanced at Frieda, as it wasn't common for her to make such a sweet remark. She was just as much in love with this little one as the rest of them, and they'd just caught her sharing her thoughts. Lucy didn't expect them to have the same opinion about much of anything. Their individuality was what Lucy appreciated the most, and it filled every spot of her bleeding heart.

Mammi stopped chopping and put her hands on her hips. "Have you heard from your *mamm*?"

Lucy cringed. "*Jah*, a long letter giving me orders about her trip down here."

Lucy bit her tongue. She'd thought Frieda had tried to bring up the subject lightly, but there was nothing about their relationship that was light. Still, she selfishly appreciated Frieda's response because it was the same as hers when she got her *mamm*'s letter. "Did she say in your letter how long she was staying?"

"*Nee*." Lucy glanced with uncertainty at Frieda.

"Well, because you're with child, I'll take her in. You

don't need the added stress; you've already got that with Sam."

The room went silent. Although Sam's verbal abuse was known to her *mammi*, Lucy knew it was against Scripture to talk against your husband, and she tried to follow His Word.

"It's all right. It might be easier if she's with me." Lucy wasn't sure if that was true, but she couldn't expect the two of them to last more than a few days before her *mamm* would be on her doorstep if she came here.

Rosy, the peacemaker, surveyed their facial expressions and stepped in. "*Nee*, we'll take turns."

Nellie stuck out her bottom lip in thought. "*Jah*, we'll share the load." Then she chuckled. "I didn't mean it that way."

Frieda grinned. "Sugarcoating things doesn't help matters. We'll all take care of what we need to do and pray that everyone's on their best behavior." All eyes were on her again. She sighed. "*Jah*, I was saying that more to myself than any of you. Now you can hold me to it."

A knock at the door made them stop their work momentarily. The *click-clack* of Frieda's shoes faded as she walked out of the kitchen. Although this was her *haus*, Rosy and Nellie had made the large *haus* their home as well. Lucy sometimes wished she lived with them; the mood and atmosphere were relaxing and soothed her mind.

Frieda came back in with someone walking up behind her. "Ladies, we have a visitor." They stopped working and greeted their guest as he came into the kitchen, but Lucy didn't respond.

When she did turn around, Manny caught her eye. She looked downward on her work, unable to hide her cheek with a dough-covered hand. He nodded to her and then Rosy, who walked over to him and guided him to the table.

Seeing him again so soon caught Lucy off guard. She compared him to Sam, as Manny was everything Sam wasn't. Gentle and kind, he was soft-spoken but even from a distance she knew he was willing to stand up against injustice or mistreatment of others. She knew how he had treated his wife; she had seen it when his wife was ill and Lucy had brought meals to them. Lucy decided to stop comparing. She despaired of ever having that kind of love, but she was grateful to have a *haus* over her head and dear friends to keep her spirits up. It was selfish to ask for more.

"Lucy, take a load off, and I'll bring you both a cup of coffee." Nellie's commanding tone made Manny grin.

Lucy could feel his gaze as she looked up, waiting for the question that people had asked over and over again when she moved here. Her community down south knew; they were there and had loved her through it.

Manny pulled out her chair and helped her into the seat. "If there's one thing I've learned from my visits here, it's that you all don't take no for an answer."

Lucy wiped her hands on a cotton towel and smoothed out the wrinkles on her dress before glancing at him from across the table.

"It's good to see you again, Lucy." His eye hitched for less than a second.

"*Ach*, it's good you were out and about. Luce doesn't get off the farm much." Rosy smiled, but Frieda and Nellie were quick to give her stern frowns.

Lucy knew she should be more social but wasn't comfortable talking to most anyone, let alone Manny, and didn't appreciate any comments about it. Nor did she want them listening in. Feeling paralyzed, she hoped someone would step in and talk.

"How about some fresh-made egg noodles?" Nellie set a bowl of noodles with chicken broth in front of him. These ladies were known for their cooking and didn't expect anyone to refuse anything they made.

Manny took in a long whiff, waved some of the delicious aroma Lucy's way, and took a bite. "It tastes even better than it smells." He motioned over his shoulder to the three ladies bustling about.

"*Jah*, sure." It was only polite to agree, but her stomach was telling her something different.

"*Gut*, I hate to eat alone." His smile was like sunshine in the dead of winter. It seemed as if a black cloud hung over Sam's farm, so the sun was something she didn't take for granted. Then she realized he had referred to the fact that he did actually eat alone. Lucy's situation was the opposite, in a way; she dreaded meals with Sam and sitting with him in silence if he wasn't complaining about something she did or didn't do.

"I hear your *mamm* will be coming for a visit." Manny gave her his full attention as he waited for an answer but never said a word about her scar.

Lucy felt the room become still, an unfamiliar experience for this group of chatty women. The more they stared, the more she felt the walls shrink in on her as the words flew around in her head, refusing to leave her mouth. She stuttered, trying to push a word out—any word—to stop the room from spinning. She took a breath and heard Manny's voice.

"Take this." He held out a napkin, but she couldn't get her hands to move and take it, and closed her eyes instead.

The darkness calmed her, allowing her breath to even out. When she felt anxiety pass, she opened them, expecting to see everyone huddled around her, staring, but to her surprise, the girls were cleaning up the kitchen and Manny was by her side.

"Feel better?"

His soft, clear voice reassured her, and to her surprise, she wasn't embarrassed that he had his hand on hers. It was a gesture of comfort she needed at that moment.

"Your color's back. I'll help you to the couch so you can rest, if you'll let me."

She thought, horrified, that he must feel her confusion regarding what was right and wrong, and probably her embarrassment for her behavior.

He glanced over to Frieda. "Maybe some water," and lifted his eyebrows at her for an answer.

"*Jah*, water, please." Lucy lifted her eyes to his. "I'm sorr—"

He held up a hand. "I understand."

"*Nee*, you see, I'm with child."

"*Jah*, but I didn't know the other day until Caleb told me. You shouldn't be walking from your place like that in your condition."

She pushed herself up and away from him. "Sometimes I just need to be away from things."

He handed her the water Rosy gave him and moved closer. "What kind of things?"

Her eyes widened as he sat there staring at her, waiting for the answer she wanted to give but couldn't. No one needed to know the life she lived and accepted as her fate.

He moved in closer—too close—so close that she moved back and pulled her hand away. Her senses were coming back to her, and she knew she was in a potentially dangerous position. Sam would never understand or accept what happened here, even if it was completely innocent. If he found out, she would be as concerned for Manny as herself…but what Sam couldn't take from her was the sensation of her fluttering heart.

ᴄᴀ *Chapter Four* ᴀᴏ

Manny's heart sank. It always did when he drove up to his farm alone, knowing the house would be empty. He slowly rode over to the barn. He'd learned to drag out every chore, repair, meal, or errand as long as he could. It helped the days go a little faster but not much.

He'd chosen another horse to go over to Frieda's place and needed to stop and check in on Sweet Pea. It was always nice to see those ladies when he made his regular trips over for a meal in exchange for some work on their farm. He would have stayed longer, but Lucy made him uncomfortable. The way she held her cheek was odd, to say the least. Still, there was something intriguing about her. She barely met his eyes when she spoke, but he sensed an inner strength, a steely resolve that seemed guarded, maybe due to her husband, Sam.

Manny didn't like to speak poorly of people, but that man didn't seem to like anyone, maybe even himself. Manny knew what it was like to lose a spouse, but he didn't take his pain out on anyone. He wondered what Sam's excuse was and whether he was the cause of her scar, but he would never be so bold as to ask her.

Manny unhitched the buggy, rolled it into the barn, and then went out to the farthest stall. Sweet Pea turned her large head toward him and stood at attention, as if waiting for him to do or say something. But then this was their ritual. Since he didn't have a spouse or therapist to talk to, Sweet Pea was the next best thing.

She nodded and let her mane flutter against her brown neck. Manny felt fatigue kicking in after a day's work repairing one of the fence lines, milking, feeding, and doing some of the chores in the *haus* when Emma couldn't make it over. He'd never thought he'd be doing women's work, but this was part of where he was.

"You think I'm a sissy, Sweet Pea?" Just hearing her name, a name Glenda had picked out for the horse, reminded him he was still outnumbered. Even his dog, Daisy, had a girlie name, but he didn't mind. They gave him some comfort and never complained. "Well, maybe I am. Glenda always liked that, didn't she?"

The horse nodded again, almost on cue. Manny would like to have thought it was a reply, but he knew she just wanted an extra scoop of oats. "Not so fast. I need your opinion about something. What can you do for somebody who's shy?"

Sweet Pea looked him in the eyes and stared.

"*Jah*, I'm talking about Lucy. There's nothing wrong with helping somebody, and that's all I'm doing." He hiked his arm over the wooden stall. "To be honest, she makes me uncomfortable, so I'm really doing it for selfish reasons." He shook his head in thought. "If only she wasn't so darn timid." He lifted one eyebrow. "Maybe it suits her, and she's more comfortable than she seems."

Sweet Pea nodded again, and this time Manny was sure she meant it as an answer to what he was asking. "Well, that doesn't leave me with much, so I guess you're telling me to leave it be." Though he didn't want that to be the answer, he didn't have much choice as to what to do. His compulsion to help Lucy was futile. "I'll butt out. But if I happen to run into her again anytime soon, I'll be taking that as a sign."

He dipped the scoop into the oat bin and then paused, listening. The *clip-clop* of horse hooves reached him.

Who could be calling so close to suppertime?

Most families were finishing up chores for the day, not out visiting. As he waited for the visitor to approach, Manny admired the sunset lit up with streaks of yellow, orange, and crimson nestled in with the clouds. A familiar buggy came down the road, and he felt the loneliness fade away.

"*Hallo*, Emma." He grabbed the reins. Emma practically jumped out of the buggy and wrapped her arms around him.

"As far as I'm concerned, you won't eat your dinner alone." She reached into the buggy and pulled out a basket. "Whether you like it or not." She slipped her arm around his and urged him toward the *haus*, strands of her brown hair blowing in the slight wind.

"I'm not your little cousin to care for; you tend to forget that from time to time." He tugged her forward to get a rise out of her. Her playfulness lifted his spirits, and *Gott* knew he needed that. With both of his parents gone now, Emma and her family were just about the only relatives he had left.

"You are to me. And you'll be eating your dinner off the dirt road if you don't stop pushing me around," she teased with a stern face.

"Paybacks for you picking on me as a kid."

She couldn't argue with that, and they both knew it. But for all their teasing, they had just as many good-hearted conversations. If not for Emma and Caleb, Manny didn't know how he would have made it through Glenda's passing.

"Well, that goes both ways." When they reached the door, she stopped and stared him in the face until he agreed with her. She'd done this for as long as he could remember, and he'd finally quit squirming when he grew taller than her. Now that she had to look up, she wasn't nearly as intimidating. There was still the problem of her flailing her gums at him, but he wouldn't have it any other way.

As soon as Emma set foot in the kitchen, a whirlwind of commotion began as she prepared his dinner. "You're gonna need more help planting this year. You should ask *Daed* and the boys to help out."

He sat down at the kitchen table, his legs suddenly heavy. He knew she was trying to help, but he didn't want to hear how different everything was now that Glenda was gone, after only one year together.

He'd been through a harvest without her, and it wouldn't matter how many others helped; it would never be the same.

When he glanced over at Emma, he saw her looking at him. His throat caught, so he didn't try to talk. Then his chest started to heave. He took deep breaths to keep the pain at bay.

"Don't get all sentimental about it, Manny, or you'll get me going." She turned completely around to check on him, and he dropped his head.

The more she saw his emotions spilling out, the worse it would be. There were plenty of thoughts going through his mind, but one stopped. He wasn't just upset about Glenda, he was suddenly worried about living the rest of his days alone. He hadn't thought much about finding another wife, but in that moment he wondered what his future held and stopped thinking about the past. Maybe. Even if it was fleeting, it made him feel a little more alive.

Emma was in a chair by his side before he knew it, wrapping her arms around him and resting her head on his shoulder. "You're gonna be all right, Manny. I promise you, you will. It just takes time, like healing a wound. You just can't keep opening it up again." She lifted her head, staring straight at him, but neither spoke.

She was right. It was time to let go.

"I don't know what I'd do without you and Caleb." He tried to smile but couldn't.

She suddenly stood and glanced around the room. "We're going outside." She set the casserole in the oven and went about opening and closing drawers, diverting his attention.

"What are you looking for?" He was too tired to stand but did it anyway. She wouldn't give up until she found what she wanted. "And what about dinner?"

"It can wait." She gave him an empty jar and kept one tucked under her arm, opening the back door with the other. The screen door slammed behind them. Emma took off running toward the dirt field, but stopped short, standing in the hip-deep prairie grass.

"You mind telling me what you're doing?" As he watched her take off the lid and creep around slowly through the grass, he knew what she was doing but couldn't believe it.

"Let's see who can catch the most fireflies." She didn't lift her head, just kept her jar level with the grass and then scooped up a tiny, glowing light. "It's hard to believe that's a living creature in there." She held it up and watched it go off and back on a second later.

Manny watched a glowing, yellow light fly by and then turned toward Emma, jar in hand. "They say the female lights up to show the male where she is."

He looked over to see Emma walking toward him. She stopped and tapped his jar with hers. He opened the lid, and she poured the firefly into his jar. "Ya got to let her go, Manny."

He nodded and put his arm around her. "What would I do without a cousin like you?"

"Find a wife."

He turned to her. "I'll find someone, someday. Quit trying to get rid of me."

"We need pie. Whoopee pie, to be exact." She looked over expectantly, waiting for his reaction.

"You made my day by saying those words."

They'd almost made it to the door when a horse with one rider came thundering up to the *haus*. It was Sam. His first thought was Lucy and the baby, but it was difficult to read Sam's face. He was a serious man without much expression. But looking at him now, Manny wondered if that was the look of a man who never got over the death of his first wife.

Sam jumped off his palomino, dropping the reins, and let it wander a couple feet away. "You have anything you want to say to me, Manny Keim?" His eyes were slits and his breathing heavy. His fists were balled and white-knuckled. Manny could feel the man's steel grip without him actually taking hold of him. Sam stood a good four inches above him and had twice the girth.

"I'm assuming this is about my visit at Frieda's place this afternoon."

"You assume right."

"If you're referring to Lucy's dizzy spell, I helped her gain her senses is all."

Sam let out a long breath and dropped his fists. "You touched my wife."

Emma stepped forward. "Now, just a minute here, Sam—"

Manny held up a hand and stood in front of her.

"She didn't feel like herself, and I helped her gain her strength back. That's all." Manny's heart beat in his chest. He didn't expect good manners from Sam, but he didn't like to be accused of doing something completely different than what he had done.

"What is it you're concerned about, Sam? There were three other people there who can tell you that we had a nice conversation and something to eat."

Sam glared at Manny long enough to make him sweat a little. "Stay away from my wife."

With that, Sam yanked his horse over and hiked himself up into the saddle. He gave Manny one last look, kicked both sides of his mount, and then took off at a gallop. When the cloud of dust disappeared, Manny looked away.

"I'm sorry, Manny." Emma's voice brought him back to the moment.

"I wonder how word spread so fast," he muttered under his breath. Then, realizing what Emma had said, he looked at her. "Sorry for what?"

"I told Sam I saw Lucy on the road heading toward Frieda's when I was out earlier. I didn't think a thing about it. I guess someone told him you were there when she had that fainting spell."

"You didn't do anything wrong. Neither did I."

"Then what's the fuss about?"

"Lucy had a dizzy spell, and I kept her from falling, is all. No matter what Sam says, I only did what was necessary." He watched Sam turn down the dirt road and slap his horse on the flank.

"I never did understand that man or his wife." Emma turned to go into the *haus*.

Manny suddenly felt protective of Lucy and resented Emma's comment. "Ya gotta get to know someone before you decide how you feel about 'em."

Emma stopped and glanced at the road. "Well, I think we both know how Sam feels about you."

Manny didn't care what Sam thought about him. What he did care about was what kind of tongue-lashing Lucy would undergo when Sam got home.

~ Chapter Five ~

There's a stray horse in my yard." Sam let the back screen door slam shut behind him.

Lucy stopped peeling potatoes and walked to the back door. She smiled when she saw Sweet Pea grazing on the small patches of green grass. "I saw her out there the other day."

"Raggedy old thing." He growled and sat down, waiting for his lunch. "You gonna serve me a meal, or do I have to get it myself?" His mood was crustier than usual, but so was she. Lucy just didn't have the courage to show it. She'd avoid him as much as possible, which wasn't difficult, especially since she was with child. He'd lost all interest in her once she'd become pregnant, and she thanked *Gott* for it as she set his lunch down before him.

"More beef," he demanded while stuffing a bite of the Salisbury steak into his mouth.

Lucy mixed the bread crumbs, ground beef, eggs and milk, and then made patties. As she placed a patty onto the skillet, some grease popped up and hit her wrist. She yelped and walked quickly to the cooler for a piece of ice and placed it on her wrist, letting the cool water run down her arm.

"My food's burning." His chair screeched across the wood floor as he stood and strode to the stove. He grabbed the metal handle without the oven mitt and hollered so loudly that Lucy covered her ears.

She withdrew, stepping back against the counter, and waited for his reaction. He stared down at her, his eyes bulged, and his body shook with rage. Lucy almost apologized, but she knew anything she did or said would only make it worse. So she waited and prayed he would calm down or leave. His work boots seemed louder and his stagger more pronounced as he headed for the back door.

Not knowing what to do, she wiped her face with her sleeve, slipped the spatula under a slab of charred meat, and threw it out for the dogs. She went out and sat down on the porch, letting her shoulders drop, feeling completely incompetent as Skip and Hop enjoyed their special meal. She didn't seem to be able to do anything right, at least when she was around Sam. She wasn't a great cook or *haus* keeper, but she could hold her own. As stressful as Verna would be to have around, she might be able to help with some of the details Lucy seemed to miss.

She looked over the large farm that Sam had built up after years of work. From what she'd heard, he and his first wife had spent so much of their time working this place that they did little else. No one seemed to really know them the way the rest of the community knew and helped one another. It seemed strange, but then most everything about this man was odd to Lucy.

She looked over at Sweet Pea, wondering whether she could take her back without Sam getting upset. Sam didn't like her to leave the farm unless it was necessary. She didn't know why, other than it might be another way to control her. But she was used to that; she seemed to gravitate to controlling people.

It was wash day, and unlike most women, she did hers

alone. She decided to finish her chores before returning the horse.

Sweet Pea whinnied, causing Lucy to stop and look her way. She smiled when the horse stamped her hoof on the ground, as if demanding attention.

"What is it, girl?" Lucy moved closer, just enough to feel the horse's warm breath. "I'll take you home soon."

The horse shook her head.

"You're going to have to wait. If I don't get something done around here first, I'll pay for it when I get back." She rubbed Sweet Pea's chest, watching the horse's eyes droop with satisfaction. "You probably get spoiled at Manny's place."

Sweet Pea grunted her response, and her eyes closed.

"I bet he talks to you too."

Sweet Pea opened her eyes wide.

"You're a good listener." She patted her one last time and let out a long sigh. For some silly reason, she felt better. Maybe Sweet Pea was good medicine.

After the clothes were washed, Lucy walked to the backyard to hang them up to dry. It had to be very nasty weather to hang the clothes inside. Sam became especially annoyed by the lines hung from wall to wall with damp clothes filling the room, but their family room was only used for a short time before bed, when they read from the Bible.

She found Sam in the barn shoeing a horse. This gave her some hope, as he didn't seem as irritated doing this task. "How is your hand?"

He jolted and turned to her. "I'm in no mood. What is it you want?" He took hold of the hammer and started in again. The noise resonated in her ears, distracting her from what she wanted to say.

"I should take the horse to her owner." She didn't know whether he heard her, as he kept pounding away. She waited until he finished and stuck the hot horseshoe in a tub of water. The steam rose to the roof of the barn.

"I won't be gone long."

"Make it quick. I'll be expecting an early dinner." He glared at her with his ice blue eyes and pulled the horseshoe out of the tub—his way of making her feel guilty, making it hard to ignore. She had ruined his lunch, so he expected a large dinner. She would be sure to give him one, just to keep the peace. Filling his belly would be a sure way to do that.

She didn't know where these thoughts came from. She'd learned that submission was the easiest and smartest way to deal with her life and her husband, especially with a baby on the way. Lately that way of thinking was harder for her to do. Maybe it was the hormones making her thoughts bolder than usual. Angry impulses crept in now and then. Even anger toward *Gott*—something she'd never dealt with before, not until the day she'd first seen Sam in action. She couldn't forget the sight of him taking out his anger on an unruly horse.

Tiptoeing out of the barn in case he changed his mind, she heard him grumble but ignored it.

Skip nipped at her heels, wanting to play. She lifted her head and kept walking. Never would she have imagined that she would be so tense over such actions. She couldn't so much as walk away from her home without worrying Sam would change his mind or that she'd be scolded when she returned.

Once in the buggy, with Sweet Pea tethered to the side, she felt freedom in riding along the road by herself. One of the many things she looked forward to was being with her little one, just the two of them enjoying the countryside as she was doing now.

As she came upon Manny's place, she noticed the dried and withered flower gardens. It would be better to strip them and have an empty garden than the dead flowers that were there now. Her hands itched to get on them and help them thrive. She could douse each stem with life-giving water and pull out the weeds that sucked away all the nutrients.

As the buggy drew closer to the farm, Lucy started to regret coming. She felt like an intruder, but she hardly got the impression from Manny that he would feel that way about her making a visit—especially with his horse in tow.

"*Hallo!*" She called toward the barn, which was where she suspected Manny might be this time of day. With the milking done and morning chores completed, he should be getting ready for lunch. As the *haus* came into view, she thought about how lonely he probably was after losing his wife. Had they truly loved each other, the way she'd hoped her marriage would be? Or was their marriage a simple business arrangement?

"*Hallo.*" Manny's voice sounded behind her. She tried to peek out the side of the buggy, but her stomach cramped, so she stayed put. She had started worrying about the baby, wondering especially about different ailments she might have. With some marrying third and sometimes second cousins, more and more babies were being born with defects. Though she and Sam weren't related, she knew very little about his forebears. She often wondered if his parents were second cousins, because that would explain much about his short temper and other traits people put down simply to Sam being Sam.

Manny appeared by her window and smiled. "Well, *hallo* there."

"Manny, I've found something of yours." She clambered out of the buggy, holding her stomach, and tried to stand straight. Her short legs made it difficult to step down, and she felt for the ground by dangling one leg behind her.

"So I see." He took Lucy by the arm to help her balance and then moved away once she was sure-footed. "Where did you find her?"

"Out in the backyard."

He untied Sweet Pea from the buggy, and she heard his voice faintly comforting the horse.

Lucky Sweet Pea. Lucy wished she had someone to talk to her in the same way. "She's a sweet horse." Lucy stroked the horse's side, listening to her whinny softly.

"That's why I gave her the name." He glanced back to Lucy and took a moment to study her.

She felt her cheeks redden. Not from Manny's scrutiny, but the fact she'd forgotten to hide her scar. She wondered why that bothered her more than usual when she saw Manny. Many times she would go into town and face the gawking, but for whatever reason she didn't want Manny to see her blemish.

"The grass must be greener at Sam's place." It still sounded strange when people called the place she lived only her husband's, but she felt like a visitor there. Although Sam didn't come out and say it, she knew better than to think the *haus* was anyone's but his.

"Would you like something to drink?" Manny offered,

but seemed a bit reluctant. With no one around but the two of them, it was a little awkward. But Sam had approved her going, and a glass of water sounded good.

"*Jah*, I'll wait on the porch." She looked up to see more steps than she'd expected. "Or maybe I'll sit on the steps."

"*Nee*, I'll bring you a chair." Manny took the stairs two at a time, grabbed a rocking chair from the porch and set it down by the bottom stair. "There you go." He looked up at the nearby tree and then the ground where she sat. "You'll have some good shade here."

He was so hospitable. Unfamiliar emotions started to well up inside. She choked them back and let out a long breath.

"Are you all right?" He squatted down. It was nice she didn't have to look up. But at the moment she didn't want him to see her face with the heat rising up her neck.

"Just a little warm." She rubbed her belly. "This little one creates a lot of heat." Then she felt embarrassed for talking about the baby. It wasn't common to mention, but it was so obvious, it seemed silly to ignore it.

"I'll get that water." He touched her hand. "I'll be right back." He slowly walked away, not looking back until he was at the door.

She scanned his farm, which was smaller than but just as well-kept as Sam's. It seemed quaint and inviting, more like a home than a business. She sat up to look closer. That was the difference. Sam ran his farm like a business. Manny's was a home first, then it provided a living. Sweet Pea was relaxed, with her head down and eyes closed, unlike at Sam's where she was jittery. The calming atmosphere seemed to affect them in the same way, confirming that the tension was a reality at the place she called home.

"You two taking a nap?" Manny's voice floated toward her as her eyelids lifted.

"Just resting my eyes," she said, although she might have had a wink or two.

He handed her the water and smiled. "I have trouble with that too when I'm rocking under that big oak tree." He squatted down by her and looked up. "Nice day."

She took a moment to admire the blue sky with white clouds rolling by slowly in the slight wind. She hadn't felt this serene since...she didn't know when. And there was something definitely soothing about Manny...but maybe it just seemed that way to her since she lived with someone so opposite.

Lucy suddenly felt uncomfortable enjoying herself when there was dinner to make. "*Danke* for your hospitality, Manny. I should go."

He stood and offered his hand. She accepted with a smile of appreciation and started for her buggy. He helped get her up and settled, as the lump in her throat swelled again. But there was no appropriate way to express her feelings other than a simple *danke*.

"If you ever want to talk, feel free to stop by."

What a lovely thought, but it would never happen. "I bet you're a good listener."

He grinned. "Actually, Sweet Pea is better than me."

Lucy chuckled, picturing him talking to the horse the same way she just had, and she didn't feel quite so foolish. She grinned at Manny. "*Jah*, I know."

∽ Chapter Six ∽

*M*anny sat up in his bed and looked out at the dark sky. It would be a long day of threshing wheat. It was time-consuming and hot this time of year, but the flour would last through the winter and then some for all the baking the women did.

He glanced at the empty side of his bed. "Not that I need as much as most now."

But his cousin, Emma, would be sure to come over and make him his favorites—cherry pie and peach cobbler.

He dressed and took slow steps down the stairs to the kitchen to fix some coffee. Rummaging through the pantry to find the coffee beans to grind, he came up short. One more grocery item he had forgotten at the store. He bent his head and placed his palms on either side of the door. Even the littlest of things seemed to keep popping up, showing him another chore Glenda had done that he took for granted. The canister of the herbal tea she liked was almost full. He eyed it before shrugging. It wasn't the same as a strong cup of coffee.

He looked out the window over at the tall cluster of trees that blocked any view of Lucy's *haus*. As he tapped his fingers on the counter, he could almost smell the roasted beans being ground. He was in need of coffee, but wouldn't it also be neighborly to stop over at her place just to say *hallo*? He had to admit he worried about her.

Not that it was his place to. There was just something that didn't sit right.

He tried to push aside his worries about Lucy and headed outside to get started on his morning chores. But once the cows were milked, his thoughts drifted once again, and he decided he needed coffee, which would give him a good excuse to check in on Lucy. The rest of the chores could wait. He swallowed his pride and got up his nerve to face Sam as he started down the lane to the main dirt road that led to their place. He stopped at the driveway. Somehow their place always seemed darker. Maybe it was the tall, thick trees that surrounded the *haus*. Or maybe it was just Manny feeling uncomfortable being there.

He stood at the back screen door, savoring the smell of the coffee and bacon. Maybe some eggs too...or was that his imagination, dreaming about them. Standing under the window, he heard Abner's voice and took a step back, listening, not wanting to intrude. Abner walked in from the mudroom and seemed to be talking slower today. Manny glanced through the window and noticed he held a letter against his chest as if it was made of gold.

Lucy walked over to the stove and stirred up something that sizzled. "Good to see you, Abner." When Abner didn't respond, she took a closer look at him. His pinched forehead and the way he averted his eyes worried Manny. "Are you feeling all right?"

Abner rubbed his hand over his wrinkled face. "*Nee*. I'm not."

She waited, and watched him stroke his beard. "Why don't you take a load off and have a seat." Lucy motioned toward a kitchen chair.

He sat down heavily. "*Nee*. I need to get something off

my chest. That's what needs to be done." He scratched his thinning gray hair and let out a breath.

Manny was eavesdropping, but at this point, he was as concerned as Lucy appeared to be and needed to know what was on poor old Abner's mind. He made himself visible, taking a step forward, but couldn't get himself to go any farther and interrupt the conversation.

"What in the world's got you so upset?" Lucy rested her hands on her belly and waited, shifting her weight.

Abner's eyes went to her hands that cradled her stomach. "I just have to say this once and for all." He glanced outside, and she followed his gaze out the window to a tree stump where Sam chopped wood. "Do you know why I bring you the mail?"

She shook her head and scooped the eggs out of the pan.

Manny figured Abner was either nosy or felt sorry for her, not knowing which for sure.

"It's 'cause I worry about you." His eyes sought and found hers.

"I'm fine, Abner, and the baby is—"

"I worry about your safety, Lucy." His stern face was taut with red blotches. "You know right what I'm talking about too." His nostrils flared when she shook her head, as if he knew what she was about to say.

Manny wanted to know what Abner had seen and heard. They were so secluded; Lucy probably thought no one could know what went on to worry about it. Thinking of all the times Abner must have dropped by, Manny was sure he'd seen and heard plenty. It seemed clear that Lucy had talked herself into thinking that was just how things were.

She looked away, and Manny couldn't bear to see the

disappointment in her eyes, her denial. "We're fine. Really we are. I appreciate your concern, Abner."

His lips tightened. "It's bothered me too much not to finally say something." His hand shook as he looked out the window to see Sam stride to the stump and grab his ax. "I know it's not common to get into another's business, but I can't help but worry for you both." He gestured to the unborn babe.

Lucy let out a lungful of air. "You're a sweet man, Abner. But I've learned how to live my life. I'd hoped for different, but the Lord hasn't brought that to be. So I'll make do with the path I'm on."

Manny hadn't heard her say so much in one breath. She knew what Abner was saying was right, but she was trying to keep him from carrying her burden. Manny didn't want him to either, so he walked up to the door and knocked.

Lucy's head lifted as she caught him staring directly at her. Abner wiped his nose with his sleeve and averted his eyes.

"Mornin'." Manny took note of the mounting silence with each step he took into the kitchen. He stopped within reach of Lucy but looked over at Abner.

"Good to see ya, Manny." Abner's shoulders dropped a little, and Lucy hadn't taken a breath, obviously uncomfortable with Manny's presence.

"Nothing will leave this room." He looked at one and then the other, making eye contact long enough for them to know he meant it and that he was aware of their exchange. "Sorry for busting in on your conversation. I've been listening, not knowing when to step in."

The flush on Lucy's neck was spreading to her face. She

glanced out the kitchen window. *Chop, chop.* The sound of Sam's ax seemed to make the color increase.

"Has he laid a hand on you?" He hadn't taken his eyes off her until now.

Abner choked, taking a hanky to his mouth as if to stifle his discomfort with the discussion.

Lucy jolted, obviously not expecting the question but knowing what he was most worried about. "*Nee.*" The air pushed through her lips, and she looked through the kitchen window in thought.

Abner grunted. "Well, thank *Gott* for that."

Manny wasn't so quick to accept her one-word reply. "I take it that's not how you feel about it."

"At times, I wish he would. Words hurt worse." She finally gained the courage to meet his eyes. "If it wasn't for the baby, I wonder sometimes if the physical pain would hurt less."

"Somehow, I knew you'd say that."

She waved a hand at him. "I can't…" That was all she could say. He understood. This was too close, and Sam was too near.

"You don't need to do anything. That's why we're here— to keep an eye out if you need us." He gestured to Abner. He decided he'd ask him to bow out, for his own safety. He didn't want the kind old gentleman to get in the middle of Sam and Lucy's marital problems any longer.

Her eyes grew round as she took in his words. Fear and anger could easily seep up and out at them for interfering. Manny got the feeling he might have overstepped his bounds.

"I appreciate your coming, both of you. But please go."

She turned away, and when neither of them moved, she walked out of the room.

"Would you mind bringing Lucy their mail?" Abner wiped his nose again and kept his eyes averted. "As long as I know someone stops by now and again, I'd feel all right about handing it over to you."

"You go on now, Abner." Manny took the letter Abner still held in his hand and dropped it to his side. "I'll take this and all the mail from here on out."

"*Danke*, Manny." Abner watched Sam out the window and lifted his bottom lip. "You know it's just a matter of time until it comes to blows, especially with the baby on the way." His lip trembled. "So help me *Gott*, if he ever lays a hand on her, I'll—"

"Abner." Manny softly but firmly cut him off. "Allergies bothering you?" Manny thought he'd save the man's dignity and the emotions that were welling up in him as well.

"Must be." Abner nodded once and walked out the back door. When he shut it, Lucy came back into the kitchen.

Manny held up a hand. "I'll go." He handed her the letter. "I'm your new mailman." He tipped his hat and turned to leave. Then he stopped and lifted his chin toward the letter she was tearing into. "Hope it's good news."

Her eyes moved over the words. And then she smiled. It was as bright as a rainbow and made him grin a little too.

"Fannie's coming!"

Manny lifted his brow when Lucy giggled. He'd never seen her so happy and wondered who this person was who made her act this way. "Who's Fannie?"

Lucy pushed a dangling strand of hair off her face. "My sister. She's coming with my *mamm*. You'll have to be sure and meet her, Manny."

"I'll look forward to it." Manny wanted this high-spirited talk to continue, such a change from the discussion they'd just had. "When will she be here?" Seeing Lucy's face light up and her animation stirred something inside him as he saw a glimpse of her true personality.

"Who?" Sam's voice made them both stop and stare as he kicked off his boots and walk toward the kitchen table. "Well?"

She should have breakfast on the table. Actually, it was past breakfast. Manny had distracted her and now felt responsible. "It's my fault, Sam. I had some mail to give her—"

Sam held up a hand and sat at the table with a fork and knife in hand. Manny wondered whether he always did this or if he was trying to make a point. The pan was starting to heat up again, but the ham and eggs weren't ready.

"Abner does that," he said.

"I'm gonna do it for a while. He's not feeling up to it, and I'm glad to help." Manny wondered how long it would be legitimate for him to bring them mail. Abner was their next-door neighbor. Manny lived three *hauses* down—not convenient at all.

Sam frowned. "Just until Abner's up to it again."

"I'll be on my way, then." The coffee smelled good, but Manny could hardly be in the same room with the man. He didn't know how Lucy could either. "I'll see you later, threshing the bishop's wheat."

"Will do."

When he shut the door behind him, he wished it was him sitting at that table, not Sam. The change in Lucy's demeanor was understandable with a man like that.

Manny got into his buggy and made his way to Bishop Atlee's. His home had two add-ons for *dawdihauses* from both sides of their families. The appearance was deceiving in that three sets of families actually lived in their own *hauses*. The bishop was a firm man. Manny preferred to go to one of the deacons rather than the bishop. Both were conservative in their thinking. Although Manny followed their rules, he didn't always agree with their adherence to the old ways.

"You're late." Caleb greeted him with a grin. "Where have you been?"

"Why?" Manny was deep in thought, and must have had a crusty look about him.

"You seem irritated. Have you been by Lucy's place?" Caleb said it like he knew what went on at her place, but he surely couldn't know what kind of morning Manny had had.

"As a matter of fact, *jah*." Manny jumped down and gave the horse's reins to a group of boys who took the buggies, unharnessed the horses, and let them out into a corral, and then put up the buggies. "How'd you know?"

"I had a feeling you'd find an excuse to go to her farm. Sounds like you and Sweet Pea have a lot in common."

Manny stopped in his tracks, wondering how Caleb had gotten so perceptive. Then he thought about it for a minute. "Emma." He shook his head.

"If you tell her something, you've told me too." Caleb grinned then turned serious. "Watch yourself, my friend. Lucy is married, and Sam is not one to tangle with."

Manny nodded, wanting the conversation to be over. He valued this time to set his mind straight and be around others. His time alone in his *haus* was nearly killing him. He felt if he didn't have that horse, he'd really be lost.

He grabbed a handful of wheat stalks that had been tied together with twine. The women stood by a large can and vigorously beat the bundles against the insides of the cans to separate the kernels from the stalks. They transferred the wheat kernels to a bucket, hoping for a nice breeze to separate the chaff away naturally. As they poured the wheat between the two buckets, they chatted about the lunch menu. The men preferred to use a wooden hammer to move the process along, beating the wheat away against a flat surface. When no more kernels remained, they threw away the stalk and started the process over again.

The young men took loads to the granary silo. The boys would back up the wagon and use large buckets like a conveyer system to load the wheat at the top of the silo.

"Make sure you sweep up that floor before a single piece of wheat is dropped in that silo," the bishop told the boys in his authoritarian manner.

The boys gave him their full attention and scrambled onto the wagon, hanging off the sides. When they were about to transfer the wheat into the silo, Manny went over to make sure the floor was clean.

When Lucy and a handful of women came up to give the boys some lemonade, he glanced over, but she made herself busy with the little ones who appeared, running around near the silo. The older boys started pouring down gallons of grain without giving a signal, and the dust and pouring grain pounded down on them. The women rushed to pull them away.

"Stop! Children are down here!" Manny yelled to the young men above them as he climbed up the stairs. The grain stopped falling, so Manny stood still and glanced up at them.

Mothers scolded and consoled the little ones, and Manny knew the older boys would get an earful for not giving a signal. He looked up at the pillar above him, thinking how dangerous the massive structure could be.

⌒ Chapter Seven ⌒

The next morning Sam walked through the kitchen without a sound except for his boots hitting the floor. Lucy entered the mudroom just as he shut the outside door behind him. She didn't understand. She'd done nothing wrong, from what she could tell, anyway. Had his former wife gone through this too? No one talked about her or what had happened to her. Lucy didn't know whether it was because of Sam's reclusive ways or whether his first wife was more like him than Lucy was, wanting solitude.

She peeked out the window, watching him walk to the barn to milk. She looked down at her swollen stomach and wished she wasn't pregnant—a horrible thing to think. She wanted her baby, but not with a man like Sam. She prayed for a boy, in hopes that someday he'd be able to take care of himself if Sam didn't treat him well. She was on her way to feeling sorry for herself when a buggy rambled down the road.

"Nellie," she whispered. Lucy closed her eyes and praised *Gott's* timing. A visit from her was just what she needed. She opened the door and stepped outside. Her forehead began to perspire, and the sun wasn't even up. Yet she waited for Nellie in the heat.

"*Gut* morning, you!" Nellie climbed out and handed Lucy the reins to tie onto the hitching post Sam had carved from an old hickory tree. She held the brown suede bag in which she kept her quilting materials. This one was larger than others Lucy had seen.

"You're here early." Lucy didn't mind, but Sam might. Anything that took time from the farm was more than frowned upon.

"I'll help with your chores." She tucked a finger under Lucy's chin and looked into her eyes. "You look tired." Nellie shook her head. "I understand your situation, but definitely don't agree with it. I have little patience for Sam's treatment of you."

"But complaining only makes things worse." Lucy whispered, in hopes Nellie would do the same.

Nellie lifted a hand. "I know. That's why I'll just bite my tongue and stay out of his path."

"I'm always tired these days, with this little one keeping me up at night." Lucy opened the door for Nellie, and they walked into the kitchen. "Sam already ate, but there are plenty of pancakes if you're hungry."

She knew the look in Nellie's eyes, and averted hers. Lucy was worn out of…well, just about everything right now. She didn't have the energy to do much but keep food on the table and try to make it through the day without taking a nap.

"I've eaten. Your *mammi* doesn't give anyone a choice." She walked through the kitchen. "Let's sit in the family room." Nellie sat and placed the bag on the floor next to her. "Are you up to quilting?" Her brow furrowed as she studied Lucy's face.

"*Jah*, I'm fine." Lucy wasn't, but of all the quilters she knew, Nellie was the best around, and she always learned something new from her.

"You can't fool me. You look exhausted." The lines in

Nellie's forehead deepened, and she shook her head. "And it's not just the baby. You're only halfway through your last trimester."

Lucy rubbed her eyes, keeping the tears away. "Why didn't you ever get married, Nellie?"

"Funny you should ask. I took a different path." Nellie glanced down, grabbed the bag, and set it beside her on the couch. The large satchel was filled to the brim.

Lucy examined it. "That's a big bag."

"It's a big story." She pulled out one of the largest quilts Lucy had ever seen.

Lucy tilted her head, thinking back to her question about marriage. "What other path is there?"

Nellie smiled. "I'll show you."

Lucy took one end of the quilt, marveling at the variety of colors, shapes, and sizes. The elaborate decoration and thoughtful design were like none Lucy had ever set her eyes on. "I could spend hours looking at this quilt. Who made this with you?"

"Only me." Nellie's smile showed pride. Even though she was not well looked upon in their community, how could she not feel proud of such an incredible piece of art?

Lucy gave her a look. "How can you have possibly done all of this by yourself?"

"I made a profession of quilting."

Lucy puzzled over how that could happen. It sounded too...English. "How can that be? We sell them at the mud sales, but do you mean a real business?"

Nellie nodded. "People came from all around to purchase them. Eventually I needed more room, and I rented a store."

Lucy's mouth dropped. This was unreal. That Nellie

could be so independent and support herself dumbfounded her. "You did? Where?"

"Right here in Lititz." She turned to look at Lucy. "I expected you to be surprised, but not this much."

Lucy shook her head. "I'm sorry. I don't doubt you could do that, especially without a family to tend to. I'm just surprised I never knew about it."

"Things got a little messy with the bishop. That's one reason why I came here to live with your *mammi*. She was one of the few who didn't judge me for what I did." She paused just long enough to take in a breath. "Your *mammi*'s a special lady."

"*Jah*, I don't know what I'd have done without her." Lucy was secretly envious of Nellie's boldness, knowing that she could never do such a thing but also that she didn't want to. A loving husband was all she truly wanted.

"Lucy, I'm telling you all this to show you how strong you are."

Lucy started to speak, but Nellie stopped her with a raised hand.

"You just don't know it yet. Do you think I knew what to do or how to do it when I started up that store?" She moved her head slowly back and forth. "I started from the ground up, and it was only by the grace of *Gott* that it all came together."

She sat back and smiled contently. "You should have seen it, Luce." She lifted her hands in front of her. "I named the shop Pieces of Life."

Lucy sighed. "That's a great name." She looked up with Nellie, envisioning what it would look like in the storefront window. "What stories, though? Our quilts usually symbolize something."

"These were different. These quilts were about the customers' lives. What they did, where they lived, the experiences they had, and whether they included it or not, I'd ask them about their faith. These quilts are like the Bible, filled with parables and stories. True stories."

Lucy chuckled. "You were a storyteller and evangelizer all wrapped up into one." She tried to imagine it but instead leaned forward and studied the quilt for the answer. "Is this one yours?"

"*Jah*, this here is one with your *mammi*." She pointed to a block with a stalk of celery in the middle, the Amish tradition at most weddings. The green color was obscure, not quite the dark color it should be.

"Is this her wedding?" Lucy frowned, knowing something wasn't right.

"*Nee*, your *mammi* can tell you her story."

Lucy glanced over at her. "You have her story in here? No wonder it's so big."

"*Nee*, not their stories, but she and Rosy were so involved in my life, they are in the quilt quite a bit."

"And your sisters are in here too?"

"*Jah*, but I didn't have the same relationship with them as your *mammi* and Rosy. As they are widows, and there are no men in our lives, we created a life of our own together." Her eyes squinted. "Do you see the beauty of the story as well as the beauty of the quilt?"

Lucy scanned the many patches and wondered what each and every one said, like pages of a book. Some were obvious, and others didn't make any sense to her at all. Maybe in code or secrets that only Nellie would understand.

"What a beautiful way to track your story, like a memoir

in a quilt," she murmured. "What is this one with the rainbow?"

Nellie grinned. "That's a memory about a young man who courted me when I was young. He was older than me, and my parents didn't approve. We went three days without talking, and I thought I was gonna burst. The very next day, he came to see me. I snuck out the window and ran through the cornfields with him until we couldn't run anymore." She stopped and took a breath and then looked up as if she saw it all over again in her mind.

"It started to rain, but we didn't care. He took my face in his hands and kissed me. The rain kept coming down and then stopped suddenly. He pulled away and looked up. There in front of us was a huge rainbow spread out over the sky." She met Lucy's eyes. They were soft and bright blue, with a contentment about them.

"What happened to him?" Lucy didn't like the ending. She wanted Nellie with this young man who was so smitten with her.

"I did as my parents told me to. They encouraged me to court with others, but no one compared." She rested her cheek in the palm of her hand. "I'll always have the memory of lying in the wet grass gazing at that beautiful rainbow. Biggest I've ever seen."

"Do you think it really was? That big, I mean?"

Nellie pointed to the patch that was one of the larger blocks. "It's a double rainbow. See the second arc outside the primary one?"

"How do you know this?" And then Lucy remembered the times she was with Nellie and how she lingered when she saw a rainbow stretching across the horizon.

Nellie folded her arms as if to protect the precious

moment. "The light reflects twice inside the water droplets." She smiled at Lucy. "We saw a two-arced rainbow that day, and I've never seen another like it."

"That's sad." Lucy's heart went out to her, although Nellie didn't seem bitter or callous in any way, so why should she pity her? "Did you ever see him again?"

"I left soon after we parted. I spent all the time I had quilting and working in town. I became lost in it to forget about him." Her face pinched for a moment and then relaxed again. "When I heard he was courting someone else, I left to start my own shop, knowing I wouldn't get married." She pursed her lips for a second and placed her hands on the quilt. "And I never looked back."

Nellie's success turned the sorrow into happiness, both with her shop and, more important, her precious quilts, which were not just quilts but life stories.

"That's an incredible gift you give to people, Nellie."

"It's been more fulfilling than anything else I could have done." She paused. "I do keep a piece of me in every quilt I make." Nellie pushed the fabric inside out to show her initials. "I sew it up so they can't see, but I know it's there." She chucked Lucy under the chin. "You can do anything you set your mind to." She put a hand to Lucy's stomach. "You're going to be a good *mamm* to that baby."

Just as Lucy was about to complain about her situation, Nellie put up a finger.

"Don't talk of the troubles. No matter what Sam does or doesn't do, you and your baby will have each other."

With no daed.

Nellie was right. And she would be a good mother, no matter what Sam said. After hearing Nellie's story, Lucy seemed to sense inward resources she hadn't been aware of before. Instead of feeling helpless with what the future held, she felt strengthened to take on whatever came her way. This baby would have the best *mamm* she could possibly be. She didn't need anyone—not Sam or someone like Manny—to make her life complete.

A soft knock at the door drew their attention. "I'll get it." Nellie stood, and when she got to the door and looked at the side window, she grinned. "It's Manny."

Lucy frowned. "Nellie, stop."

Nellie opened the door wide and let him in. "Good to see you, Manny." She pointed to an envelope he held. "Are you the new mailman now?"

"For the time being. Abner's not been feeling well, so I thought I'd help him out."

"No one needs to bring us the mail. Sam can fetch it." Lucy stood, more clumsily than she would have liked, especially while making a stand to be more self-sufficient.

Manny walked quickly over to help her, but she found her balance and stood tall. "You all right?" Manny's blue eye caught the sun, making her think of the little lesson Nellie had just shared with her about colors in the sky.

"I'm fine, *danke.*" There was no good reason to look into a man's eyes, knowing what she knew. Her life was here at Sam's farm with their new child. Manny was a neighbor, but not one she'd known until recently. Going to two different churches on Sunday had kept them from getting to know each other. Maybe there was a reason for that too.

"How's Abner getting on?" Nellie smiled at Manny and glanced at Lucy.

As Nellie watched Manny talking, with his one blue and one brown eye and messy blond hair, she pressed herself away, and when he smiled at her, she pushed farther still.

᪥ Chapter Eight ᪥

*L*ucy stood on the porch of her two-story white clapboard house taking in the bright sun as she waited for the buggy rattling down the dirt path. She didn't recognize the driver, which made her eyebrows rise in question.

"*Hallo.*" A young Amish man quickly brought the horse to a halt and stepped out. "This is the first time I've been out this way." He looked around while walking to the other side of the buggy. "Nice place you got here."

"*Danke.* And you are?" She bobbed her head to see what he looked at and took a step forward out of curiosity. His eyes were fixed on the tall silo standing out like a beacon— a gluttonous symbol, in her opinion.

"Sorry. I provide transportation for folks visiting local family." He offered his hand, and Lucy hesitantly complied. "The name's Jeremiah. I'll grab the bag and bring it around." Lucy had heard of this but had planned on picking up her *mamm* once she got word. Leave it to her to make a surprise entrance.

A woman's voice drew Lucy's attention as the buggy squeaked and leaned to one side. Her *mamm* stepped out.

As she came around the front of the buggy, Lucy took in a sharp breath.

Mamm smiled. "I knew you'd be glad to see me."

"*Mamm!*" was all Lucy could think of to say. Maybe all those thoughts she'd just pondered were in preparation for this surprise. She'd expected a letter or word from the bishop, who had the community phone, to give her the news, not this unexpected arrival.

"You know how I like to keep people on their toes." *Mamm* thanked the young man and then looked around the place with pensive eyes. Lucy and her *mamm* didn't look anything alike, with her *mamm*'s dark hair and eyes, and especially her height. She stood almost a foot taller than *Daed*. Lucy had her *daed*'s features and small build and his meek—"not weak," he'd say—temperament.

"Well, you sure surprised me. I didn't know you were coming this soon." She moved forward and reached out to offer a hug. *Mamm* bent down and patted her back. Lucy wished she had gotten the *haus* ready. She could already imagine the expression on her *mamm*'s face when she saw the lack of a woman's touch in the *haus*—especially in the kitchen. Not to mention the bedroom that Lucy hadn't gotten together yet. Three of the bedrooms weren't in use and were probably collecting spider webs.

Mamm moved back and examined Lucy's belly. "It's hard to believe you're in your last trimester. You always were a petite little thing."

Little did her *mamm* know about the constant stress she lived with. That alone hindered her appetite, not to mention her cooking, which was mediocre on a good day.

"This babe can't come fast enough. I'm already worn out." Lucy felt tired just thinking about the chores ahead of her, with her *mamm* there adding stress to it all. Maybe it was good to have her *mamm* nearby, at least for a little while, to get her ready for what was to come.

"How's *Daed*? Feeling any better?" Lucy was almost scared to ask. For him not to come and spend time with her told her he was not well. She had hoped he would show up with her *mamm* but wasn't surprised that he hadn't.

"*Nee*, he doesn't have much energy. I know you were hoping to see him. Maybe after the baby's born." She let out a breath. "To be honest, I think it might be you coming to visit once you and the babe can travel. It's just too much for him."

Mamm's look of sorrow was such an uncommon reaction, it made Lucy pause. "I so want to see him." Her *daed* was the only one who truly knew her. She looked down at the rich soil beneath her feet, reminding herself of the reason she was there. Her *mamm* had been sure she would need to leave the community to find a husband. She had always been shy and more interested in working with her *daed* than being in the kitchen with her *mamm*. She stroked her belly, worried for her unborn child, but then pushed back the emotions and lifted her head.

"Lucy?"

When she looked up at her *mamm*, she decided to be grateful for what she had instead of complaining about what she didn't have. *Mamm* was there. Although stressful at times, it would be good to have a helping hand. "Sorry, *Mamm*."

"What a large farm." *Mamm* put her hands on her hips. "And well kept." She grinned. "I can see my handiwork in you."

Lucy wished she had added her own touches with more of a creative bent than the stringent ways of her *mamm*. Once they walked into the *haus, Mamm* would be singing a different tune. But Lucy was prepared for anything now that she was here. "How was the trip?"

"Not too long. You don't live that far away, my dear. Your

sisters will try to visit once the baby comes." She stopped to get Lucy's attention. "And from what I'm told, Fannie will be coming out when I leave." Her *mamm* told Lucy about the schedule she had put together as to who was coming out when, but Fannie had bumped up her visiting time to be there when the baby was born. *Mamm* meant well, but Lucy would rather her sisters came and went as they saw fit, or all of them at once. She knew that would never happen, but it would be wonderful-*gut*.

Mamm watched Lucy's face as she chattered. "This is a large farm. Hopefully you'll have a boy to help Sam run the place."

Lucy took a step back. "*Jah*, I suppose. I miss my sisters, so it would be nice to have a girl."

Mamm shaded her eyes with her hands. "It's so still and quiet. Does that bother you?"

"*Nee*, I'm fine." Lucy didn't want to complain. If she did, she knew her *mamm* would give her reasons not to be bothered by the silence. It was a twist she put on things to make her girls stronger, or so she thought.

"I'm surprised after reading some of the letters you sent home to the girls." She rubbed what must have been a dirt smudge on Lucy's cheek. Lucy didn't miss the jab. The girls corresponded through a round-robin. Each wrote a letter and sent it to the next person in the order, who added her letter, until it went full circle. Their *mamm* was not included.

"It's hard to adjust, but it's starting to feel like home." But she overstated. Though she had made great strides, home was where her sisters were. "Sam should be at the *haus* soon for lunch."

Her *mamm* frowned, maybe expecting a more formal

welcome when she arrived. "Why don't you show me around while we wait for him?"

She started walking, so Lucy followed. "A greenhouse?" *Mamm* glanced at Lucy and then walked toward the structure. "I prefer to work outdoors myself. You can't get away from the heat either way." She took long strides to reach the small building Sam had made. The foundation was cement, with a brick base halfway up, and then sealed with thick plastic on all sides.

"Do you want to see the house first?" Lucy watched for Sam. She already didn't know how to handle *Mamm* with her determined ways. With the surprise early visit, she didn't know if she could handle both Sam and her.

"*Jah*, sure." But she stayed the course, and they soon stood in the middle of the greenhouse. *Mamm* inspected each flower, fruit, and vegetable. "Hmm."

Lucy knew the sound; *Mamm* disapproved of something. "There's a lot more to it than I realized, and this is my first attempt." Lucy stopped. She was already giving *Mamm* her excuses for failing at something. It was a common conversation between them whenever Lucy tried something that *Mamm* felt was above her abilities. She knew her mother was only trying to help, but she wasn't. Each time her *mamm* told her she couldn't do something or do it well enough, it took a piece of Lucy.

Skip and Hop came alongside them, threatening to jump up. "Stay." *Mamm* lifted her pointer finger at the dogs, and they obeyed. "Such silly names."

"They're verbs, *Mamm*." Lucy started to smile, but stopped when she realized that was Sam's response when she'd suggested the names. They might not have had names at all, if it was up to him.

Mamm waved a hand as if to dismiss Lucy's reasoning. "They're animals, nothing more." She told Skip, "Down!" and scowled at the dog until he caved and lay down with his nose between his paws.

Lucy looked skyward to see the sun shining brightly, but Sam wasn't anywhere in sight. "Are you hungry? It must have been a long ride."

"Actually, I'm famished. I haven't had a decent meal since I left." She cupped her hand under Lucy's chin. "Your scar." She studied her cheek. "It seems darker, and you look exhausted. Let's get you something to eat and some rest." Without waiting for an answer, she started the walk to the *haus* just as Sam came out of the barn.

When he saw *Mamm,* he stopped for a moment and then lowered his head and kept walking. Lucy could feel his irritation from twenty feet away but didn't know what to do about it. He'd known *Mamm* was coming, just not today.

"*Hallo,* Sam," *Mamm* called out to him.

He didn't respond until they were all close to the *haus.* "Verna, I didn't know you were coming today." He eyed Lucy with a quick flash of his dark eyes and then shifted them back to her *mamm.* "How was the bus ride?"

He opened the white wooden gate and let it go for Lucy to catch before it shut. She was more aware of these small things now that *Mamm* was there and wondered how she would react. It would be interesting to see how they got along, as they had met only twice—once when he came up to get her and once at their wedding, which was over so fast it made Lucy's head spin, not to mention *Mamm*'s.

They walked into the kitchen, which was fairly tidy, though lacking some charm and color. Lucy watched

Mamm scan the room, taking mental notes as Lucy expected. She told herself to take *Mamm*'s comments with a grain of salt, and anything she or especially Sam didn't like, they could change after she left. It wasn't worth anyone getting upset. It was just what *Mamm* did, to decorate.

"This is a large room. I can see why it's been difficult to spruce up things—where to begin and whatnot." She clapped her hands together.

Lucy felt the tension coming from Sam, knowing the only thing he was concerned about at the moment was food. "I'll start on lunch. First, I'll show you to your room, if you like, so you can freshen up."

"We'll eat first." Sam sat down hard in his chair at the head of the table and looked straight ahead.

Mamm squinted as she stared at him.

Lucy stepped in quickly. "Go on up; any of the empty rooms are fine." They hadn't been together five minutes, and already Lucy was deflecting them from each other. Her stress level shot up, and the baby responded.

She started in on the meal, working quickly while Sam read the Budget paper to catch up on the Amish from all over the country. She'd never been so happy to see him read the paper as if she weren't in the room, though many times she'd wished he'd talk to her while he read it.

As she diced potatoes to go with the roasted chicken she'd made, for the first time, she wished she had her English friend's microwave oven.

~ *Chapter Nine* ~

*M*anny thought he was going to bust. "This chicken pot pie is good, Emma." He put his hands over his belly, waiting for her to say what she always did.

"*Gut*, you need to put on some weight. When Caleb gets in here, you'll have to have some more." She gave him that pitying look she had about her and then turned away from the table to clean up. "You can't mourn over Glenda forever. And she would want you to be fat and happy." She smiled as she looked over at him.

"*Jah*, well, I don't cook as *gut* as you do, but I make do." He smirked. He'd actually learned a thing or two about cooking but didn't like to eat alone. It wasn't worth the effort to cook for one. Sometimes Manny just needed to be around people, and since Emma was the one who lifted his spirits the most, he usually ended up here.

She frowned. "I've told you to come over for breakfast, lunch, and dinner every day, if you like. Why don't you come?"

"Good question, you ol' mule," Caleb said as he came in from the barn, where he'd been cleaning up a bit more after the milking. "Why don't ya come over more often?"

"Milking went twice as fast with me helping." Manny winked at Emma and turned to Caleb. "So what took ya so long to get in here?"

"I thought I'd let you two talk." Caleb washed up and sat

down across from Manny. "You seem better." Caleb gave Manny a knowing look.. "Any special reason?"

Manny scoffed. "Tell me what you're really asking."

"All right. Have you been out to Sam's place again?" Caleb held his gaze on Manny.

Manny drummed his fingers on the table, pondering what to say. "Why do you ask?" He couldn't find the right words, so he answered with a question to avoid saying more than he should.

How honest could he be without feeling disrespectful? He saw not only her pure heart but also her need for someone who truly cared about her. He shook his head at how ridiculous he sounded. She was married, and he was still in mourning, but Caleb was right: he needed to move on. The draw he had been feeling toward Lucy had taught him that much at least. Now he was beginning to hope that someday he would have a relationship again, but he couldn't imagine how that would happen or with whom.

"Don't encourage him, Caleb," Emma snapped at him. "She's a married woman, ya know."

Caleb snorted. "I'm not trying to cause trouble between her and Sam, but Lucy's got to be the unhappiest person I ever met. Surely there's no harm in her having a friend in Manny." He leaned back in his chair and stared at Manny. "Emma's right. Lucy is a married woman. So who else is there that you enjoy spending time with?"

Emma walked over and slapped his leg with her spatula. "You're making Manny uncomfortable."

"*Nee!*" Caleb sat back in his chair, tipping it up on two legs. "You're not uncomfortable, are ya, Manny." He said it more like a statement than a question, knowing Manny wouldn't tell him even if he didn't like the conversation.

"Can I use that spatula?" Manny teased, making them all laugh.

"It's the only thing that works when he starts flapping his tongue." Emma handed it to Manny for fun.

"I'm armed now. So change the subject." Manny whipped the spatula around and caught Caleb on the arm.

Taken off guard, Caleb reared backward and lost his balance. He fell with a slam to the floor, cradled his head with one hand, and pushed himself up with the other. Scrambling to his feet, he stared at Manny. "I give!" He held up both hands. "I'm done teasing you for today."

Emma had her hand over her mouth in shock, but now let out a loud laugh. "Are you okay?" She stroked Caleb's cheek and then felt the back of his head.

"I'm *gut*. I was probably asking for that." His face was a bit pale, but he was in good humor, so Manny decided he was right. His teasing had gone too far, and Manny was glad Emma got on him about it. He couldn't tell anyone how he felt—not now, probably never.

"Sorry, friend." He stood and clasped Caleb's hand. "No hard feelings?"

"*Nah*. Now I don't need that extra cup of coffee. 'Cause you woke me up!" Caleb grinned, letting him know he meant it, and walked over to Emma to give her a peck on the cheek.

"*Danke* for dinner, Sis." Manny headed for the door as Emma patted Caleb's cheek. The endearments they shared were too much for Manny. He was happy for them but selfishly jealous he didn't have what they had. It wasn't right to pine over it, so he tried to occupy his mind with something else. He hadn't had a good talk with Sweet Pea in a while. Maybe he'd head home and have a heart to heart with her.

Manny took his time going back to his farm, deciding to check and see whether the mail had come yet. He looked up at the blue sky. The sun was straight overhead. His mail should be there waiting for him. It would be a slow ride because he'd brought Sweet Pea. He liked to get her out now and then, not wanting her to think she was going to be sent to pasture.

He'd been delivering the mail to Lucy for over a week now, but he felt a little unsteady inside each time he rode down the path to her place. Sam wasn't usually around, so the awkwardness was at a minimum. The best part was, she seemed a bit more relaxed around him. But because of her concern that Sam might not approve of him dropping by, Manny stood in the mudroom, never entering the *haus*.

Manny took in a long breath and gave himself a minute to scope out the surroundings as he pulled on the brake. Sam was nowhere in sight, and neither was Lucy. The path to the main road was lengthy, so they had time to see who was coming long before a visitor actually got to their farm. Lucy usually greeted him at the door and asked him if he wanted a drink of tea or lemonade, but today no one could be seen.

He looked down at the two letters he held and wondered whether he should shove them under the door, but he didn't want to take the chance they might get lost. He decided to take a walk around to see whether he could find either of them.

As he strolled along, he started thinking he had chores to do and should be getting back to his own place, but something about Lucy drew him to her. He didn't know whether it was an attraction or a need to make sure she was all right. He'd never seen anyone so forlorn…at least until he got her talking. Then another side of her came out that he enjoyed very much.

He was deep in thought when he heard Sam's voice. The sound grew, and soon Sam was yelling…no, screaming.

Manny's first thought was for Lucy, but he held back the thought, thinking it could be a horse just as easily as a human on which Sam was taking out his wrath. Still, he found himself running, following the growling force that seemed to surround him. He tried to decipher where exactly the noise was. There were a number of buildings to pick from—the bunk *haus*, chicken coop, barn, and shed, to name a few. Sam's farm was so big he could get lost in it.

A woman's cry, shockingly loud, made him stop in his tracks. It directed him to where he should go, and he was at top speed within seconds. His boots felt like concrete, they were so slow and heavy. He drew up as he neared the door, smacking into it to stop his pace. The large garage housed farm equipment, which he maneuvered around to find the source of the sobbing he now heard. Lucy stood against a flatbed covering her face with her arm. Sam paced back and forth in front of her with balled fists, squeezing and releasing them.

"Sam!" Manny didn't recognize his own voice. It was calm and louder than usual.

Sam lifted his head and squinted at Manny. "Who's there?"

"It's Manny."

Sam stopped and looked at Lucy, who straightened with

palms against her thighs, but didn't lift her head. "What brings you here?" He growled at Manny.

"Just dropping off your mail." Manny was glad he had a reason to come and now understood why Abner was concerned. It wasn't clear what was happening, but whatever it was, it was not good.

"Take it from him."

Sam didn't have to ask Lucy twice. She was by Manny's side before he could lift the letters up to her.

Manny tried to look in her eyes, but she put her head down and kept walking. He watched her go, and then turned to Sam. He was back to work repairing a manure spreader. It was a bold move, but Manny couldn't let this go, and he took his time walking down the aisle filled with everything from plows to carts. "Is there anything I can help you with?"

Sam continued to bang out a bent piece of metal, but he didn't speak.

"Lucy seemed upset." Manny shifted his boots.

Still no response.

To his surprise, Manny was prepared for whatever Sam said or did. It might have been less than he thought, but after looking into Lucy's face, he was pretty sure what had transpired between them was not right; she wasn't herself. "Do you want me to check on her?"

Sam turned his head away from the spreader and slowly stood without taking his eyes off Manny. "Why are you still here?"

"To deliver your mail." Manny wished he had the two envelopes.

Sam glared at him. "Don't bother yourself with the mail."

Manny scoffed. The few times he'd brought the mail to them, there was nothing for Sam, but he knew how important it was for Lucy to get correspondence.

"It's no problem." He felt like he'd blown it. That was his excuse to check in on her, and after what had just happened, he felt the obligation even more. His mind raced to find what to say. But when he looked up at Sam, he knew nothing he said would change his mind. "I know you don't like to bother with it, and I think Abner's on the mend, so I'll see if he's able to."

Sam's lips pinched together as he stared him down. "We'll manage." He took a single step that put them nose to nose. "*Gut* day, Manny."

His words weren't rude, but his tone was.

Manny felt useless at this point. Worst of all, he'd put Lucy in the middle. He'd overstepped his bounds, and when he thought about it, he was probably making it harder for her. Had he heard what he thought he had or was he thinking the worst? This was the overprotective side of him that he had no right to indulge.

He was out of line; the Amish kept family issues within the family. The bishop would consider this a private matter, yet Manny thought it was hard for him not to do anything when there was some sort of verbal abuse going on. He was involved just because of what he heard and saw, whether that was wrong or right.

Manny walked away from the barn deep in thought, wondering where his place was in all this, if he had any at all, and noticed Lucy sitting on the porch swing reading a letter.

"One of those from your sister?" He understood why Abner was so nosy now and was glad that he was. It was nice to know she had family who loved and cared about her.

Lucy jumped a little and nodded. Her freckles looked brighter today, but then, her face was also paler. He wondered whether it was because she didn't feel well or because of Sam.

He took slow steps to the gate and stopped. "Is everybody good back home?"

Her eyes rose over the top of the paper she held, and she nodded.

"Are your sisters coming down anytime soon?"

"*Nee*, my *mamm* came yesterday, but she went to fetch some more coffee."

He relished hearing her voice at an even level. "That's nice. You enjoying spending time with her?" That seemed like a stupid question, but he was so glad she was talking to him that he didn't care, and she didn't seem to mind.

She put the letter down and turned her head toward the barn. "Sort of."

Manny couldn't hide his surprise. He waited for her to continue.

"She's...hard to please." She immediately put a hand to her lips, as if to lock them shut. "I didn't mean it in a bad way."

Manny smiled, tickled she was worried about what he thought when all he cared about was having a conversation with her. "Family can be like that at times."

She gave a short laugh. "Or all the time."

He listened to her laugh in his mind again and smiled with her. "I know what you mean."

"She'll be a big help, though." Her eyes lost their sparkle, and Manny looked over his shoulder to see Sam with a bucket of milk in hand to separate.

"I'm sure she will be. I look forward to meeting her." He

knew he should leave; she was obviously nervous with him there and Sam wishing he was gone. But when Sam moved out of sight to finish his chore, Manny turned around on a heel and stuck his hands on his hips. "Are you all right?" He didn't know where his courage came from, but he couldn't leave without asking.

Lucy's face turned pink. "Manny—"

"I won't do or say a thing. I just need to know." He waited a beat and then another, thinking he wasn't going to get an answer. He was about to turn around when she said his name.

"Manny, *danke*." When she stood and walked into the *haus*, he'd never felt so helpless.

ᴇᴀ Chapter Ten

The women took their places at the large table around the quilting frame in Frieda's kitchen. "It's about time we all got together to quilt. I thought I was gonna end up making this whole quilt myself." Frieda's tone wasn't pleasant, but she had reason to be a little frustrated. They had been increasingly busy. With the beginning of fall harvest around the corner, they were hopping from farm to farm, threshing, cutting, and baling as much as they could before the more time-consuming crops would need to be tended to.

"Now, Frieda, you know I'll always get us together and work double-time if need be." Nellie took two stitches, using her thimble to push the needle back and forth through the fabric. "Lucy's little one isn't due for a few more weeks now. Remember in the days when we used cotton? It was like quilting through butter."

Lucy admired Nellie's gift of quilting and wished she could do half as well. She made it seem effortless. Nellie's hand was poised above the quilt as she watched the others work. It was as if she had two sets of eyes—one stitching and one overseeing others' work. After hearing Nellie's story, Lucy admired her even more, not only for her love of quilting but also for her independent nature, something rare among the Amish.

"That's when we were down south, and the cotton was plentiful." Rosy wiggled her fingers to get the knots out of them. "Those were the days, weren't they?" She looked up as if seeing that time all over again. Her bright-blue eyes gazed upward as if she were there.

"You missing Tennessee, Rosy?" Frieda took a back stitch and then pushed the thread under the quilt and snipped off the head. Lucy watched and learned more than she quilted. These women had experience on their side, spending many years making the most difficult stitch look easy.

Rosy leveled her head to meet Lucy's gaze. "You miss it there, don't ya, hon?"

A lump formed in Lucy's throat as she recalled the pain of leaving there. Being the youngest to find a husband had become a concern, not so much for her as for her *mamm*. But Lucy hadn't been happy since she'd moved away and figured she wouldn't ever live there again. Sam would never leave even though his family was up north, and she would never ask him to. With his *mamm* and *daed* gone and only one surviving sister that he didn't speak to, he had no reason to go. But in Lucy's mind, he had little reason to stay, especially since her family was down south.

Lucy watched Rosy cut a length of thread, lick its end, and then pick up a magnifying glass that *Mammi* had wired to the quilt frame to thread the needle. "What will we stuff this one with?"

Lucy hadn't used anything but old dresses, old quilts, or worn-out pants. She wanted only the best for the little one, something that she'd made. Lucy knew the babe would have plenty to rest her head on, but the one from her would have to be extra special.

"Something warm." *Mamm* had been quiet until now and looked over at Lucy. "So you'll have something to keep you and the baby warm."

"Well then, we might have to put some cotton in there." Frieda winked at Lucy and grinned. "We wouldn't want you or little Joe to catch a chill."

"Little Joe?" Lucy stared at Frieda. "You've decided it's a boy and named him already?"

Frieda nodded. "*Jah*, I know you want a girl, but I'm thinking that by the way he's sitting down low, it's a boy."

"Huh-uh." Nellie chimed in. "Lucy wants a girl, so that's the way we're thinking." She peered over at Lucy's bulging belly. "Although Frieda's right about how low that babe is."

Verna was unusually quiet about the whole conversation. She must have something on her mind, but quilting was the best medicine, no matter what ailed a woman. "As long as the baby doesn't have Sam's eyes, I don't care if it's a boy or a girl."

Nellie, Frieda, Rosy, and Lucy all stared at her. But *Mamm*'s eyes were on her needle as she stitched like she was punching a bag of corn. The room was silent for a long moment.

"Why do you say that?" Frieda asked with a frown. Lucy was just glad she hadn't had to ask. She was curious as to why her *mamm* would say such a thing, at least out loud. There were many things she thought about her own husband but never had the nerve to say. She worried that Sam and *Mamm* might set each other off, but so far they'd done their best to ignore each other.

"I've never seen such cutting eyes. And the color, it's a mishmash of something I haven't seen before." She tied and snipped a piece of thread and reached for a patch. She glanced around the room quickly. "Don't tell me you haven't noticed."

Now that Lucy thought about it, that was what made

his stare intimidating and his eyes unfriendly. It matched his personality to a T.

The room quieted again, and Lucy found she needed some air. She'd expected awkward moments with her *mamm* coming to visit, but it wasn't any easier to deal with. She appreciated her mother's concerns about Sam, but her *mamm* was an opinionated woman around opinionated women, and it was a tough situation to be in the middle of when they were all talking about Sam.

"*Jah*, I guess I have," Rosy responded, which surprised Lucy. She was usually the last one to get into a controversy. But then Rosy was probably the most honest as well. Not that the others weren't, but Rosy had complete loyalty to the truth.

"Aha. I'm glad to hear someone say it." *Mamm* looked over at Frieda, whom she probably expected to comment about anything concerning Sam. Frieda normally made it obvious that she didn't like the man and never had. Verna probably didn't either, judging by her comment about him, but would never admit that.

Verna had encouraged the match between him and Lucy when she heard that a wealthy widower was looking for a young, strong wife to help him farm. Lucy wasn't sure then why Sam looked for a wife outside his own community, but Verna convinced her that she would enjoy working alongside him, just as she'd enjoyed working with her *daed*. And it didn't hurt that Sam didn't seem to mind her scar. But even now that she could see what Sam was really like, Verna was unlikely to own up to the fact that the match hadn't turned out to be a happy life for her daughter.

"This isn't the time." Lucy didn't look directly at her

mamm but hoped she'd know not to continue the conversation. It wasn't likely Sam would be walking through the door, but in case he did, this wasn't the time to talk about him. It never was. This was her cross to bear.

Nellie reached for a patch and needle and began quilting, which was a wise thing to do. It was as if a cow was in the room, but no one admitted seeing the creature. "You're looking a little peaked, Lucy."

"*Jah*, I think I'll take a walk." She noticed her *mamm* shifting in her seat. "Alone, if that's all right." She looked away before her *mamm* could speak. The usual warm conversation she shared with Rosy, Nellie, and Frieda was interrupted by her mother's presence.

Chapter Eleven

*B*oom!

Lucy sat straight up.

Sam jumped out of bed. He grabbed his clothes from a chair, hopping on one foot, stuffing his other leg into his pants.

Lucy held her belly and turned to the side of the bed, placing one foot down and then the other. She felt like a snail, moving in slow motion. Heat filled the room, and when Lucy went to the window and opened the shade, she gasped. Yellow, orange, and red flames engulfed the seventy-six-foot silo.

"Move, woman! My farm's gonna blow!" Sam screamed and ran down the stairs.

The top of the silo shot into the air, hurling chunks of concrete across the road. Smoke poured from the silo, rolling out of the structure like a white cloud.

Lucy lifted her arms to cover her face and pulled the curtain down. The back of the *haus* shook as if a boulder had smacked into its wooden frame, knocking out the mudroom downstairs. Lucy moved as quickly as she could, holding her belly with each step. Tears flooded her cheeks as the heat scorched her flesh.

"*Mamm!*"

No reply.

"*Mamm!*"

As she passed *Mamm*'s room, she poked her head inside

but saw no one. Lucy hoped she was already outside. It wasn't the smoke so much as the heat that made her eyes spring with tears and pain crawl on her flesh as if she were in a living hell with no mercy from the scathing heat.

What about my baby? How will he be affected by smoke filling my lungs?

Getting to the front door opposite the silo's location seemed to take forever. Her bare feet hit the wood planks of the porch. She fell but got up, dismissing the pain in her ankle. All she could do was run fast. She took in a breath and coughed on the soot and bits of flying debris filling the air.

When she was in the middle of the yard, she stopped and turned to take in the scene around her. All she could do was stand and watch as the silo burned. Relief washed over her when she heard the wail of the fire truck in the distance. A few minutes later the firefighters arrived and they leapt out and took to the hoses. There were no hydrants, only the water in their vehicles. One fireman ran over to her and motioned for the medic. "Is there anyone else in the house?"

Lucy shook her head but then nodded.

It didn't take long for word about the fire to get around the community. Soon buggies and wagons and a couple of riders on horseback filled the road. A stream of Amish came prepared to help with whatever they had. The men went as close to the fire as they could, which wasn't close due to the heat. The women came toward Lucy with hands full of food, drink, and, she hoped, something to cool her skin from the blistering heat. She looked for Sam and *Mamm* but saw neither of them.

Lucy felt hands on her...water on her lips...salve on

her face and arms. She looked at faces, but they were only a blur. Drops of water fell from her eyes. She was weeping. Then she heard her own voice, crying out, asking about her baby.

Hushed tones and whispers calmed her. Frieda and Rosy loomed over her with wide, pensive eyes. Nellie rubbed her back, and Lucy flinched as hot debris flew around her. Lucy looked through the blur to see Rosy crying. Then, all went black.

Manny jumped out of bed at the sound of a knock at the door. He pulled on the clothes closest to him and grabbed his boots. More pounding spurred his pace. When he opened the door, Caleb had his hand on the doorknob, ready to burst in. Manny's eyes stung from smoke.

"There's a fire." Caleb started down the porch steps with Manny right behind him.

"What happened?" Manny jumped into Caleb's buggy and braced himself.

"Hi-ya!" Caleb's driving had Manny hanging on and his foot pressed against the foot rest. "Silo exploded. Didn't you hear it?"

"*Jah*, but I didn't think it was something like this. Where?" Manny wrestled with his shirt, trying to hold on and still brace himself so he wouldn't go rolling out of the buggy. Manny looked at Caleb, wondering if he'd heard the question. "Whose place?"

Caleb turned toward him. "Sam's."

Manny's *gut* churned. "Is anyone hurt?"

"I don't know. I came and got you and haven't had a chance to find out anything more than I told you." By the way he looked at Manny, it seemed Caleb knew he'd be more upset than just any other neighbor, and it made Manny wonder if his concern for Lucy showed more than he thought.

"Can't this nag go any faster?" Manny felt like jumping out and running. He could blow off steam, and it would at least feel as if he was getting there faster.

"Should have thought to hitch up two horses, but I was in a hurry to come get you." Caleb glanced at him. "You're no good to her upset this way. Keep your head together."

Manny paused in surprise. He didn't think he'd been around her enough with Caleb there to observe his concern for her. He overlooked the comment and kept his eyes on the inferno before them. "I just hope she's...they're all right."

The closer they got, the hotter the air grew around them. The wind had picked up, blowing smoldering debris around the area. Sparse groups of people walked past them, going the opposite way. Manny leaned out the window. "Where are you going, Elam?"

"*Ach*, Manny. The firefighters are telling people to leave, sending us home. They say we can help best tomorrow when things are under control." Elam patted Manny's arm. "You younger men might be of some help to them, but for most of us we'll be doing what we can some other way."

"Did you see Lucy?"

He shook his head. "*Nee*, but her *mamm* was looking for her."

Manny nodded. "*Danke*." They went a few feet forward but drew up when the heat became too much for the horses. He jumped out of the buggy, with Caleb on his heels. They both stopped short when Manny saw Lucy on the porch. A medic held an oxygen mask over her nose and mouth.

He moved forward, but Caleb stopped him, clasping him on the shoulder. "Take a breath, friend. She needs to see your strength, not your concern." Caleb let go and slapped his back.

Manny took in a breath and nodded, coughing out the stinging air. When he got closer, he saw Lucy's head fall to one side, eyes closed. She didn't move. He ran the last few feet, hovering over her, waiting to see her chest rise. "Is she all right?" he asked the paramedic, keeping his eyes on her.

"Are you family?" The young medic didn't look up, monitoring the oxygen intake.

Knowing he might not give him the information if he wasn't, Manny said the first thing that popped into his head. "*Jah.*"

"Husband?" The medic stood then waved over to the ambulance.

Manny fingered his beard. He was lying and knew it, but Sam wasn't there, so someone should be. "They're both okay?"

The paramedic stuck a pen in his shirt pocket and almost smiled. "She's exhausted, but her vitals are good. She should be just fine."

"And the babe is well?"

"I got a strong heartbeat."

The *ding-ding* of an ambulance backing up ended the conversation as the medic motioned for the driver to approach carefully so they could drive straight out. "Excuse me, sir, we need to load up a couple of the injured."

"What hospital?" Manny stepped forward, but the medic stopped him. "Pomerene Hospital."

Manny raked his hand through his hair, knowing it would take much longer to get there in his buggy. "My buggy can't keep up with you."

"She doesn't have to go in, but I think she should get checked out. It's three others."

He lifted his hand up flat to stop the vehicle.

Manny looked back over at Lucy surrounded by Frieda, Rosy, and Nellie along with a handful of others, all fussing over her. Her eyes were open, but sleepy. "Thank *Gott*."

He turned back to the medic. "Who are you taking in?" He didn't think he'd get an answer, but it was worth a try.

The medic was called away by another paramedic. He nodded toward the news teams driving down the road. "Someone around here might be able to tell you." He turned and jogged to the ambulance, and then hopped in as the siren blared.

He walked over to the ambulance where they had moved Lucy, selfishly wishing he could be the one to comfort her, care for her, and take her home. He had no right to have those feelings, so he tried to stuff them away—but he couldn't because when he had those thoughts, he felt whole, if only for a moment.

He stopped, almost to the cot, and scanned the area. Sam was nowhere to be seen. Knowing him, he helped the others who were cleaning up the heaps of rubble that his farm had now become. He looked back at Lucy and the three older women who stood nearby. She couldn't be in better hands, but he thought he'd try to horn in and at least see her face.

When he got closer, she turned her head and gave him a tired smile. The ladies turned around and called him over.

"What a sight for sore eyes…" Frieda put her hands on her hips.

He moved closer and studied her. "How is she?" Her fair face had been wiped clean and her reddish hair combed out and tucked behind her, something he hadn't seen since before Glenda passed away.

"It's not me I'm worried about. It's *Mamm* and Sam." Lucy's eyes closed again, and he thought she might have passed out or just fallen asleep. He knelt down closer to see her chest rise, and then her eyes fluttered.

Her color was ashen, and her hands shook. "You don't seem okay." He was just as worried about the baby.

"I'm just tired."

"What did the medic say about the baby?"

"Said he's fine."

Nellie chimed in. "She needs some sleep."

"And water." Rosy held a bottle up to Lucy's mouth and watched her drink.

"I'll go see what I can find out." He patted her hand.

"*Danke*, Manny." Her eyes lingered on his. He took two steps backward and then turned to go find out what had happened.

The first police officer he saw was on his phone, but he stopped the next one he came to. "Excuse me. I'm looking for a couple of people. Can you help me find them?"

"Sure. I'm Officer Jeff Streeter. What are their names?" He took down the information. "You're family?"

"I told the friends and family I'd look into it." He felt guilty skirting around the question again. Something inside him told him he was supposed to take care of this family, at least until other family members could do the job.

"I'll ask around for you, but I can't promise anything. Unfortunately it's a matter of priority."

"*Jah*, I understand. The woman in the ambulance is who I'm asking for—Lucy Wagner." He glanced toward the ambulance. "You've probably explained this a number of times, but what happened?"

"This one's the worst explosion I've seen."

Manny had heard silos blowing before, but not to this extent. It could be that since Sam's silo is the largest, it would be more of an issue with something like this happening, but it seemed to be more than that to do this kind of damage. "What made this one so bad?"

"There have been many cases of silos and the associated ducts and buildings exploding. If the air inside becomes laden with fine granulated particles like grain or dust, it can trigger an explosion."

"I didn't know how powerful one of these could be, until tonight." Manny watched the firefighters' futile attempt to stop the fire.

"Oh, yeah, powerful enough to blow a concrete silo and adjacent buildings apart, usually setting the buildings on fire like it did here." Officer Streeter checked his phone.

"How can some dust do this?" Manny bought as much time as he could, hoping he'd hear something over the officer's radio from another officer.

"It's often triggered by sparks caused by metal rubbing against metal ducts or due to static electricity produced by dust moving along the ducts when they're extra dry."

Manny couldn't stand it any longer. He took a deep breath. "Would you tell me if there were any fatalities?"

"If you are family." He nodded toward the vehicle. "I just got here, but I can try and find out for you, if the lady there is able to vouch for you. It's all protocol."

"I'd sure appreciate it."

The officer stepped away and spoke quietly to another officer. Manny stood, taking in the scene. He figured he would have heard by now if someone had died, but there was something eating at him. It wasn't right that Sam was not around. Manny would have been more worried about Lucy than his farm if he was in Sam's shoes. It also bothered him that Lucy's *mamm* wasn't with her. It sounded like her *mamm* was a take-charge kind of lady, but he was beginning to think she might not be able to be with Lucy. Something might have happened, that he hadn't heard of; his suspicions were increasing.

The officer came back to Manny and nodded toward Lucy. "Let's take a walk over to the ambulance."

Manny didn't say a word while they walked to the ambulance where Lucy sat on a stretcher drinking out of a white paper cup. When she saw him, she looked up expectantly.

The officer stepped forward. "I'm Officer Jeff Streeter. And you are Lucy Wagner?"

Lucy nodded, and Frieda quickly added, "I'm her *mammi*, her *mamm's mamm*."

He tipped his hat to Frieda and turned his attention to Lucy. "How are you?"

"We're fine." Lucy rubbed her belly, and the officer looked down.

"Ma'am, your mother was taken to the hospital due to smoke inhalation."

Lucy put a hand to her chest. "Is she going to be okay?"

Frieda held Lucy's hand. "She'll be all right. You know how strong she is."

Manny hadn't met the lady, but from the little he'd heard about Lucy's *mamm*, he felt their assessment about her was right.

Lucy held Frieda's hand so tightly that it turned white. "*Danke* for letting me know, officer. And Sam?"

The officer looked her in the eyes. "Your husband suffered extensive burns. I'm sorry to have to inform you that he passed away."

Chapter Twelve

Gasps and murmurs filled the air, but Lucy remained still and wordless, as did Manny.

"I'll give you all a minute and wait over here in case you need me." The officer walked a few steps away and stood at attention.

Lucy's eyes turned to Manny, who stood staring at her. Her first instinct was to go to him, so he could console her as she knew he would and as no one else could at this moment. There was something about him that pulled at her, telling her she'd be safe with him. And that he would know what she could do, since he too had lost a spouse. She was at a loss. But even more than that, she had harbored horrible thoughts about her husband, and now he was gone. She would have to live with those harsh feelings and great regret. She closed her eyes and said a wistful prayer for forgiveness, knowing she would say many more as long as the guilt clung to her.

"Lucy." Manny's voice instantly stopped her feelings of disgrace, even if it was just for a moment, but she couldn't meet his eyes. Not after everything that had gone through her mind.

"I'm so sorry."

She nodded and stood up from off the stretcher. Then Frieda stepped forward and wrapped her in an embrace. As she closed her eyes, she felt more arms surround her. Rosy's touch was butterfly-light next to Nellie's bear hug.

One by one, they pulled away, their warm bodies leaving a chill that penetrated deeper into her core than the heat all around them.

"You're going to be all right, Luce." Frieda bent over as far as her rickety, worn-out body would let her.

Nellie came closer and lifted Lucy's head with a single finger under her chin. "Look at me. I'm here for you. All of us are. We won't leave your side, darling. We're all right here for as long as you need us."

They were clearly filled with emotion. Rosy could only hug Lucy, unable to speak. Frieda finally took Rosy away so she could stop hiccupping, her usual reaction to anxiety.

Lucy sat back down, and Manny squatted in front of her. "Lucy, what do you need right now?" His eyes glistened, especially the blue one, reflecting the small fires that lingered behind her.

She shrugged. "I can't think..." She held her belly, causing him to look down as well.

"Then I'll tell you. You're going to the hospital. They've taken in those who were in a bad way, and now they're taking some who they suspect were affected by the smoke." He squeezed her hand, giving her warm shivers. "Do you want me to go with you?"

She was unable to look him in the face after the emotional turmoil she'd just felt about him moments ago. It felt right but was so wrong that she had to say no. She shook her head. "You shouldn't." A cough racked her throat; she wanted to go and make sure the baby wasn't affected.

"You need someone to go with you." He moved closer. "If you're worried about me going with you, I won't, but after what's happened, I would think it's understandable with no...without a husband to take you." He looked over his shoulder at Frieda consoling Rosy and at Nellie's droopy eyes. "They may need some rest."

"It's just not right." She paused, wanting to say more, explain why, but her throat was burning, and she didn't know the right words to say. "But *danke* for offering."

She wanted to ignore the rules of her upbringing and what people might say. He was the person who could care for her best, and if there wasn't a flickering fire in her heart, she'd say yes. But she couldn't in good conscience let him be beside her with questionable motives.

"Ma'am, the ambulance is ready to take you now." The officer seemed to be nearby at every turn. Grateful for his assistance, she touched his arm, knowing he'd be able to answer a question she didn't want to ask. "Where is my husband?"

The officer bent down and put his arms on his thighs. "I can take you to him at the hospital, but I need to warn you, because of your condition, it might be difficult for you to see him."

She nodded. "But I have to. I have to see him to know what's really happened...that he's truly gone." The way it came out, she sounded like any wife who'd just lost her spouse, but it wasn't that way. She wanted to see that he was really gone—forever. No more looking over her shoulder or flinching at his sharp words and harsh ways. She wanted to see her deceased husband for all the wrong reasons, and nothing could stop her. She couldn't move on if she didn't.

The officer nodded. "I'll escort you to the hospital." He pointed to his police car and helped her stand.

"I can do that for her, *danke*." Manny held one of her hands and wrapped his arm around her waist, something that would never be allowed in any situation but one such as this. When they got to the ambulance, they both tried to help her in.

"I'll take it from here." The medic glanced at Manny and then at the officer. He helped Lucy into the vehicle and strapped her in. When he went to close the back door, they were both still there waiting until she was ready to go. "We'll see both of you at the hospital, I take it."

"I'll be there," Manny promised as the paramedic grabbed the door handle.

Lucy watched the officer walk to his car and Manny stand stock still until the door shut, cutting off her view. A buggy ride would take a while for Manny to get to the hospital, but she selfishly hoped he would come. Maybe the *Englischer* nearby would give him a ride.

She leaned her head back against the gurney and closed her eyes. She shouldn't be thinking about him now, of all times. What kind of a person had she become? Had her life with Sam tarnished the good in her, making her so callous she had to make sure he couldn't come back to haunt her?

"We assumed you'd want to go to the Pomerene Hospital since it works with the Amish." The medic checked her chart as he waited for her response while he strapped a heart monitor around her middle.

"*Jah*, I was there once when a friend had cancer. They're good people." She felt a little better already. She had no idea how much money Sam had or what to do with medical expenses, so she was glad to be going to a place that accommodated the Amish, giving the community time to gather the money to pay one another's bills.

The medic sat back and typed on a small keyboard,

keeping an eye on the monitor. "There used to be a problem with pesticides on your crops causing cancer. It seems to have gotten better now."

"*Jah*, we made some changes, and many went back to some of the old ways of doing things, I hear." Fatigue was setting in, causing her eyes to droop.

"You can rest, but it's a drive, so no power nap." He grinned, and that was the last thing she remembered until he shook her arm.

"Ma'am, we're here." He tidied up the ambulance, and as soon as the back door opened, she saw Frieda, Nellie, and Rosy with Manny, talking to a Mennonite who must have given them a ride. When Manny saw the ambulance, he finished the conversation, and they all walked closer as the medic rolled Lucy out and to the emergency entrance.

"We'll see you inside." Manny walked away as the ladies waved and followed him. He looked back and smiled—one gesture she hadn't seen tonight. The thought of him there at the hospital created mixed emotions. It was a horrible night. Some were hurt, and two had lost their lives, from what she'd heard. And many others were probably being treated for burns or smoke inhalation.

This feeling of needing Manny wasn't right, not now, maybe never. But no matter what the future held, at this moment, she was a widow, something Manny could relate to. Still, their situations were completely different. He had been with someone he truly loved. She'd had someone who made her life miserable. So where did she stand? She wasn't sure if she was expected to be a widow mourning her husband. That felt hypocritical, and she worried she'd turn shallow.

Some of the Amish were leaving after being discharged.

Others roamed the lobby, waiting to be seen, and still others were being admitted. Once in the exam room, Lucy waited for what seemed an eternity. When she let out a painful breath, the burn in her throat seemed petty compared to the condition of some she'd seen at her farm and here at the hospital.

A bustle of noise drew closer, and then Frieda came through the door with Rosy and Nellie at her heels. "Oh, Luce, you're so pale."

Nellie took one of the paper cups and turned on the faucet. "How are you feeling?" She handed the cup of water to Lucy.

"I'm *gut*. I don't even need to be here, taking up space when there are others who need attention." She took a sip and coughed, sending needle pricks down her throat as she drank.

Rosy handed a tissue to Lucy. "It's better to be safe than sorry. And it's good to check on the baby, even though there's not a single thing to worry about."

The nurse came in, took Lucy's vitals, and looked down her throat with a small flashlight. "I'll have the doctor come and look at you, but you're in good shape. Just some soreness, but it will pass."

"A nice cup of warm tea with honey is all you need."

The nurse grunted a laugh. "What you all make probably works better than what the pharmacy has downstairs."

"Oh, I'm sure of that." Rosy was adamant about her herbal remedies, and as far as Lucy knew, most of the time they did seem to work.

"Have you had an ultrasound?" The nurse typed the information into her small electronic device, waiting for her answer.

A shot of concern sent a chill through Lucy. "*Nee*, you said the babe was fine. Why do you think we need to?"

"Not at all. I just thought you might want to. Most mothers do." She stopped typing and turned to glance at the three women with *kapps* on. Lucy was the only one without a *kapp*, having rushed out the door when the explosion happened.

"*Nee*, but thank you." Lucy didn't know what kind of a financial situation she was in but couldn't rationalize undergoing a procedure if she didn't have to. She thought of Sam and tried to gather the nerve to ask about him. She was hesitant because bringing up the reality that he was actually gone would stir up all kinds of emotions that she couldn't deal with.

"Wouldn't that be something to see the little one in Lucy's tummy?" Rosy grinned at the thought.

Nellie shook her head. "Then we'd want to see if it's a darling little boy or girl."

Frieda looked over at Lucy. "We have more important things at hand, ladies." She went over and took Lucy's hand, seeming to know what was on her mind.

After a few long minutes the doctor walked in and pulled up a stool with wheels. "Mrs. Wagner." He held out his hand and shook hers. "I hear your throat is bothering you." She nodded as he flipped through the chart, wrote something, and set it down on the bed next to her. "Open for me."

The wooden taste of the tongue depressor stayed on her tongue when she closed her mouth. Then he put the stethoscope on her belly and looked to the floor for what seemed forever.

Nellie wrung her hands. "How are they, Doctor?"

He pushed away and grabbed the silver chart. "You seem to be in good health, from all I can observe. But I'd like you to see your doctor. " He glanced at Lucy. "Rest up and take care of that baby." He tapped the pen on the chart and looked around the room. "Looks like you'll be in good hands."

"*Jah*, I am for sure." Lucy smiled at the nice but rushed doctor, feeling guilty for taking up his precious time on such a busy night.

He stopped at the door and talked to the nurse about prescriptions, which Lucy didn't think she needed. The nurse came in with forms to fill out and instructions concerning Lucy's throat. "You're ready to go. Just check out at the window." She paused. "If you feel up to it, Mrs. Wagner, I can arrange a time for you to see your husband."

Lucy shivered. "*Jah, danke.*" Her mind went numb, and she felt unable to speak or do anything. "What needs to be done?" It sounded cold coming out that way. Was it obvious, the way she'd said it?

"Someone needs to make an identification, but it doesn't have to be you if you're not comfortable." The nurse turned to pull the paper sheets from the exam table and get ready for the next patient while Lucy tried to make a decision.

"I might wait, if that's okay." Lucy didn't know what the typical procedure was, but then, nothing about their marriage was normal.

"Maybe tomorrow, when things have settled down. There are others here who can do that, if needed." The nurse finished sanitizing the area, and Lucy slipped away, wanting to leave as quickly as possible.

She whisked past Frieda and Rosy, with Nellie looking

on. She'd had enough, couldn't function anymore. The baby kicked when she stood still, watching Manny pacing across the waiting area. For whatever reason, she felt better just watching him roam the room from side to side, not having seen her yet. When he did, his dark eye caught hers and lightened against the fluorescent lights, but he didn't move.

Lucy took slow steps to the closest chair while Nellie, Rosy, and Frieda went to the admissions and checkout counter.

Manny sat next to her. "What did the doctor say?"

"Everything is fine." She twirled her hair self-consciously when she remembered she didn't have her *kapp*. She wanted to say much more, and probably would have, if they weren't sitting in a room full of strangers.

"That's *gut*, Lucy." He leaned over and put his elbows on his knees. "I'm so sorry." He looked at her.

"I don't have the courage to go down to that morgue." She looked away and then back to him. "Does that make me a bad person?"

"*Nee*, it means you'll do what you need to when you're able. No one knows when that is, only you." He sat back and offered his hand. Proper or not, she needed him. "I have a driver whenever you're ready to go. Where are you going?"

"To Frieda's, but not for long because I need to tend to the farm." It seemed nothing stopped on a farm—especially one as large as theirs.

"I can help with that. Stay at Frieda's for as long as you want to." He leaned back but kept his eyes on her. "That's something you don't need to worry about—especially with the damage and cleanup that will be going on. It's best you stay away until it's safe."

"*Danke*, Manny. You don't know how much that means to me." And as she looked into his eyes, Lucy felt a huge burden slowly slip away.

❧ *Chapter Thirteen* ❧

*L*ucy woke up slowly, feeling an exhaustion she hadn't known in a long time. Then she remembered. The fire. Sam. Even though her bed was warm, she shivered. She would have to go back to the morgue today and see him one last time. Perhaps Frieda or *Mamm* would go, and she could stay curled up in her new nest.

She sighed and flung the covers off. *Nee*, it was her responsibility, and she'd never shirked her duty before. She'd see this through too. The smell of bacon tickled her nose and made her mouth water. It felt strange not to be in her own *haus*. Not that she missed the farm. It comforted her to know Manny was watching over things there, but she couldn't expect him to do it for more than a few days. He had his own place to care for.

Sitting on the bed, she gathered the energy to put her feet on the wood floor and pulled her dress on. She noticed the calm that came over her when she realized she wouldn't be chastised or told she was ignorant, lazy, or dumb. There were times Sam would scold her for doing something that he'd asked her to do or tell her she'd done the task wrong. Every corner she turned seemed to be a dead end.

She walked down the hall to the room where *Mamm* had slept last night. She opened the door slightly to see her fast asleep and then left it cracked open in case she needed assistance. She had been discharged from the hospital in exchange for the promise that she would get a lot of rest.

The familiar creak on the stairs made her smile. This place was her refuge, and she relished it. There couldn't possibly be a better place for her to be than right there, right now.

When she stepped into the kitchen, each of the three women was at her own work station. Nellie cut up the ham, her hips swaying with the rhythm of her chopping. Frieda scrambled fluffy eggs to perfection, and Rosy pinched a little of this and that into a boiling pot, making some herbal remedy. The smells mixed together into a plethora of mouthwatering *gut* eats.

"Morning. How can I help?" She walked past Frieda, picked up a piece of ham, and stuck it in her mouth. It went down hard, a reminder that her throat still needed time to heal.

Frieda gave her a one-armed hug, careful not to use her messy hands. "How did you sleep?"

"*Wonderbar.*" She stopped her thoughts, feeling guilty for indulging in a good, long night of sleep when such a tragedy had brought her there. "*Mamm* is still sleeping, so she must have slept well too."

"I'm glad you're both here." Nellie brought over a plate of steaming eggs and toast with a sprinkle of ham. Then she sat next to Lucy with a plate of her own. "Come on, ladies, the food's getting cold."

Rosy brought two mugs of tea and then went to get two more. "This will calm the nerves. I don't know about all of you, but I'm still jittery." Rosy was always at least a little nervous it seemed.

The stairs creaked, and *Mamm* soon came through the

door. Lucy had never seen her in such disarray. Her hair was plastered on her neck, and her pajamas were beyond wrinkled, as if she'd slept in a knot. Her usual cutting eyes drooped with dark circles underneath.

"*Mamm*." Lucy leaned forward to stand, but Frieda put a hand on her arm. "You eat. I'll take care of her." She stood and walked over to Verna. "You look terrible."

Mamm's head moved slightly back as she focused on Frieda's face. "Well…" She frowned, maybe too tired to respond. She let Frieda help her to the table, where she accepted a cup of Rosy's tea. She took a sip and then another.

"You should go back to bed," Nellie offered as she took a bite of the eggs, encouraging the others to eat. "This ham is delicious. Is this from the Mullets' farm?"

Rosy sat down with her plate and nodded. "*Jah*, but I don't feel like eating."

Lucy stood before anyone could stop her and went upstairs to *Mamm's* room to get a brush and her *kapp*. She knew her *mamm* well enough to know that she wouldn't want to be seen without her head covered, even if it was with her own family in their kitchen. Then she went to Frieda's room to borrow a *kapp* for herself. It was shameful enough that Manny had seen her without one last night. She wouldn't let that happen again.

She was careful walking down the stairs, holding her belly. With one more month to go, she wondered how she could go about her usual chores. Planting her flower garden would be much more difficult this time around, but at least she could have one. Sam wouldn't let her plant flowers until the fruit and vegetables were showing above the dirt, and even then, the amount of room left for flowers was hardly worth the effort. But she did because she loved the beauty they brought to her ugly life.

She walked to *Mamm,* who sat with her eyes shut, sipping on her tea. Lucy sat behind her and started brushing her long, dark brown hair.

Mamm startled and turned to the side to smile at Lucy. "Are you and the baby well?" Her scratchy voice sounded the way Lucy's throat felt. She hesitated to ask her anything that would make her speak.

"We're fine. It's you I'm worried about. What happened to you last night?" Lucy had been scared to the point of almost getting angry for her *mamm* to leave her and go off doing who knows what. But there was surely a good explanation.

"You know what a light sleeper I am. I heard popping and a sort of sizzling sound coming from outside. So I got up to go look. The air was hot and thick with humidity. I knew something was wrong, but not enough to know what to do." Her eyes filled with tears, so foreign to Lucy that a lump developed in her own throat.

"Where did you go? I didn't see you anywhere." Lucy offered her some toast to dip in her tea, as she so often did.

"Just as I turned to go back inside to wake Sam and tell him about the noises, the silo exploded. The blast took me off my feet, but it was the hot fumes that caused the most pain. Thank the Lord I wasn't any farther from the *haus.* Before I knew it, I was in an ambulance going to the hospital." She closed her bloodshot eyes and took in a long breath. "My biggest concern was that I couldn't find you. I felt so helpless in that automobile taking me away from you."

Lucy had never heard her *mamm* talk this way and

wasn't sure what to say or do. *Mamm* must still be in shock to say such things. She twisted the hair in her hand and made good use of the few pins she had, unable to find any words to reply.

"Makes you appreciate life a little more and love on your family more often," Nellie said, looking at the floor.

Frieda picked at her food. None of them seemed to have any desire to eat, even though the food was delicious. The room was quiet except for Rosy tapping a fork on her plate as they all digested what had happened, and even more so, what could have happened.

A knock on the door brought them back, and Frieda got up to answer. Lucy felt the fear she was accustomed to whenever Sam came looking for her when she was gone too long. She cringed at the thought of the tongue-lashings he'd lay on her all the way home. Sometimes he'd made her walk beside the buggy. A couple times it was so hot that she'd collapsed and woken up in the buggy.

She tuned out the voices of the women around her. Her heart beat loudly in her ears, blocking out any other noise but the man at the door.

"Look who's here!" Frieda's usual expression calmed Lucy somewhat. She was never that jolly when it was Sam at the door. Lucy squeezed her eyes shut.

Sam's not here. He can't hurt you anymore.

The voice was not hers, but a calming man's voice. Her *daed*? Not exactly the same as his, but definitely a familiar, safe tone that slowly made her heart stop racing. When she looked up, Manny stared straight at her. They all did.

She put a hand to her forehead. "I'm not feeling well." She glanced up as Manny took off his hat. "I'm sorry—"

"No need to apologize. I just wanted to check in on you

ladies. How's everyone this morning?" Manny asked them all but still had his eye on Lucy.

"Tired but I can't complain."

One side of his lips turned up into a small smile.

"*Mamm* is the one to worry about."

"I'll be fine. It could be a lot worse." She set her empty mug on the table and looked into Manny's face. "Have you heard anything about what happened?"

Rosy stood, ready to keep the cups filled.

"An officer explained it to me. It comes down to the dry air and dust igniting a spark that can get hot enough to start a full-blown fire. It's not that unusual, but one on this scale seems to be. With a silo that big, it made for a mighty-size explosion."

It was unreal to hear them talking about the place where she'd lived for the last two years. It didn't seem possible that this had really happened. As much as she didn't want to, she might have to see the farm to believe it. With that would come all the bad memories, which seemed even worse now that she didn't have to live there. She had gotten in the habit of blocking it out of her mind. There was too much to process, and if she did, she thought surely she would disappear into a crack in the floor, unable to function.

Manny's eyes flickered back to Lucy. "When you feel up to it, I'll take you over to your farm. A few people are starting the cleanup. It'll take some time to get things cleared away, but I thought you might want to see what's going on."

Lucy tried not to look at him. She was too fragile, and he was everything she needed at that moment, but she couldn't accept. "I need to go to the hospital today."

All eyes went to her as the women were reminded of the responsibility Lucy had to take care of. "But I would like to go to the farm later. I don't know what I'll be up to just yet." She hated to be so weak and indecisive, but her emotions were unraveling at the sight of him, not to mention the thought of taking care of the huge mess ahead of her.

"Don't worry yourself about any of this. It will all get taken care of in due time. I just wanted to offer my help when you need me." He was done talking, but his eyes didn't move, and neither did Lucy's.

"You know you can't leave until we feed you, so pull up a seat." Frieda offered her chair and went to the stove to make him a plate.

Mamm stood, and he took her arm. "If you'll excuse me, I'm going back to bed. *Danke* for coming over, Manny. We'll be taking you up on your offer."

Rosy took over for him and headed for the stairs. "You're an angel, Manny Keim."

He grinned and took Rosy's chair next to Lucy. "I have to be honest. I do come for the food as well as the company."

Frieda let out one of her bellowing laughs. "Well, there's no shame in that."

"We're always glad to have you, Manny." Nellie went to help Frieda, but Lucy knew full well they would be listening.

Manny averted his eyes and fiddled his thumbs. "I hope I'm not bothering you by coming around." He tilted his head toward Frieda and Nellie. "You have plenty of help. I feel like I should be taking care of you…but you can tell me to jump in the lake whenever I become a nuisance."

Lucy laughed, hurting her throat, and she put a hand to her neck and reached for her cup.

He handed it to her. "See, I did it just there by making you laugh."

She took a drink of the lukewarm tea. "You could never be a nuisance, Manny."

"Get to know me a little better, and you'll change your mind." His grin made her smile. She was glad he had no idea of the demons she lived with.

Chapter Fourteen

As Manny walked to Lucy's farm, he couldn't get the vision out of his mind of Lucy in the ambulance the night before. Even more, he was embarrassed to admit, he couldn't forget the sight of her long, red hair tucked around her—a light color, like fall leaves, soft and pleasing to the eye. He shook his head; now was the worst time possible for him to be thinking such thoughts.

When he got to the *haus,* he switched gears and refocused on the task at hand, which was to take care of her farm. He wondered how Sam had gotten along doing everything by himself. He had only enough Holsteins to provide them with the milk they needed, and they didn't have much livestock. What Sam did have was crop. He'd had a lot of money in that silo, more than he could ever use. Manny wondered why he hadn't sold more of the precious grain and seed. From what he'd observed, they lived conservatively, in contrast to his income.

This was the time of day when the chores were done and breakfast was over, so there would be people stopping by to help clean up Lucy's farm until around noon. Not all were Amish; some from town came by to offer what they could, from physical work to meals and machines that would do the work of a dozen Amish men. Bishop Atlee was arriving today from the Amish community, where he spent a good deal of his time, to help decide what needed to be done and observe the situation. Manny wondered how he would respond to their using English machines. The locals deemed the area unsafe, which was why they'd stepped in. Manny understood both sides and was eager to learn what would be decided.

As he walked up the path to Lucy's, he heard a buggy approach. He waited to see who was coming up to the *haus*, as most went down the path that led to the silo, or what was left of it.

"Morning. You here to help out?"

Caleb's presence made Manny feel better. Not only would they be working side by side, making decisions together, but he could tell him about Lucy. He didn't know what to say or how to explain what was happening. If anyone could set him straight, it was Caleb, and he was one of the deacons, which could work to Manny's advantage to get things done around here.

Emma poked her head out from beside Caleb. "And we brought you food!" Emma was one of the most down-to-earth young women Manny knew. He thought a lot of her—especially at that moment, hearing she had food.

"You know you don't deserve her, right, Caleb?" Manny grinned and went around to Emma's side to help her down. She stumbled a little, and he maneuvered around her so she didn't lose her balance. "What did you make me?"

"Are you more interested in my cooking or me?" she teased and took the arm he offered. "I know how you like whoopee pie, so that's for dessert." She wagged a finger at him. "Not before." He'd been known to take a bite or two as soon as the pie was within reach.

"I can't promise anything, but I'll do my best." He slowed down to her leisurely pace and looked over at Caleb, who seemed overly happy today—strange, considering what they were there do to. "What are you smiling about?"

"Who, me? Just grateful for what I have and what's to come." He winked at Emma and took the basket from her. "You making good progress?" Caleb scanned the area, shading his eyes with one hand.

Manny heard the skepticism in Caleb's voice but didn't blame him for asking. "*Jah*, it doesn't look like it, but actually we are. I don't think anything can be salvaged to the point anyone could live here…at least not for a while…until the ground is restored and the debris hauled away."

The grass was torched black. So was the soil where acres of crop had been burned to the ground. Cornstalks were scattered in disarray, along with tobacco, wheat, and other crops. Large chunks of cement had been set aside in a heap so crews could get to the silo, which was almost ground level. The *haus* wasn't safe, and not much beyond the kitchen and mudroom still stood. As he looked at it now, quite a few areas were exposed, the main reason for any demolition. The job he hated the most was trying to salvage what they could to give to Lucy. He wondered how much she'd be able to take without opening wounds.

"That's such a waste. Sam was running an incredible farm here." Caleb stopped talking abruptly. "I'm sorry. I should be asking about Lucy and how she's dealing with all of this, and about Sam's funeral and all."

Manny gave Caleb an understanding nod. "Abram got caught up in the fire. He didn't make it to the hospital."

"Good man, Abram…" Caleb looked at the ground, and they all paused for a moment.

Manny cleared his throat. "It's hard to know the right

thing to say and do. When I offered to help Lucy look over the farm, I thought it would be giving information and helping to keep things organized, but the emotional end of this has been a lot harder than I thought. Most people want to know how to help Abram's family and Lucy—more than worry about this place. It seems to have become a sad memorial for what happened here, and no one seems to want it back the way it was." Maybe that didn't come out right, but Manny felt the need to tell someone what he had observed.

"You're doing what you can, and that's all that's expected of you. I'm sure Lucy really appreciates what you're doing here." Emma gave him a peck on the cheek. "You've always had a soft heart."

Manny shrugged, unsure how to accept what was meant to be a compliment. He didn't always believe what Emma said was true as she tried to lift his spirits, but in this case she was right. Manny's bleeding heart never seemed to cease, especially for someone like Lucy.

"Where's a good place for us to eat, Manny?" Emma scanned the area and stopped when she saw a picnic table in the middle of nowhere. "Where did that come from?"

"It's one of the few things that was salvaged. There are some personal items that were collected that you might want to give to Lucy." Manny was tempted to open the box marked with Lucy's last name and sift through her belongings but then stopped the thought. Something that wasn't right came over him when he thought of her, but try as he might, he couldn't keep the thoughts at bay. The more he learned about her and the battles she'd been through, the greater he felt the need to protect her.

She was shut up like a clam that he wanted to open, sure to find the pearl inside.

"Manny, come eat." Emma frowned and put her hands on her hips. "I think you're losing your hearing." She set down a plate filled with deviled eggs, minced-meat sandwiches, baked beans, and pie.

"This makes my mouth water just looking at it." After spending the last year alone, Manny had learned to appreciate whatever food he was given. Having someone cook for him was a real treat.

"I love feeding you, Manny."

"Hey!" Caleb shot back around a bite of his sandwich.

"I love to feed you too." Emma pecked Caleb on the cheek and poured them some fresh-squeezed lemonade. She put the jug in her basket and sat next to Caleb. "So what are you two going to work on today?"

Caleb looked over at the *haus*. "Looks like the *haus* has to be leveled pretty far down to the ground. Too bad. It was a nice one. Big too."

Emma nodded. "It appears that Sam had a lot of everything. I didn't realize how much until this all happened."

"Didn't seem like they had much company, with most of his family passing away." Caleb reached for another sandwich, and a chunk of minced meat plopped onto his pants.

Emma handed him a cloth napkin. "He was the oldest of a small family, right?"

"Think so. I only saw him on Sundays coming home after church meetings." Manny hadn't given Sam much thought. He knew little about him, as did most of the community. Sam had been one of the few who liked his privacy. He didn't talk much, and Manny couldn't remember ever seeing him smile. But then he hadn't been around him enough to make any judgments about him…until he met Lucy.

"If we tackle that pile of wooden slats, this place will be pretty much done." Caleb was scanning the mound of lumber that had once made a home.

Manny wondered how Lucy felt about losing her home. Devastated, he was sure. But was there also some sense of relief? She'd had something hanging over her head, something that might make her glad this place was no longer her home. He wished he could get her to open up and tell him everything he wanted to know.

"Let's get to it. Thanks for lunch, Emma." He kissed her on the top of the head and started clearing the table.

Emma put a hand on his. "Go on. I'll take care of this." She shooed him away and glanced at Caleb. "I'll be back before dinner. Manny, you're welcome to come over and eat with us. You'll be tired and hungry after you're done here." She put the rest of the utensils in a plastic bag and put them in her basket.

"You don't have to twist my arm."

Emma waved and got into the buggy, turned around, and went down the dirt path from Sam's *haus*. Manny put on his work gloves and started hauling charred beams and siding over to a pit they would use to burn the useless wood.

Caleb got the fire going, just big enough to do the job, and gave Manny a hand with the larger pieces. After about an hour, they decided to take a break and got out their water bottles, drinking to cool their parched throats.

Just as they were finishing up, a buggy that was starting to look familiar to Manny came down the lane. He pulled off his dirty gloves and tucked them into his pants, took off his straw hat, and ran a hand through his hair.

"You're primping like a girl." Caleb smiled over at him. "I take it that's Lucy."

Manny tried to ignore Caleb's remarks by keeping his eyes on the dirt road. "Hello." Manny took the horse's reins and then went to help her out of the buggy.

"Manny, Caleb, how's it going?" Her gaze wandered from what was left of the silo to the leveled *haus* that she had called her own for nearly two years' time. He thought he saw her eyes water, but she moved past him quickly enough that he couldn't tell for sure.

Caleb pointed to the *haus*. "We're almost done here. Once they get rid of what's left of the cement, we should be finished."

Manny tried a softer touch, wishing Caleb had been less direct. "How are you and the baby?"

"She's not kicking so much." Her face was strained and her forehead drawn.

"Maybe she's tired today." Manny wondered if that was a fool thing to say. He had enough experience from his cousins going through a dozen babies or more, but it still felt a little awkward to talk about with Lucy.

Her head lifted, and she stared at him. "Maybe so. It's a tight fit in there now too." She rubbed her belly and almost smiled at him, realizing she'd started thinking of the baby as a girl. What he'd said must have put her at ease.

"I brought you something to eat." She pulled a basket out of the buggy and plopped it on to the picnic table, which was getting good use.

Caleb glanced at Manny with a grin and then at Lucy. "Emma's coming down the road right now to pick me up for dinner. Thanks, though." He brushed himself off and started down the road, looking back once with a smile at Manny.

Manny was still full from lunch but couldn't say no to Lucy.

Chapter Fifteen

Lucy walked behind what was left of the barn, avoiding the chunks that looked like charcoal covering the ground around her. She found a tree stump—the only section of wood that wasn't torched.

The fields were half burnt; the rest wouldn't be enough to bother with. It would be the first year she'd ever had without a harvest. A strange and lonesome feeling came over her. This had become her hideaway, a place where she could disappear, at least for a while. Sam had never looked for her once the chores were done and his belly filled. She'd spend hours reading the Bible and books that some of the Amish bought from the local store, the ones that she wouldn't have to be ashamed of if the bishop found out about them. Sometimes she'd sit and watch the sun rise and glory in God's creation. And she felt safe, at least for a little while.

"Lucy." Manny's voice startled her back into reality, something she often did when Sam's boots would clunk down the cement floor of the barn. The noise gave her a minute to scatter to another area so he wouldn't know where she spent her quiet time. Lucy would poke her head out of one of the stalls and greet him in a casual way so he wouldn't suspect anything. A couple of times, he'd look past her into the stall but never said anything. She wondered what he'd do if he found out she'd spent hours there, reading and praying. Maybe he knew all along but didn't care enough to find out how she spent her time as long as she made his meals. She quickly stood and came through the stall. Manny was right in front of her. "Is it time?"

"*Jah*, are you ready for this?" He stared into her eyes, waiting for her answer.

"Are you ever ready for something like this?" She'd already put it off a couple of days. No more excuses. She should have gone to the morgue first thing, but after bringing Manny a bite to eat, she couldn't pass up his offer to take her once he finished up at her farm.

"I suppose not. It's one of those things that you're glad you did, once it's over." He looked down at his dark pants and blue shirt. "I tried to wash up a little. I did the best I could."

"You look fine." She gave him a small smile.

There was nothing she wanted more than for this to be over. It would bring back a lot of pain and sadness, not like typical mourning. With Sam, it was mental anguish that grabbed her from the beginning of every day until she laid her head down each night. She would not have the emotions people commonly have when one of their family members has died. For Lucy, it would be a sense of freedom, a long-awaited release from the prison that held her captive.

Manny helped her up and into the buggy, and as he walked around to the other side, she thought of how much she was coming to depend on him. He was the last to offer, but the first one she accepted to take her into town. She could use the excuse that all the others who might have taken her were women who could drive a buggy just as well as most men, but she felt better going into town with a man. There were times when the locals made her a bit uncomfortable, staring or teasing about her clothes or form of transportation. And Lucy knew she was more reclusive than was healthy. It came from pressure Sam created, but also she wasn't comfortable leaving the farm except to visit Frieda.

Before she knew it, the pleasant drive had ended, and they were at the edge of the growing township. "Lucy." Manny's tone was soft as velvet, pulling her out of the circles racing in her head. "What's on your mind?"

"I guess you could say I'm not too comfortable going into town." She looked both ways, watching the sidewalks full of people walking past too many stores for her to count. The town of Lititz had become a popular tourist site and was often congested, especially on the weekends.

"No worries. I come down often for supplies. You get used to it after a while." He turned to her with a confidence she couldn't imagine feeling in the bustle of the busy town. The brick chocolate factory sported a huge banner celebrating their hundredth anniversary. Tourists carried bags full of Amish trinkets and asked them for a photograph, which was against Amish culture. Lucy wondered why there was such fascination with her people but didn't bother to ask when a young girl waved her camera as they rode by and snapped a picture just in time to capture Lucy's face.

"It can be an irritation at times. Sorry." Manny put a hand on hers and then pulled away.

"How much farther?" Lucy had had enough, and they were only halfway through town.

When they arrived, Lucy's stomach flipped. She hurried out of the buggy, accepting Manny's assistance, and walked into a new wing of the hospital. She filled out a form, and Lucy gave the clerk her birth certificate for identification. That's when her chest started to flutter. This place and what she was there for, plus all the people, made her heart pound.

Manny guided her along. "How about some water?" He pulled her aside to a water fountain and kept hold of her arm.

The cool water gave her some relief, as did his touch against her arm. "*Danke.*"

"Better?" He smiled, studying her face. "Are you sure you're up to this?" His concern seemed to be in sync with her to the point she felt he knew everything she was feeling and going through. But of course, he'd endured this with Glenda not much more than a year ago. How selfish of her not to think of his emotions at such a time.

"You don't need to go any farther." She couldn't let him. Not after being so insensitive to the grief that was probably fresh in his heart.

He pursed his lips. "You'll be all right?" He gave her a sideways glance as if not believing her.

"*Jah*, I want to do this alone." That was a lie; she wanted him there more than anything, not only because he understood, but also just because it was Manny.

"Okay, then, take your time. We're not in a hurry." He pointed to a gray plastic chair. "I'll be right here."

Lucy wanted to grab his hand and pull him into the cold steel room she was about to enter, but she resisted. She had been selfish enough. She closed her eyes and whispered a prayer for strength before walking into the room.

The attendant greeted her. "This way." He walked past what looked like large drawers. The chill in the air fit the quiet, colorless room, which smelled of sanitizer. He slowed by one of the pale gray metal drawers, pulled out a clipboard, checked the numbers, and pulled open the drawer. He pulled down the sheet and turned to her. "Mrs. Wagner, I'll give you a few minutes." He stepped away.

Lucy held a hand up. "Will you stay for a moment?" She didn't know whether she could do this, didn't want to, but it was her last duty as wife to this man. The cold chilled her heart and mind into a place of submission, a feeling she knew too well. She would never again allow a man she didn't love to be in her life. She'd most likely be a widow for the rest of her days. It didn't matter.

The attendant, his eyebrows raised, hadn't moved and looked firmly into her eyes. "Do you want me to take you out, ma'am?"

Lucy shook her head. She wanted Manny in there now. She was foolish to be so proud as to leave him in the waiting area. But she didn't want the attendant to leave her there alone. "Can I...?" She covered her arms due to the cold or maybe her nerves, probably both. "Bring in—?"

He cut her off. "Your friend. I'll get him for you." With that he turned on his heel and headed for the door, leaving her alone.

She panicked and glanced down at Sam. Anxiety overtook her as she tried to suck in air. His naked body, covered with blisters, black, charred down to his waist, seemed small and insignificant. There was no longer anything to fear from this man. The apprehension she'd once felt when seeing him was sifting away by slow degrees.

A soft touch to her shoulder made her shudder. She turned to see Manny standing behind her. "I'm ready to go." She instinctively took Manny's hand and led him out of the sterile room and out the front door. Once out-side she stopped and took in the fresh air and sunshine. Adrenaline rushed through her, filling her with strength and a sense of liberation she'd never felt before. The experience had been awful, but she needed to know Sam was really gone.

Manny gave her a questioning look.

"I'm fine. I really am. *Danke* for coming in when you did. It just hit me wrong, seeing him that way, but it's okay. I'm okay." Lucy realized how fast she was rambling on and lifted her eyes to Manny's.

He smiled a half-grin with his head cocked to one side. "I've never heard you say so much at one time." His smile widened. "I didn't expect you to be sad, but not this, either."

"It probably isn't respectful of me, but no one can judge me. No one knows what I've been through." As soon as she said it out loud, she wanted to take it back. That was too much to tell anyone, especially Manny. The others couldn't understand what she'd been through and didn't need to know. It was over, and that was all that mattered.

"I'm not judging you, Lucy." He looked straight at her. "And I do have some idea of what you've been through."

Staring at him in that moment, Lucy felt vulnerable. For some reason she felt he did understand, but that brought her no comfort. She didn't want someone around who felt sorry for her or wondered why things happened the way they did or questioned her doing or not doing something in the situation.

She shook her head, with all the thoughts rushing through her mind. "I know. I didn't mean you. I know you wouldn't judge." She looked down at her black boots. "I don't think you'd ever do anything to hurt me, Manny."

The tears welled up, and she felt the urge to push them away. Sam would scold her when she got emotional, so she'd learned to keep them at bay. She looked up to see Manny's face consumed with concern, his eyes wide and lips parted as if he wanted to speak but could not find words.

She paused for a moment, waiting for him to break the silence. She could almost feel his affection for her, but not enough to take the chance she might be wrong. Besides, she couldn't be carrying on about him when her husband had just passed. Later today Sam's body would be taken to her *mammi*'s home, and visitors would come to pay their respects. The funeral tomorrow would last all day long as she received food and guests. Thank goodness she'd have her *mamm*, *mammi*, Rosy, and Nellie there with her. A little voice in her head told her who she wanted there the most, but it was so wrong that she shoved it from her mind.

"*Danke* for bringing me, Manny." She took slow steps to the buggy with him close behind.

"It seemed only right to take you. I can walk back home."

Lucy was amazed at how much comfort she felt sitting next to him.

"Luce?" Manny stared at her, waiting for a reply.

If he only knew my thoughts.

Her face heated just thinking about it, the silliness of it…it circled around in her head. He was a nice man who understood what she'd gone through. That was all there was to it.

"You called me Luce." She smiled. It was nice and made her feel a little better.

"*Jah.* I guess I did. Your *mammi* calls you that."

"She knows it will get my attention."

"It worked for me." He studied her for a moment. "Are you ready to go or is there something else you need to do?"

"*Nee*, I should get back and start preparations for tomorrow."

"Okay, then, let me help you." He assisted her into the buggy, and they started for home.

She didn't even want to think about it yet—all the work to get ready, and people coming in and out all day long as she stood and accepted condolences for a man she was glad to put to rest. What a horrible person she was, and an even worse wife. She must be, for the Lord to give her such a horrible man as a husband. But she had paid her penance now, put up with the words, so many harsh things said. Lucy wondered whether she would ever rid herself of Sam's voice.

"Hey there. I'm losing you again." Manny's soft voice was barely audible, but enough to bring her back into the moment. "Are you all right?"

"*Nee*, I'm tired. So very tired." She sighed and wished she could sprawl out and rest. The baby felt so tight in her belly, she wondered whether it would be sooner than the midwife had told her. Everything seemed like more of an effort.

"Lucy, get comfortable on the bench seat. "You're exhausted. I can see it in your eyes. Understandably, you've had a stressful day." He looked down at her belly. "And you're working twice as hard." He smiled.

"She does take a lot out of me these days. Seems she's growing faster than ever." Sometimes, Lucy wondered whether there were two little ones in there. Not having an ultrasound or regular checkups meant anything could be going on, and she wouldn't know until she delivered. She closed her eyes and rested her head against the side of the buggy, letting the sound of the horse's hooves hitting the street lull her into a restless sleep.

Chapter Sixteen

The next morning the crunch of wagon wheels over the pebbled dirt made Lucy open her eyes. Deep in prayer, she'd been unaware of her surroundings. She needed to confess, ask countless questions, and plead for direction. But honestly it was strength she needed more than anything—strength for the baby and for her own health—to make it through this day.

She walked downstairs and watched Manny and Caleb unload the six-sided coffin and then the "rough coffin," the outer wooden structure that the coffin was lowered into before the whole thing went into the open grave.

"*Danke.*" She motioned with one hand toward the funeral director. His reply was only a nod, which Lucy appreciated, as she didn't have the energy to say a single word more.

Manny eyed her as they took the wooden box into the great room of Frieda's *haus*. She had taken full advantage of her *mammi's haus,* for which she would always be grateful. Going through these events without *Mammi* would have been unimaginable. Lucy felt sure she would go back to where her extended family lived at some point, but after all she'd been through, this felt more and more like her own *haus.*

The men arranged the coffin, carefully setting it on a wooden stand. Lucy took slow steps until she stood within touching distance. Sam's pasty, gaunt face was as white as the simple undergarments he was wearing.

Caleb shifted his eyes. "Do you want these doors open or closed? Visitors will be coming by after seeing the wagon with the coffin."

Lucy looked up and shrugged. "That's fine. But what I really need is for you to pray for this day and the funeral tomorrow to be over and done." She paused. "I know that sounds terrible, but I can't ask you to pray for something that's not in my heart." She tried to smile.

Caleb didn't say a word to her; he just nodded and closed his eyes to pray. His words were as kind and thoughtful as she'd expected them to be, and her soul felt a little lighter.

"*Danke*. It helps to have the words to take me through the day." She twined her fingers with Manny's. Proper or not, she needed to feel the warmth of his hand before the first of the mourners came. She imagined those in the community would come in and out all evening.

A moment later Lucy pulled away and glanced at the two wooden pieces on hinges that folded down to reveal the body from the chest up. Sam's eyes were shut, but she could picture the coldness in them. How selfishly glad she was not to see the coldness in those piercing eyes anymore.

She was ashamed of these conflicting thoughts, but only for a moment. Sam had made her feel worthless, no matter what she thought or did. His power over her had died with him. She resolved to be stronger and not let anyone tell her what kind of person she was or what her worth was.

Manny came up behind her and put a hand on her shoulder. "Maybe this is enough for now."

She felt his hot breath against her cheek, and her nerve

grew a little stronger. She nodded. "Can you shut those?" She pointed to the two pieces of wood, not wanting to be face-to-face with Sam ever again.

Manny obliged and then led her out the door. "Let the others do everything today. You know they want to, and it's easier on you if they take some of the burden."

She smiled, and he frowned.

"I didn't expect to see a smile from you today. Am I that interesting?" A smile flickered on his lips and then disappeared as if he didn't feel it was appropriate.

Most others would be consoling her for a life event she had secretly been hoping for. She'd been a hypocrite long enough. It was time to admit the truth to someone, and who better than Manny? He knew some of it already, but probably didn't know what to do with the awkward situation. Now that Lucy thought about it, neither did she.

"Do you think I'm awful for not mourning as I should?" There, she'd said it. But she didn't feel any better. Her confession put a damper on his effort to lighten the conversation. But she knew well enough that he would understand. He always seemed to.

"There is a time and place for everything, even in your case. It's not honest to pretend something you're not, but not everyone understands what you've been through—especially those from other communities." The twinkle in his blue eye warned her to watch her actions and words. No matter how much had happened to get her to this place, she needed to remember that counsel, today of all days.

"I understand, and *danke* for telling me. I've had a difficult time working through my emotions anyway, but now, with the way everything happened, sometimes I feel responsible." She was saying too much and probably not making any sense, but she had to get it off her chest. She guessed she was telling him because he was safe, not part of anything that happened, oblivious to what her life had really been like.

But when she looked up and into his eyes, she rose to attention. His jaw tightened, and his face was intense. "Don't ever say that, Lucy. Nothing was your fault." He took her hand, which caught her attention. "If anything, *he* should have gotten you and his baby out of danger's way, not tried to save his precious farm." He squeezed his eyes shut. "Sorry, I get angry when I think of how things could have gone."

"Manny, you ready?" Caleb gave them both a serious stare. Lucy knew they shouldn't be so close, whispering, with him holding her hand. But it was innocent. Caleb would know that.

As Manny and Caleb left, Rosy walked into the room and glanced at the coffin. She asked, "Does Sam's family know about his death? Do you think anyone will come?"

"He never spoke much of his family. I haven't heard word from anyone." Lucy wouldn't know what to do with Sam's family, people she'd never met. Certainly she wouldn't recognize them if she saw them.

Frieda walked in with a determined look on her face with the *Budget* newspaper in hand. "They were up north, but not that far. I had heard Sam's first wife speak about how she only saw them one time at a wedding and never again."

Rosy took the newspaper and started reading the latest news from all over the country. Word had gotten around over the past few days, and the *Budget* was a sure way to share news of any kind, especially about a death. "Well, I see the announcement, but if they have read it, they haven't made contact that we know of, *jah*?"

"I doubt they would. Unfriendly people, or maybe they were just not happy with Sam for some reason." Frieda turned to Lucy. "You never heard a word about them, eh?"

"*Nee*, I asked only once, and he gave me a look I never forgot. From then on neither of us talked about his family." The more she opened up about these things, the more she realized how bad it truly was. She had gotten used to it, brainwashed, maybe, into believing this life was what she deserved.

"Well, I guess we wait and see what happens tonight and tomorrow. They might show up." Rosy's positive attitude was a good balance with Frieda's negative one, and Lucy was somewhere in the middle. She couldn't imagine not going to a sibling's funeral, but then this was Sam. Nothing surprised her when it came to him.

Lucy went to bed early, exhausted yet again. By the time she woke up next morning the *haus* was buzzing with commotion. Lucy quickly dressed and prepared herself mentally for the day. It was a strange experience to go to a funeral for someone she disliked. And what was worse, that person was her husband.

A knock on her door vaulted her into the moment.

Her *mamm* stood at her door attired in black from head to toe. "Are you ready?" She took a step back. "You look fine. Grab your shawl. You never know if you might get a chill sometime during the day. Unpredictable weather..."

She went on, but Lucy's thoughts were elsewhere. Few had come to view the body. Only the deacon, minister, and bishop came, along with a couple who offered their condolences. It made her realize how isolated she and Sam were, and she was saddened at the time she'd lost. As she walked through the great room with Verna, she saw a sprinkle of people there with others still coming in.

"This is what community is about," *Mamm* told Nellie, who had a dull look on her face. Due to the day's meaning, their community was faithful to one another.

"*Jah*, there have been a few others. I'm glad to see that, no matter what the circumstances."

Nellie was right—there was no denying it—but it was an awkward situation for her any way you looked at it. Lucy didn't know these people like she should. A visit to church once a week with little conversation wasn't what it should have been, but Sam was set on doing his own farming and attending church like a revolving door. But this was how it was supposed to be. This was what she'd been missing.

Benches were set up in rows that filled Frieda's large home for visitors after the funeral. Minister Eben followed the bishop, with the deacons behind them. "My condolences" and "I'm sorry" were repeated over and over again. Lucy was glad to have her *mamm* by her side accepting support from many people Lucy didn't know. They most definitely didn't know her, simply because she hadn't been allowed to reach out to them, to join any quilting bees or do anything with the other women in the community.

After the last amen, the mourners filed out. The buggies were filled and following one after another. When they arrived, each was marked with chalk, and the coffin was placed in the hearse.

Her *mamm* walked up and stood beside. "By the way,

Manny and Caleb took care of dressing Sam. I thought you'd want to know."

Lucy lost her breath for a moment. "*Danke*. I'd forgotten. How sad there is no family for Sam." She dropped her hands on her lap, actually feeling a bit of remorse for the man.

Her *mamm* looked out the window without batting an eye. "I'd say I'm sorry, but that would be an untruth, so I won't. We reap what we sow."

As they made their way behind the horse-drawn carriage, Lucy felt the solemn, impressive weight of buggies following them. She was touched that these people had helped after the explosion and now were showing their presence during this humbling time in her life. She wondered how much influence her *mamm* and *mammi* had in it, but it didn't matter. Her heart fairly burst with gratitude as her body warmed with the thought.

When they reached the cemetery, the grave was already dug, and all was quiet. The bishop usually read a hymn, but he was under the weather, so Minister Eben gave the sermon, ashes to ashes and dust to dust. No one spoke of the dead. The Creation story was told, and the resurrection of the dead—all good thoughts—but nothing stirred Lucy's heart, and her guilt got the best of her.

She drank in every word. She could feel the ice melting away...that guard she'd put up to keep her safe from Sam. Maybe at some point she could forgive him, and the ice would turn to harmless water and trickle away.

"Amazing Grace" filled the air even though it was prayed in silence. Then all separated back to their buggies to share a meal at Frieda's *haus*.

Lucy caught Manny's eye as he strolled along with

Emma. He nodded and kept walking. Then she realized her *mamm* was talking to her, and she appreciated what she was saying.

Mamm straightened her black *kapp*. "These are the times we are reminded that our focus should not be so much on this world as on what is yet to come."

∽ *Chapter Seventeen* ∽

A *blast of hot fire shot down the aisle. Horses whinnied, stamping to get out of the stable that would become their coffin. Lucy leaned forward, tried to run, but her feet were heavy as sacks of corn. She felt her belly, aching with child. This couldn't be happening again. She didn't have the strength. The baby didn't either.*

A rafter broke away. The supporting beam came crashing down as spitting fire hit the cement. Lucy turned to run, leaving the animals. How could she? It was her and the baby or the livestock. Hot tears streaked her face. A blur ahead formed into a man's figure, standing tall, but he didn't move. She screamed to him, but he didn't respond. The fire drew close, enveloping him until he turned to ash.

Lucy sat up, leaning on her elbows, unable to sit straight with the babe. Putting her hands on either side of her, she pushed herself up and looked around. *Mamm* was first in her room. She instinctively put a hand on hers.

"You're all right. Take a breath." *Mamm* squeezed her hand, and she let the air out of her lungs. Frieda, Rosy, and Nellie came in one by one. *Mamm* stared into Lucy's eyes and then looked her over from head to toe.

"Bad dream, honey?" Rosy's soft voice drew Lucy in.

Lucy rubbed her throat. The lingering ache sent her mind going through the entire dream all over again.

Rosy stroked her hand. "You need some warm herbal tea."

"Nothing hot." Her voice sounded perfectly fine. It was all in her head. That horrible dream had not only taken her back to that horrid night but also mystified her with the man, as if he was waiting for her or for something to happen. The bigger question was who was he? Sam came to mind. It was too easy to accuse him, but it fit, with him standing there waiting for her to be swallowed by the fire.

Frieda moved in closer. "You're sweating. Must have been some dream."

Nellie gave Frieda a cold cloth to wipe Lucy's forehead. "And you're pale as a ghost." She tilted her head and smiled. "What can we get you, hon?"

"Just some water is fine." She couldn't help but think of Manny. As much as she loved her *mammi* and her friends, all she wanted was to be with him. The dream had exhausted her as if she'd actually lived it. Her heartbeat finally slowed to a normal rhythm.

"I'll make you some cold tea." Rosy gave her a comforting smile and walked out with Nellie and Verna. Lucy leaned back as she listened to their boots tapping on the hardwood floor.

She watched Frieda bustle around in her room, pulling up the shades and rummaging in a dresser drawer for a hanky. She walked over and handed it to Lucy. "Why did you move here with me, *Mammi*?"

Mammi stopped and gave her a long look. "When you left to live with that godforsaken man—"

"*Mammi*, you shouldn't speak about Sam that way." She sighed, knowing what a hypocrite she was. She didn't say it out loud, and *Mammi* was bold enough to say what was on her mind, but they were no different.

Mammi glanced over at her. "You hated that man, and

who wouldn't, the way he treated you?" She pressed her palms together and laid them on her lap as if to keep in the anger she must be fighting, judging by the color her cheeks were turning.

"We shouldn't talk of the dead this way." Lucy bent her head in hopes she would stop. It wasn't that anything she was saying wasn't true, just that it went against everything their religion told them to do.

"The whole community let out a deep breath when Sam died, I can promise you that. We're all so polite, no one would ever say it, but you know as well as I do that he won't be missed." *Mammi* let out a breath through her nose and pursed her lips. "I'd say I'm sorry, but I'm not, and I will not lie."

Lucy didn't know what to say. There wasn't a word *Mammi* said that Lucy hadn't thought at one time or another, but to hear it out loud, with Sam only gone for a few days…it just didn't sit well. "It's disrespectful, *Mammi*."

"You're a good wife even to the end and past it." *Mammi* leaned over and kissed her forehead. "You're a better person than me. For that matter, better than most." She stood and peered down at Lucy. "How about some toast with my plum jam?"

"That sounds *gut*."

It didn't help—nothing did—but she knew her *mammi* wanted to do something to make her feel better. They all did. If she was to follow custom, there would be a year of mourning, lasting until long after her baby was born. She had *Mammi*, Rosy, and Nellie, but that wasn't what her heart desired. Lucy wanted to be normal, or at least as normal as possible, which meant having a husband. She didn't remember what that felt like or looked like any-more. The life she'd lived those couple of years with Sam seemed like an eternity, full of strife.

The thought of raising a child with no father in the pic-ture saddened her. Her *daed* would be a wonderful *dawdi*, but with his health, how often would he see the baby? Once she starting thinking about it, what did she have to keep her here? Now that Sam was gone, she and her *mammi* could go back to Tennessee.

"*Mammi.*"

She stopped at the door and turned back to Lucy.

"Would you ever want to go back to Tennessee?"

Mammi turned completely around and took a few steps closer to her. "I hadn't given it much thought; we've settled in here pretty well." She studied Lucy's eyes. "I should say that *I* have. Maybe you will too, now that things are dif-ferent." She lifted a finger and closed one eye. "You might have more of a reason to stay than you think."

Lucy nodded, feeling defeated, but her spirits lifted at the thought of being with her sisters. Maybe she was being too hasty. She would miss the girls, friendships that her *mammi* had made with two incredible women. But even though they had each other, it seemed lonely not to have a husband to grow old with.

"Lucy!" Her *mamm*'s voice carried up the stairs. "You have company."

The *tap-tap* of her shoes coming closer had Lucy won-dering who had come to call. Nellie peeked her head through the door. "Manny's here." She smiled brightly and then glanced at Frieda. "Well, help her get ready."

Mammi jumped to attention and started gathering Lucy's clothes. When she got to the bed, she turned sideways at Lucy. "I told you there might be a reason to stay."

Lucy's jaw dropped. Why these three women thought she and Manny could ever get together she didn't know. He'd been over mourning for some time and surely had someone in mind. The added attention he'd given her was just his way. He was kind to everyone she'd ever seen him with. She would not get her hopes up, and she wouldn't let the girls either. It wasn't proper. Not right now, anyway.

"What are you daydreaming about?" Verna had come back upstairs, and her voice brought Lucy back to a reality she didn't want to be in. As much as she wanted to see Manny, maybe it was best not to grow any more attached to him than she already was.

"I'm not feeling well. It might be best if he stops by another time." She played with a stray thread on the quilt.

"Your color's coming back. Are you sure? He's such a nice young man." Her *mamm*'s comment surprised her a little. But then Manny did have a way of gaining people's approval, and that wasn't easy when it came to *Mamm*.

Lucy heard boots scuffing up the stairs. She reached for her *kapp,* but it was gone. She'd lost her borrowed one from *Mammi*. Pushing herself to the side of the bed, she grabbed the robe lying at the foot of the bed and put it on. When she turned to stand, Manny's hand came around and handed something to her.

"Looking for this?" He grinned and held up the *kapp.* "One of the police officers came by your place today, and he gave it to me. This is yours, *jah*?"

"*Danke*" was all she could get out of her mouth. She suddenly felt embarrassed, always seeming like the fragile woman at a man's mercy. But considering the circumstances, it seemed rare to catch her when she didn't need nursing from some horrific life event or another.

He held his hat loosely with one hand and stared at her with smiling eyes. "Are you ill?" His docile voice soothed her—so different than what she was used to.

"*Nee.*" Her eyes flickered up to his quickly. She felt like a young girl complaining about a bad dream to her *daed.* "A dream is all." She waved a hand as if it was nothing, even though it had made her heart pound and her body sweat. It was as if she'd seen a ghost, that frame of a man standing in the fire.

She went about putting her *kapp* on and setting the pins in place. She felt him watching her. She was covered just as much as her dress would cover her, and fixing her hair didn't really matter at this point. Her *mamm* had offered for him to come up and see her without question, which was uncharacteristic of her. But since the fire, *Mamm* had seemed to change. Her prickliness was down to stubs. Even her eyes seemed softer. Lucy supposed that sort of thing could happen when something so horrendous happens to a person. Even her choice of name to call her *mamm* had changed. Maybe now she would feel more like a *mamm* to Lucy instead of Verna.

Manny's voice brought her away from her thoughts and over to him. "Where were you just now?" She paused a moment to look at the blond wisps falling into his eyes—one eye blue, the other brown—glistening in the sun rising outside the window. He stood a head taller than her, tilting his head slightly, just enough to look directly at her.

"In a scary place." Talking about it made her feel worse. The negative feelings she bottled up kept her from forgiving Sam and moving on. She took in a rough breath and turned away, not wanting him to leave but not wanting to go through the whole thing again—not this soon. The hope was that this dream was telling her Sam was truly gone. But she held her story inside.

"I gotta go. I just wanted to give that to you." When he blinked, she glanced at his eyes, thinking how unique this man was in many ways. First in his appearance, but also his patience, love for God, and compassion, which were not usually seen in a man of his emotional strength.

Lucy fumbled for an excuse to make him stay. "Aren't you hungry?"

"*Nee*, and I have chores to finish."

"Did it set you back, taking care of Sam's place?" She squeezed her eyes shut. She'd always called it his, but she knew it sounded strange. And she hated using his name. It was if it brought him back to life in her mind, summoned by her guilt at not mourning for him.

He shook his head. "Don't you worry about it, not one bit." He glanced at her belly and then back up to her face. "I'm just sorry you don't have your own *haus* to live in, even if you're taken care of here." He grinned and waved toward the kitchen.

"*Jah*, but now and again I do miss my own things and time alone." She'd been more alone living with Sam than she ever wanted to be. She couldn't help wondering what it would be like to live with a man like Manny. "*Danke* for coming by."

"It's no bother." He pursed his lips and turned to leave.

Lucy scrambled for something to say that would keep him there, even for just a second more. "I'd like to go by and see the place."

He stopped instantly and turned back to her. "I can

come by after lunch and pick you up." His eyes widened as he waited for her reply, making her feel a little better about how eager she was when there was any excuse to spend time with him.

"I'll see you later then." He lifted one side of his lips into a grin and walked out the door.

Lucy dressed and went downstairs just as Abner came to the door, his face not as jolly as usual, his fuzzy gray brows drawn tight.

Rosy greeted him, "*Gut* morning."

"It's not so *gut*." He held up a letter and turned to *Mamm* and then to Lucy. "This is for you." He stuck out the envelope, but neither of them took it.

Verna slowly moved her hand forward, and Abner handed it to her. She flipped it over to see Fannie's handwriting. Lucy watched her rip open the envelope and close her eyes as tears fell down her cheeks.

"*Mamm*?" When her *mamm* didn't respond, Lucy took the letter, but she couldn't make sense of the words.

She looked at Abner, knowing he often read their mail. "What is it, Abner?"

Abner's face turned pink. "It's your *daed*."

ᦼ Chapter Eighteen ᦾ

As Lucy woke to a streak of sunlight coming through her window, her first thought was of her *daed*. She got up and dressed. She wished she could talk to him, hear his voice, and know he heard hers. There was no other voice she wanted to hear. Lucy would go to the bishop and ask to use the community phone, if only her *daed* might answer.

The door creaked, and *Mamm* walked in. Her ashen face told Lucy she'd had a rough night, much as Lucy did most of the time now, with the baby growing and the image of the silo blast waking her in the middle of the night. Now she would worry about her *daed* too.

"How did you sleep?" Verna's voice was unsteady, so different than what Lucy remembered from her childhood.

"The thought of one more tragedy is…just too much." Lucy looked down at her apron and picked at the edging. She was more worried about her *mamm* than herself or even her *daed*. The illness the doctor had described wouldn't get better. With no timeline to go by, they prayed and waited. What would *Mamm* do without him?

Mamm tried to be strong, wiping a tear away hastily, not meeting Lucy's eyes. "I have to go back." She slowly turned to Lucy. "I wanted to stay until the baby came." Her face tightened as if in physical pain, and Lucy knew her emotions were getting the best of her.

The automatic response she'd always given her *mamm* was "*Jah*, me too." The proper response, but it was far from the truth. This time with her *mamm*—especially with her *daed* not there—seemed to have brought the two of them closer.

"I wanted you to stay." She nodded. "I really did." Her eyes swelled with tears, and *Mamm* wiped them away. "I worry I may never see my *daed* again."

Mamm shook her head. "We'll continue to hope that he can fight through this, at least a little longer."

Lucy glanced down at her bulging belly. "How I wish he'd see my baby."

Mamm made an effort to grin. "He would like to have a little redhead grandbaby like you and him. The only two in the family." She laid a hand on Lucy's belly. "This little one might make three."

"Sorry to barge in." *Mammi* rapped on the door as she walked in. "We'll figure out how to get you to the bus station." None of them spoke. *Mammi* finally nodded. "No hurry. Today, tomorrow…whatever suits you, Verna." *Mammi*'s eyes shifted from *Mamm* to Lucy. Being such a talkative woman, her *mammi* didn't know what to do with the silence. She let out a grunt. "You two act like you're going to a funeral."

Lucy's eyes widened at her *mammi*'s brash comment. She usually took her in stride, but now with this involving her *daed*? Lucy glanced over at her *mamm,* who seemed to have gained her composure. She sat up straight, stoic, her eyes on her *mamm*. So maybe *Mammi*'s words were helping.

"Ezra's still kicking, and you should appreciate every second of it, Verna. You know how hard it was for you when your *daed* passed." She said it like a question, but clearly it was an answer. "The doc told us he was gonna go long after his time actually came."

She wagged a finger. "Make some special memories together, and stop mourning when there's still life to be lived."

Lucy turned her head toward *Mamm*, hoping she was taking it the right way. But then *Mammi* was Verna's *mamm*. This blunt way of talking was what she'd grown up with, and she was much the same way. "I think she might be right."

Mamm slowly bobbed her head with her eyes fixed on Lucy's belly. "*Jah*, I believe you are, *Mamm*." She stood and ran her hands over her apron, a habit Lucy was accustomed to. "Downstairs." She held out a hand to Lucy, and they walked down the creaky stairs.

"What's this all about?" *Mammi*'s patience had worn thin.

"We're cooking something"

Mamm was as good a cook as she was with everything. She had a secret ingredient for most everything she made, but it did no good to ask her what it was; she said she'd go to her grave with the information. "Blueberry French toast."

Frieda gasped, causing Rosy and Nellie to pay attention. Lucy smiled warmly, knowing how rare this was. Lucy's older sisters had surely figured out how to cook like their *mamm*, but this particular dish was extra special. It was bittersweet watching her *mamm* cook, the women peering in to catch every move. This was what her *daed* would want them to be doing—doing what they did best, making people happy with fine food.

Nellie cut the bread into cubes while Rosy chopped

the cream cheese. *Mammi* went down to the cellar to get some canned blueberries, and Lucy cracked the eggs, stirring them as she watched this group of godly women she loved dearly.

"Milk…that's the last ingredient," *Mamm* said as she looked around in the cooler. She stood. "Half a cup, but we need two cups." She held up the glass jar.

"There are some bottles in the cooler in the barn." Lucy started for the door.

Rosy grabbed her hand. "Let me get it. You rest."

Lucy chuckled. "All I did was scramble eggs. Besides, I could use the walk."

When she looked around the room, they were making quick glances her way. "I'm fine." She wondered whether she looked more pregnant today and laughed at the thought. This baby did seem to be taking up every bit of room, stretching her belly to an uncomfortable level. No sooner did she get to the barn than she heard the door creak.

"I don't need any help," she sang as she closed the cooler, balancing two bottles of milk in her hands. When she turned, Manny was walking toward her. She felt her cheeks heat a little but could blame that on her hormones. "Manny?"

"Didn't mean to surprise you. You okay?" He studied her the way everyone else was doing.

She waited for his suggestion or opinion about what she should or shouldn't be eating or drinking, whether she should be resting, even though she was the only one who knew what was good for her and the baby. Still, living with those precious women enabled her to do much less than living on Sam's farm.

When it came to Manny, though, she'd agree to anything if it meant being with him. She felt he'd know just the right thing to say regarding her *daed*. The thought of him tightened her heart.

"*Jah*, just worried about my *daed*." She watched his head tilt to the side as he listened to her. "I want to talk to him. It's been so long since I've heard his voice." She stopped to hold back the emotions. She missed everyone back home and wished she could be there with all of them in that moment, when her *daed* needed them the most.

Lucy wished she was more like Fannie, able to talk their *daed* into or out of whatever he asked her to do. Fannie was strong-willed and feisty at times, which got her into trouble but also got her what she wanted. Like when she married a beau to her liking, while Lucy was passed over time and again, ending up with Sam. Lucy knew her *daed* worried about her with Sam; even without being around much, he knew something was amiss.

"I thought it might do you good to talk with Minister Eben, if for nothing else but to ask for prayers your *daed*'s way." He quickly held up a hand. "I don't want to overstep my ground. I know your *mamm* will have her own plans."

Lucy almost smiled. "You're getting to know her pretty well."

"She's hard to ignore." He grinned.

Lucy nodded her agreement. "She's not herself. In all my days I've never seen her so…weak, and…well, kind."

"Hard times can bring out the best or worst in a person. Sounds like she's taking the high road."

"I think it's more the hard road. With me in my…condition…and *Daed* in poor health, it seems to have softened her. It makes me realize how glad I am that she came to visit, even if it was only for a short time." Lucy suddenly saw spots dancing around and closed her eyes.

"Lucy!" She heard Manny's voice, but she didn't want to open her eyes. She felt lightheaded and worried she might fall to the ground. Then strong hands wrapped around her shoulders, holding her up. "Look at me, Lucy."

She blinked several times and looked into Manny's eyes. He glanced down at her lips and then drew his head back, helping her gain her balance. "Come sit down. Are you all right?"

She sat on a wooden bench and caught her breath. "I don't know what got into me." She lifted her eyes to his. "But I'm fine now." His face was inches from hers as he knelt in front of her. She couldn't help but enjoy the comfort she felt when she was with him, hearing him talk or watching him smile at her. Everything about him pleased her in what seemed to be every way.

"*Jah*? Well, you don't look as good as you might feel." He moved back as if he realized what he said might offend her. "I mean, you don't look yourself. You should get some rest."

She managed a quiet giggle. "I just got up not too long ago."

"Well, maybe you should still try to rest." He chuckled. "Really, you just got up?"

She nodded and wrinkled her nose. "Don't tease. This little one takes up all my energy."

"It must be a boy." Manny grinned.

"No doubt. But I'm hoping for a girl."

"*Jah*, why is that? Don't you have enough women in your family? I think you need some boys to even things out." He stood and looked down at her.

"That's the problem. I don't know what to do with a boy."

He crossed his arms over his chest. "Well, I could help you with that. I would have enjoyed having a boy to play baseball with and help me with the farm." He closed his eyes and tilted his face up toward the rising sun. "There's no better time of the day than right now. Nature comes alive when the sun touches the earth."

"Hmm." Lucy looked over at the bright beams of light and closed her eyes, letting the warmth touch her face. "I believe you're right."

"About having a boy or the sun?" He smirked.

"About a lot of things. *Mamm* is taking the high road. Nothing is too hard for her. Letting her guard down and not trying to control me has brought us closer together."

"I've noticed that myself." His eyes rested on hers.

"Actually, I think it came from you." She tried to look away but couldn't. She wished she could say more without exposing the feelings springing up inside her. "Manny—"

"*Jah?*" His voice was just above a whisper and his eyes grew wider.

"I think we should go to the *haus*." She didn't want to. Her lips were moving and she was speaking, but her mind was thinking something completely different. She wanted to stay just as she was, with him looking at her the way he was right at that moment. She knew she wasn't beautiful or shapely, and her hair was a dull mix of red, but she felt beautiful in his eyes. It was as if he could look through her flaws and insecurities too.

"I suppose so." He offered his hand to help her up. "There is something I thought I should ask you about."

He held her arm as she walked, as if expecting her to lose her balance again. "*Jah*, what's that?"

"That day I took you into town." He paused. "And you

were in a quiet place in the barn. I noticed you had some things in there."

"You mean the reading material?" Besides the Bible, she also had a diary but was sure it was burned to ashes. The books she could do without as well, though she hated to see them go.

"*Jah*, there wasn't much left. Everything was ashes. But I did find this." He pulled out an engraved piece of metal and handed it to her. "It's in pretty bad shape. I couldn't make out what it was at first, but thought you might want it anyway."

Her bottom lip trembled as he laid the object in the palm of her hand. "*Danke*, Manny."

He nodded but didn't ask what it was, having the good sense to know it was something special.

"My *daed* gave it to me. It's a little bookmark he made out of a horseshoe." She swallowed the lump in her throat. "He knew how much I like to read and let me hide away once my chores were done."

"Sounds like a *gut* man."

"*Jah*, he is." She took quick steps, not wanting to see his face as she responded. "You remind me of him." And for the first time Lucy admitted to herself that she was helplessly falling in love with this man.

~ Chapter Nineteen ~

For a second time within the last month Lucy stood waiting for an unfamiliar buggy to stop in front of *Mammi*'s home.

Jeremiah hopped out and greeted her. "Mornin'." He tipped his hat in a gentlemanly way and proceeded over to the other side of the buggy. The door popped open, causing him to move back. The passenger's dress covered a long leg that stuck out, and then another. Jeremiah tried to take a step forward, but a delicate hand waved him away.

"Sure you don't want some help out?" Jeremiah kept his distance. Lucy knew who the visitor was. He had that look on his face folks always did, especially men, when she was around them. The independent touch of not accepting his chivalry confirmed it as she handed him his pay and then stepped out of the buggy. Her shapely figure made Lucy wonder if her own body would ever be the same again. She'd never been one to notice or care, but after being away from her sister for so long, she noticed more about her family back home.

"Fannie!" Lucy waddled as quickly as she could but stopped short when Fannie hopped down and stared at her.

She dropped her bag and held out a finger. "Don't you dare rush over here!" Her jaw dropped. "I can't believe how big you are!"

Lucy laughed out loud. She knew her sister meant it in

an endearing way. It was surely a shock to see her so much larger than her usual thin frame. As they embraced, Lucy felt safe and content. Just being near her sister brought her back to the person she was, loved and cared for by a sister who truly knew everything about her—her favorite food and flower, and they both liked the same hymn, but differed on color. Lucy favored more subtle hues, while Fannie liked vibrant colors.

"It's so good to see you!" Fannie pulled back and frowned. "But you look ex*haus*ted." She brushed away a wayward lock of Lucy's hair and looked into her eyes. "Should I be sorry about Sam?"

Lucy flinched. It wasn't a question to be asked, but she would respond properly. "Fannie!"

"I won't apologize. He was an awful man." She tucked her arm around Lucy's and tugged her along slowly. "I'll never forgive *Mamm* for getting you two together."

"I'd tell you not to talk that way, but I know it won't do any good." Lucy had heard so many comments about him that she really didn't know what to say anymore. Most said what was expected, with the exception of those who were more truthful, but none were as blunt as Fannie. "How was the ride?"

"No small talk. How many days do you have?" She nodded to Lucy's bulging middle. Fannie was all business—one thing Lucy loved about her sister, as it wasn't a quality she had, and she needed it at a time like this. Not only would Fannie help her get prepared, but she would also make sure everyone around her would be helpful or not be involved. She was even more forward than their *mamm*, but in a positive, non-condescending way. Lucy was curious whether Fannie would notice the difference in *Mamm*'s behavior. She wondered whether it was just a passing thing, and their *mamm* would soon be her old self again.

"I have a little over a month left."

Fannie groaned. "You need to be more specific. When was the doctor here last?"

"There is no doctor."

Fannie paused. "All right, the midwife, then."

"The closest midwife lives in a different community."

"So let's get her over here to see you." She rested her fists on her hips, and Lucy knew she was getting frustrated. *Mamm* wasn't one to ask for help, even if it was birthing a baby. She was very confident she could do anything a midwife could do. Lucy tended to agree.

"She lives pretty far away, a good day's buggy drive. *Mamm* said we'd wait until closer to the day to fetch her if needed."

"What's the point in that if she's that far?" Fannie shook her head. There would definitely be some tension while both of them were there. But *Mamm* would be leaving soon, so Lucy told herself to take it in stride. She was so close to having this baby born, there was nothing that could keep that from happening, not even her strong-willed mother and sister.

Fannie brushed her hand over her *kapp*, rearranged it, and adjusted the pins—a gesture that told Lucy she was frustrated. She would do her best to keep the peace, but no one listened to her anyway, so it probably wouldn't do much good. Regardless, Lucy couldn't be happier to have her sister by her side again.

"Well, I see what my first project is." They started walking again. "To find you a doctor."

"We'll be lucky if *Mamm* agrees to a midwife, let alone a doctor." To be honest, Lucy wasn't comfortable with a doctor, but she would hate for a ride to keep her from getting help if she needed it during delivery. Although some of the Amish were starting to use doctor's methods, most of their community hadn't, unless it was absolutely necessary due to a serious matter.

Fannie squinted at her sideways. "*Mamm*'s concerns should be on *Daed*. That's why I'm here—so she can go take care of things at home, and I will take care of you two." She smiled and put a hand on Lucy's belly. "I'm so excited for you. But I have to admit that I am torn when I see my sisters with their babies." She looked down at the road, unusually silent for a moment. "I love being an auntie. I'll especially enjoy it with your little one."

Fannie was much prettier than Lucy but was humble about her looks, as most Amish women would be. But she did have the potential to be downright beautiful. Lucy only dreamed young men might glance at her the way their eyes lingered on Fannie. But Fannie didn't give them any attention—except the one who broke her heart, creating her reluctance to let a man court her. "You'll come home once the baby is born, won't you?"

"I asked *Mammi*, and she said she'd stay, along with the girls. She has a good life here. I've grown so fond of them, I don't know if I could leave now."

"I can't imagine they'd be more like family than your own," Fannie said, a hint of resentment in her voice. Lucy expected she'd feel much the same if she hadn't experienced the threesome in action.

"And Nellie and Rosy are like second aunts to me. You

just have to meet them, and then you'll lose that stubborn face." Fannie, she was sure, would fit right in.

Fannie stopped in front of *Mammi's haus*, her eyes gliding over the place Lucy called home. "What you must have gone through when that silo blew." Fannie stared at the ground and then looked straight up as if picturing it in her mind. "When I first heard, I started hating Sam ever more—"

"How can you blame him?"

But Lucy herself had done so, over and over again. If anything had happened to the baby, she didn't know what she'd have done. There was no way, at least not in her thinking, that she could ever have forgiven him for leaving her and tending to his precious farm. Maybe it wasn't rational, but it had run through her mind many times.

Lucy had prayed thanksgiving for the child growing inside her more than ever after that fire. And Sam was no longer there for her to fear. She'd felt the tension melt away soon after the funeral. More shame always loomed for her to take on, but because of the baby she could keep the guilt away.

Fannie was watching her as she gathered her thoughts. "The same way you blame him. Don't deny it. But I don't expect you to say it out loud, either." At times Lucy felt her sister could read her mind and that she could do the same in return. Although they were very different, they seemed to complete a whole.

"Why are you so bitter? It happened to me, not you." Lucy knew the answer but had to ask in hopes Fannie would stop taking about this. She didn't have the strength to be angry or sad anymore.

Fannie let out a breath. "I guess it's the way I deal with the whole thing. From the day you first met him until right at this moment, I still can't forgive myself for not stepping in before you ever said, 'I do.'"

Those weren't the words Lucy had expected to hear. Being taken under her sister's wing had always been a good and positive thing, but at the moment Lucy felt for the first time that maybe this time it wasn't. As she looked back, she realized she had grown inwardly. She'd had to in order to survive. Although she avoided his hurtful tongue and threats of physical harm, she had built a shield to protect herself and, even more, her baby. "You don't need to be my protector anymore, big sister." She smiled to show her she meant it, and Fannie gave her one slow nod.

"I don't know if I'm ready to give that up just yet," she said, rocking back and forth.

"Someone's coming this way." Lucy held a hand up and let her face drop. She wasn't ready to tell her sister about Manny. She was trying her best to hold back any feelings she had for him. It wouldn't be acceptable, even if things were different. She had months yet to wait before even considering marrying again, and that would happen only if the bishop granted her the request. She was relieved when she realized it wasn't Manny.

"*Mammi!*" Fannie walked quickly to the approaching buggy. The buggy stopped, and Fannie gave her *mammi* an embrace then turned to hug *Mamm*. It would feel like a small family reunion—one she wished her *daed* could be a part of.

Lucy waited for them to come closer. She felt like a heifer, waddling around. The talk she'd had with Fannie worried her a little. She'd made Tennessee sound more important than necessary. Her baby would be just fine in *Mammi*'s home, getting all the love and attention she needed.

Mamm gestured to Lucy. "Come around."

It was almost as much work to get up and into the buggy as it was to walk, but she was tired from standing, so she accepted the short ride to the *haus*. "Where have you two been? I thought sure you'd be here when Fannie got here."

Mamm clasped Lucy's hand. "I'm sure you're glad to have your sister here." *Mamm* understood in a way, but the bond between Lucy and Fannie wasn't something their *mamm* had the pleasure to experience. Her bullheaded pride made a close relationship difficult. It seemed only their *daed* could fill that void.

"*Jah*, it's been much too long."

Mammi kept her eyes on the road, not making eye contact with anyone. "I was just telling Fannie, I found an old quilt I've been meaning to mend while she's here. Your *mamm* will be leaving soon, so let's work on it while all of us are together."

Working on these quilts often made Lucy think about her babe. She found herself making plans in her head, especially about the name. As much as she wanted a girl, she thought it would be nice to have a namesake for her *daed*. It was all in *Gott*'s hands.

"Where did this mysterious quilt come from?"

"It's one I made for your *dawdi*." *Mammi* kept her eyes forward, leaving a heavy silence in the air.

Lucy glanced over at Fannie, who was unusually quiet. There was something in *Mammi*'s tone that seemed serious or maybe it was emotional. One made sense to her, but the other didn't.

"You all right, *Mammi*?" Fannie lifted her eyes to hers

and waited. It took *Mammi* a moment, but she finally spoke.

"I hadn't thought about this quilt for ages…not until the baby…and now that Fannie's here along with your *mamm*, I think *Gott* was giving us something that will tie us together for the short time we all have." *Mammi*'s cheeks were pink, and her voice wasn't as loud. Whatever this quilt was, it meant a lot to her.

Once in the *haus* and Fannie had settled in, they pulled the quilting frame away from the wall and began the process to repair and revive the old quilt. They carefully looked it over for holes, frayed threads, rough edges, and moth damage. Then they repaired loose seams by turning them over, using a fine thread for better strength before adding pieces to the top of the quilt where it was most worn. When they had worked for an hour or so, it was time to prepare dinner.

"Verna, Fannie, you two go on. Rosy and Nellie will be here soon to help." *Mammi* kept working on the quilt, not looking away for a moment.

When Lucy also started to stand, *Mammi* held up a hand. "I've been meaning to tell you about your *dawdi*."

Lucy sat back down. She didn't know her *dawdi*. He had passed away before she was born, and *Mammi* didn't talk about him much. "What is it, *Mammi*?"

"I see the conflict in your eyes, worried about raising the baby without a husband. But I have to tell you, Luce. *Gott* knows what's best; I know that much is true. But it took something tragic to happen for me to understand that." She lifted a piece of thread and snipped it off with her teeth.

"I do worry. But I am relieved that Sam won't be raising

my child." She looked up when *Mammi* did. She wanted to see her unguarded reaction to those words. She knew better than to feel bad about it. It was for the best, for everyone involved.

"Your *dawdi* was a weak man, the opposite of what you had with Sam, but just as difficult."

Lucy couldn't picture her *mammi* with a weak man, but then maybe it was what kept them together, opposites complementing each other. "I can't imagine that."

"He meant well, worked hard, but when the woman has a stronger personality, that makes things hard for a wife, especially an Amish one. He died young, and sometimes I feel the blame for that." She grunted. "Not that I did anything unkind; I just didn't have much respect for the man...Now that I think about it, he probably didn't have much respect for me."

Lucy laid her hands on the small area in her lap. "I'm the weak one?" She whispered. She might as well admit it. She understood what her *mammi* was referring to. It did surprise Lucy that she would marry someone so unlike her *daed*.

"*Nee!* You have a strong spirit. I just want you to know that, and no matter what anyone says, you do what your heart tells you to do. Your *dawdi* and I had a decent life together. But I want you to have more. You can give your babe a good life without a husband, but *Gott* may have a different plan." She patted Lucy's cheek and pointed with the needle. "Do you see that block right there?" It was a square with no name or symbol like most of the others had.

Lucy nodded.

"That's the square I have under your family tree." Lucy

turned her head to see the quilt from *Mammi*'s point of view. There were four blue squares and one pink.

"What does it mean?"

"I know you said you want a girl, but from what I created all those years ago, I have always thought you'd have boys, lots of boys."

Mammi's words caused Lucy's heart to leap. At that moment she realized that because of Sam, she had buried her desire to have a happy home filled with a large family. Talking with *Mammi* had caused her to hope again. She wondered if her dream could ever come true. Immediately, one image came to her mind: Manny.

Chapter Twenty

Manny stood in the mudroom stock still. He'd come to see Lucy but was now watching an argument between her *mamm* and another woman who must be Lucy's sister. The younger woman looked too similar for him not to assume this was a family relation. The two arguing were both attractive and obviously strongheaded. They both continued to feed off each other's comments, with no hope of reconciliation. Manny thought it best to get Lucy's attention and slip outside.

Lucy sat at the table, oblivious to Manny watching her. The only time either her sister or Verna looked her way was if they wanted her to validate what they were saying. Lucy would shake her head or shrug with hands lifted. Her wide eyes and hunched posture made it seem like she was trying to disappear. He decided to step in and get her out of the uncomfortable situation.

"Morning, ladies." He took a step closer to test the waters. "How are we today?"

Lucy whipped her head around to look at him. Her shoulders softened, and she gave him a tired smile.

Fannie rubbed the back of her neck, and Verna cleared her throat. "Manny, would you like some breakfast?" Verna didn't miss a beat as she walked to the kitchen as if nothing had happened. "I was about to make some pancakes." She turned around to look at him. "I can add blueberries, if you like."

"I doubt there are any left for picking." The tall young woman crossed her arms over her chest and stared at Lucy's *mamm,* who ignored her and started cracking eggs emphatically. The sister took a step closer and held out her hand. "Hello, I'm Fannie, Lucy's sister." Manny wasn't used to pumping a woman's hand but did so anyway.

"It's a pleasure. You can call me Manny." The tension was still so thick, he just had to slice it. He wasn't used to loud, arguing tongues. Though his family sulked at times, they didn't say hurtful words. But these were strong, outspoken women, something he wasn't used to. It was probably what drew him to Lucy. She was one who would tell him her thoughts, but not harshly. "Is everyone all right?"

"Actually, *nee.*" Fannie's arms folded over her chest again, and her eyes moved toward Verna. "You see, my *mamm* and I don't agree often, and unfortunately you got caught in the midst of one of our conversations."

"Well then, we'll leave you two alone to work things out, and I'll see if I can't find those blueberries." He caught Lucy's eye and couldn't help but grin when she stood, ready to bolt out the door. He could feel the relief he saw in her eyes. "Do you know of a good blueberry patch close by?"

"*Jah,* of course. Come with me." As she passed by her *mamm* and sister, Lucy grabbed a basket off the counter. Manny was glad she didn't stop walking. It would be easy to get caught up in helping, to stay in the kitchen and cook. Not only would it be awkward to be in the middle of a family argument, but he couldn't talk to Lucy about what was on his mind.

When they got outside, Lucy stopped and let out a long breath. "You have the best timing, Manny!"

"I guess so." The women's voices grew louder once again, so Manny started walking.

Lucy glanced back at the door as her cheeks grew slightly pink. "They're not always like this. It's extra hard right now with my *daed*'s health and the baby coming soon. They're both doers, and they can't do anything right now but wait."

Manny nodded and kept a slow step beside her. Neither of them was in a hurry, and he was content just to be by her side. He had a lot on his mind and didn't know whether he should share his thoughts with her now amid all the ruckus going on. As he glanced over his shoulder toward the *haus,* he debated whether to talk of anything serious. It might be nice to just enjoy the warm sun on their faces while picking berries together. "How are you doing?"

"My body is ready, but not my mind. It's overwhelming to think of raising this little one alone." She held up a hand before he could reply. "I know you're thinking that because I have a dozen women around me, I don't have anything to worry about, but ultimately this is my baby, no one else's. I'm solely responsible for the little one. Dressing, sleeping, feeding, and not to mention keeping her in good health."

She stopped for a moment, and he noticed her scar. He had gotten used to seeing the light pink color, but something was different about it. Was the color fading? Was the scar smaller? But when he thought about it, he wondered whether it was simply because she wasn't trying to hide it like she used to.

Lucy looked over at him and immediately covered her cheek when she noticed he was staring.

"I didn't mean to stare. But believe me, I'm used to it

myself." He pointed to his blue eye and then his brown one. "It's funny how people stare, isn't it?"

She smiled and dropped her hand to her side. "You usually don't…at least, not to me."

"It doesn't matter to me. If anything, I think it makes you more interesting." That was true, but he hadn't thought he'd ever tell her and hoped he hadn't offended her.

"I guess we're both misfits." She gave him a bright smile, so he knew she was okay talking about the subject. "It's changed over the last few months." She wrinkled her forehead in thought. "Or so it seems, anyway."

"Either way, it's what makes you special. You just don't like to stand out for any reason." He watched her intently to see how she was accepting his words.

"*Jah*. I don't, but it doesn't seem as important as it used to when…he was around." She looked straight ahead.

"He still bothers you?" He was digging deep now, and maybe it was out of line, but he wanted to know what she was going through. It hadn't been that long since he'd met her, and he was amazed at how his feelings for her had grown. The two of them had a lot in common, and she had always responded openly to him, so he thought he was safe with the question.

"*Jah*, he does still bother me. Some days I expect him to walk through the back door." She cringed and looked over at a large green bush spotted with berries. "Here's a good blueberry bush."

They were almost a month too late for many of them to pick. Most were dark blue, overly ripe. He walked around to the back of the large bush where the sun was not as intense. "There are quite a few back here." He pointed to them as she walked to where he was standing.

"All we need is a few to put on the pancakes. This should be more than enough. If nothing else, it was a good excuse to take a walk." She didn't look at him as she said it, but he detected a smile before she bent down to pick some berries from near the bottom. When she tried to stand, she stopped and put down a hand to lift herself up. He grabbed her by the arm and helped her.

"*Danke*, I didn't realize how hard it's become to stand up."

He chuckled. "I think you're more pregnant than you realize. It might be time for you to just rest until the baby comes."

She started shaking her head before he could finish the sentence. "That would make the time go too slowly. And besides, I couldn't let everyone wait on me day and night."

He shook his head. As meek as Lucy was, she was just as stubborn. "Then you leave me no choice."

"And what's that?" She stopped picking and put one fist on her hip.

"To be your personal escort." The adrenaline began to flow just thinking about what he had planned to say to her. Excuses started springing up before he could stop and think through a single one.

"Manny?"

Her sweet voice broke the string of words bouncing around in his mind, and he let out a long cleansing breath.

"Are you all right?"

He wiped the sweat from his brow and nodded. "I'm…fine." With the moment gone, he decided it must not be the right time. Nothing good could come from the anxiety he'd just felt. It had to be *Gott*'s time, and he would have to wait. To distract her from his strange behavior, he took a few steps away and grabbed a handful of lilac. He came back and handed them to her. "I get a little out of sorts when I'm around you."

She had taken a long whiff of the purple flowers and now looked up at him. "What do you mean?" Her face tightened as if concerned.

"Not in a bad way. I'm not sure what I feel." His eyes met hers. "What about you?" There it was, out there, at least a little something to find out how they felt about each other. But her expression concerned him. Either he had taken her off guard or she didn't like the question.

"I like to be with you, Manny." She opened her mouth but then shut it as if she'd bitten her tongue.

That was a good start but not quite what he wanted to hear. On the other hand, he wasn't giving any better answers.

"I do too." He was relieved when she smiled and took in another deep smell of the flowers. Then she started for the *haus*.

He took their basket and followed her, not sure whether there was anything else he could say at this point. His original reason for visiting her this morning was to talk about the future, but her hands were full, and her mind was on the baby, as it should be. He could wait.

When they got closer to the *haus,* the voices of her *mamm* and sister were still raised but not quite as badly as before. "What are they upset about?"

"*Mamm* is in torn between my *daed* and me. Fannie is upset that *mamm* doesn't think she can take care of me while she goes home to take care of *Daed*."

"So what's the answer?"

"My *daed*'s a gentle man, but if he were here, he would

put a stop to their bickering and tell them what was to be done, and that would be it." She sighed. "I wish he was here right now."

The wheels started turning, and Manny justified getting a little outside help. "Would a phone call suffice?"

Lucy lifted her brows and nodded once. "*Jah*, if the bishop agrees."

Manny wasn't particularly looking forward to asking permission for Lucy to use the phone, but technically Deacon Ruben could give him the nod. Manny knew from personal experience that the bishop doesn't easily bend the rules. Even when Glenda's life was at stake, the bishop wouldn't bend the rules to accept the *Englischer*'s way of treating cancer. It was probably futile now for Manny to think that yet another round of chemo would have saved Glenda's life, but he felt the decision should have been his and no one else's. In the end the doctor confirmed that chemo would not have helped, but the bishop's reaction was still something Manny struggled to forgive.

"All right, then, I'll talk to the deacon." He watched as her eyes filled with tears.

She wiped them away as quickly as they came. "*Danke*, Manny." She pressed her lips together as if to keep more words unsaid.

"I didn't mean to upset you." He let Lucy get herself together. "Even if it is for a good reason, I don't want to be known for making a pregnant woman cry." He grinned.

She laughed through the tears and nodded. "Don't worry. I won't tell anyone." Then she put a hand on his shoulder. "It would mean a lot to me to hear my *daed*'s voice about now. I haven't talked to him in weeks. And the letters are sparse, with him feeling poorly."

"Well, it's time to talk to him again then. It'll be good for all of you." He started walking, holding onto her elbow. She was out of sorts, and he didn't want her to stumble. "As a matter of fact, after I walk you to the *haus,* I'll head over to Deacon Ruben's."

She nodded, seemingly overwhelmed by the sequence of events that had just taken place. The unusual small talk between them helped make the walk back seem a little shorter. But when they got to the *haus,* Verna was flipping pancakes so furiously, it was a sure bet she and Fannie had gone head-to-head again. Before anyone got a word in edgewise, Manny announced he was going to set up their use of the phone.

"Fannie and I had just decided the same thing." Verna wiped her hands on her apron and turned off the stove. She stormed out with Manny and Lucy following. When they got to the barn, Fannie had the buggy hitched up and was about to take the driver's seat. Verna grunted and got in the back with Lucy.

Manny wasn't about to sit shotgun. There were some things he wouldn't do, and this was one of them. Fannie and he stood staring at each other until she let out a sigh and moved over. He climbed in, and they were on their way. The drive wasn't far, but it seemed longer due to the tension between Verna and Fannie. Manny knew not to ask, and Lucy didn't utter a peep.

"Here we are, ladies." He set the brake and hopped out to help Lucy, and then took the lead up to Ruben's *haus.* "How was the ride?" he asked as Verna and Fannie started in again.

"We don't all need to be here," Fannie said offhandedly but directing the comment to her *mamm.*

Verna glanced over her shoulder. "You don't have to be here for this nonsense, Manny."

"*Nee*, but it turns out I'm here, so I may as well stay." Once he knew Lucy had a moment with her *daed*, he'd bow out. This was too much for him and for Lucy, in his opinion.

As soon as the deacon opened the door, Verna and Fannie started in. He held up a hand. "Ladies, please step inside." He winked at Lucy and took her hand. "You look radiant, Lucy."

Lucy smiled slightly and then leaned closer to him. "I'm sorry for this. I just want a moment on the phone with my *daed*, is all."

The deacon grinned. "Then that's what we'll do straight away." He nodded to Manny. "I'm so very glad you're here, Manny. Will you distract Verna and Fannie, and I'll take care of Lucy."

"Most definitely. *Danke* for stepping in." He went over to the two women, who were being greeted by Ruben's wife, and Manny joined the conversation. He watched as Ruben took Lucy by the hand and spoke briefly with her. Then he directed her to the office where he worked and gave her permission to use the phone. Time seemed to stall, which was good for Lucy, but not so much for Manny. The one good thing was that Verna and Fannie had to be polite to each other while in the deacon's home.

When Lucy finally came out of the office, her face was relaxed and her color was good. She walked over with ease but let Ruben do the talking.

"He was in good spirits, but not able to talk long. He did have a question for you both." He gestured to Fannie and Verna."

They both grinned, waiting.

"What was it?" Verna asked.

"He asked if he had to come down here in order for you two to get along." The deacon said, waiting as they looked at each other and then back to him.

Verna grunted. "He's not in good enough health." She waved a hand as if to dismiss the suggestion.

"I believe that's his point, Verna, Fannie." Ruben looked from one to the other. "Did he make himself clear?"

They both nodded like unruly schoolchildren being scolded. "*Jah*, he did," Fannie said, shaking her head as if disgusted with herself.

"Are you going to get along, ladies?" Ruben asked them as his wife walked into the room with some coffee and peach pie. They both nodded as Ruben ushered Lucy to the table and pulled out her chair. "There we are. Manny, are you hungry?"

Manny had started grinning as soon as the deacon told them what Lucy's *daed* had said. "Starving. How about you, Lucy?" He was still smiling as he sat down next to her.

She looked over at him with wide eyes, obviously still absorbing what had just taken place. "*Jah*, I believe I am."

He squeezed her hand and then picked up his fork, looking forward to a bite of peach pie in some peace and quiet.

Chapter Twenty-One

*J*f Lucy hadn't been so uncomfortable, she wouldn't have agreed to have the midwife come to check on her. Her belly felt stretched to the limit. The only way her *mamm* would leave was if she had the last word. *Mamm* was insulted that Fannie had asked the midwife to come, but neither was surprised that they didn't agree. Both women had their own way of "helping" Lucy along with her pregnancy, whether Lucy liked it or not. It didn't bother her enough to complain or add her own advice. She was just glad they were there with her.

Rosy brought Lucy a cup of tea and sat down next to her on a kitchen chair. "Chamomile. It will help calm your nerves."

"Who says I'm nervous?" But she was. She just didn't like admitting it, which made it seem more real. Only a few more weeks and she wouldn't have to wake up to an uncomfortable night of sleep, backaches, and using the outhouse constantly. She felt her body had aged, worn out over the months. She couldn't imagine how women had half-a-dozen children or more. She dropped her head and stopped complaining, thankful she wasn't going through this with Sam. Then she added a prayer of forgiveness. He was the *daed* of her child after all.

"Someone's here." Nellie had been watching through the window and now stood. She glanced back when *Mamm* walked into the kitchen. "Midwife has arrived."

BETH SHRIVER

Lucy hoped her *mamm* would behave herself. There were no guarantees, but it didn't hurt to hope. Maybe this would give her *mamm* a little more confidence in someone other than herself, since she wouldn't likely be here for the birth of the baby. Her *daed*'s unexpected spring of energy to set them all straight the other day seemed to have made everyone a little more open to suggestions. How she wished he were here with her now.

Mamm crossed her arms over her chest with a straight face. She looked serious, but not as stricken as Lucy expected her to be. *Daed* giving her such a firm direction must have settled her down a bit. The last thing anyone wanted, including her, was to get him upset.

When the door opened, Lucy leaned to one side to see who was there. To her surprise, she heard a man's voice. Must be a neighbor, or Manny, she secretly hoped. Lucy wondered what it would be like to have a man be the one taking care of her. She didn't think it likely—not in a world of women midwives.

She grew more curious with each passing minute. "Who is it?" She didn't want to get up until she had to but couldn't abide not knowing who was there.

A handsome, blonde-haired man walked into the kitchen. "You must be Lucy." He glanced at her middle and then to her face. He set down his bag on the table and pulled out a stethoscope. "I'm Doctor Daniel Kauffman." He placed the cold scope on her chest and held up a finger when she started to speak.

Lucy waited until he was done moving the metal disk from place to place and had just opened her mouth when Fannie stepped in. "*Hallo.* We were expecting a midwife."

"Yes, your father called and asked for me...which was surprising...but I'm willing to be your practitioner."

"Willing? You're willing to be our doctor?" Fannie was obviously annoyed, but there was also a gleam in her eyes. She always did like a challenge, especially with men. She was a smart one who could keep the conversation going—the more so if it was something she was passionate about, like her sister.

Without hesitation the doctor took out a glass tube and long piece of elastic and directed his attention toward Lucy. "Have you come in contact with anyone with chicken pox, the flu, or rubella?"

"The Zehr boy came down with the pox." Manny walked into the room, answering his question. After taking one look at the goings-on, he turned around and left.

"Are you immune?" He wrapped the elastic around her arm and nodded toward Fannie to hand him the cotton and syringe by his bag. She frowned but did as he directed and watched as he drew a vial of blood.

"*Jah*, she's had the chicken pox and been around the others." Her *mamm* answered. *Mamm* was watching his every move, but not with her usual puckered face. She seemed to be making sure he was doing what he was supposed to, but with favor, if Lucy was reading her correctly.

"My *daed* called you?" Lucy finally got a word in edgewise. It was a good distraction from all the prodding and poking. Although his bedside manner wasn't the best, he seemed to be confident about what he was doing, and he could handle her sister.

"Yes, I met your father years ago when I was speaking to the community in Tennessee." He took out a rubber instrument and tapped her *knee*. He stuck out his bottom lip and tapped the other knee. "Any itching, dizziness, or heavy breathing?" He pulled out a small flashlight and looked in her eyes, one after the other.

"*Nee*. Do you always ask this many questions?"

"Yes. You have swelling in your face and around your eyes, hands, and ankles. How much weight have you gained during your pregnancy?"

"She eats like a bird, always has," *Mamm* cut in. "What are you saying, Doctor?"

"Cramping and burning irritation are common symptoms for edema, which is excessive amniotic fluid. If that's all it is, it will pass after delivery. But it could be pre-eclampsia, which can cause complications."

"What exactly are you telling us, Doctor?" Fannie's voice faltered slightly. Lucy didn't know whether it was because of the diagnosis, but she was looking at him in an odd way.

"There is no tenderness, and the swelling is equally dispersed, so I'm not going to treat Lucy in that direction, but I will be making frequent visits to make sure it doesn't elevate."

Mamm and Fannie glanced at each other and then at Lucy. They must have expected a good report the same way she had, to judge from the same surprised look on their faces.

She was about to ask him another question when he chimed in again. "Keep your feet up as much as possible and when you rest, lie down on your side, preferably on the left. Don't cross your legs."

Lucy uncrossed her legs, making him grin. It was the only emotion she'd seen from him, and she decided she liked his smile.

"Anything else I should know?" He stared into Lucy's

eyes intently, patiently waiting for her answer. For the few seconds she had a good look at him, she realized how good looking he was, now that his curtness was not distracting from it. "I'd like the room, ladies."

"Is there something wrong?" Lucy sat up, giving him her full attention.

He took a step closer and let out a breath. "I am being overly cautious, but I want you to know there was a slight change in the heart rate. It's common, but I wanted you to know."

She was flustered, unable to think, having expected a clean bill of health on top of what she was about to ask him. Then she thought of what was most on her mind. "Will this hurt the baby?"

"You and the baby are in good hands. I want you to come in once a week from here on, starting as soon as possible."

Lucy instinctively put her hands on her belly. "I wish it just affected me."

"Take care of yourself, it's the best thing you can do for the baby." He said as the ladies came back into the room.

"Take care of them." He looked from one of the women to the other, as if asking their commitment to care for Lucy. He was curt, but at that moment she realized he really cared.

"Both of them," Doc said to Lucy, under his breath.

He lifted one eyebrow and placed his utensils into his bag, oblivious to the gasps and jaw-dropping.

"You mean there's more than one baby?" *Mammi*'s voice was the loudest, so her question was heard first, as *Mamm* and Fannie looked at the doctor.

Lucy's heart skipped as she waited for his answer. This was all too much to process. The bed rest and now this?

"Two heartbeats." He snapped his bag shut and walked to the door. "Good day, ladies." He turned to Fannie, a few steps away. Lucy caught random words that she couldn't put together. Fannie's reserve visibly dissolved. Her eyes never left his as he spoke. Whatever it was, he had her complete attention.

Mammi was the first to come out of her shock. "Pay him...we have to give him money." Her broken sentence only made the situation stranger.

Lucy heard him refuse payment, saying they would work out the details after all was said and done. *Mamm*'s eyes were misty, and Fannie couldn't stop smiling. Nellie and Rosy walked out of the kitchen, where they were cooking something up.

Nellie stepped into the room first. "Is the doc gone?" She wiped her hands on a towel and threw it over her shoulder.

Rosy was right behind her. "How's the *mamm*-to-be?"

"She's having twins," *Mamm* informed them with pride. "First ones in the family. Your *daed* will be thrilled."

Rosy's jaw dropped, and she turned to Nellie. "And all this happened while we were in the kitchen starting to make scripture cake."

"Well, that's a good way to celebrate the two little ones." *Mammi* was right behind Rosy and Nellie.

They all went into the kitchen, Lucy included, and settled in. Each one of them would find her place in preparing the special cake—all but Lucy. She found a comfortable chair to sit in, put her feet on another chair, and watched the women getting all the ingredients together. *Mammi* handed Lucy a piece of paper with Bible verses and the directions for the cake.

"So how does this work again?" Lucy had watched her *mamm* make the cake a couple of times as a child, and only remembered how good it tasted, not how to make it. Both *Mammi* and *Mamm* started in to explain at the same time. But *Mammi* was the one who gave the explanation Lucy thought was appropriate.

"As you add the ingredients to make the cake, you read a verse from the Bible for each item."

Mamm couldn't help but chime in and added a little more to the process. "The whole idea behind the scripture cake recipe is to find out the ingredients by looking up the Bible passages and reading them. That's how you know what goes in the cake. See here?" She handed the recipe card to Lucy and then took her place between *Mammi* and Rosy.

¾ cup Judges 5:25, last part of verse (butter)
1½ cups Jeremiah 6:20 (sugar)
2 tablespoons 1 Samuel 14:25 (honey)
One whole Isaiah 10:14 (egg)
2 cups 1 Kings 4:22 (flour)
1 teaspoon Amos 4:5 (baking soda)
1 pinch Leviticus 2:13 (salt)
1¼ cup Judges 4:19, last part of verse (milk)
½ cup Numbers 17:8 (almonds, chopped)
1 cup Nahum 3:12 (figs, chopped)
1 cup 1 Samuel 30:12 (raisins)
Season to taste with 2 Chronicles 9:9
(cinnamon, nutmeg, and other spices)

Directions: Proverbs 23:14. (You can look up
at least one!)

Lucy smiled when she read the line in parentheses that was in her *Mamm*'s handwriting. It fit her personality so perfectly. No matter how controlling her *mamm* was, Lucy would miss her when she left. But she would still be in good hands. And she prayed that Doctor Kauffman would take good care of her babies. He was so thorough and knowledgeable that she was confident in his abilities and advice. She stood to help with the cake.

"*Nee*, you sit and rest." Nellie put up a hand to stop her from walking closer to the kitchen counter that was strewn with flour, eggshells, and a half a stick of butter.

Mammi wagged a wooden spoon her way. "Don't be stubborn, now. You tell us the directions, and we'll do the baking."

Rosy just looked over and smiled when she started beating the eggs again. She hummed a hymn while she worked, and the others bickered over what temperature the cake should be baked at. Lucy appreciated Rosy's deliberate lack of concern.

She looked around the kitchen, taking in everything around her—the hardwood floors with paths worn from the counters to the large tabletop in the middle of the room, warmth from the oven that was heating to bake the cake, and the two little ones inside her who would share all of it with her and these wonderful women.

ᲙᲐ Chapter Twenty-Two ᲙᲝ

*M*anny made a full circle around Sam's farm. It was really Lucy's, but it didn't seem that way. She hadn't so much as set her big toe on the place since she brought food to him back when it all happened. The place had such bad memories for her, he understood how she wouldn't want to be here. But it did need to be taken care of. The animals had been transported to his place and Caleb's, but Lucy hadn't asked a thing about any of it. Not the farm, the livestock, or even the money, which still hadn't been dealt with. If she wanted to sell the place, it would take a mighty well-off buyer to offer what it was worth.

When he thought about Lucy, he didn't worry about her. She was far from being alone, even with her *mamm* leaving. The women in her life doted on her around the clock, to the point he was starting to get annoyed. He wanted time with her, which was unpredictable considering he wanted that time with her *alone*. With her time to deliver so close, he knew it was now or never. He had to follow through with his plans. If she said *nee*, he was prepared now, unlike his last attempt. He didn't have time to wait and wonder any longer.

"I thought that was your buggy." Caleb walked up behind him, still a ways away. Caleb slung his horse's reins over the fence rail, slipped the leather through a loop, and gave a tug. That horse wasn't going anywhere. He strode toward Manny. "Is Lucy here?"

"*Nee*, I don't think she wants to come back here, so I thought I'd see what was what."

"She's got to decide something sooner or later. We've done all we can to get it cleaned up." He stopped and turned to Manny. "She is selling it?"

"She hasn't said. I guess she needs more time to figure things out."

"*Nee*, she needs you to decide what to do."

"It's not my place. I'm willing to help with whatever she decides, but I can't tell her what to do. The minute I do, someone or something will step in, and I'll be the scapegoat."

Caleb shook his head. "I don't think so. She's not used to making decisions, more so than most wives I've come across. Sam was an intimidating guy. She probably doesn't have a clue about what to do." He took a long look around the place. "That goes for more than just this farm."

Manny ignored his last comment. He knew he was referring to their relationship, but didn't want to go there. "I suppose there's something to that, but I don't feel right making decisions for her."

"You are too much alike. Nothing's gonna get taken care of if you don't encourage her to take care of things." He scanned the place again. "Somebody's gonna get a good deal for this farm."

"For Lucy's sake, I'd just like it to be over." Manny meant that, but he worried about how things would look if he did go through with his decision. He thought about waiting until the farm was taken care of but shook it off. It was just another excuse not to do what he not only wanted to do, but also felt *Gott*'s urging to do. "How's Emma? Haven't seen her around."

Caleb grinned. "I didn't want to say anything just yet, but she's had some morning sickness."

Manny's head whipped around to him. "Emma is having a baby?" He chuckled. "She's still a child at heart herself."

"It'll be nice to have our children grow up together." Caleb said without even blinking.

Manny thought about saying something to Caleb about his plans but decided he didn't want anyone else to know of them before he'd talked to Lucy.

They turned to each other, both deep in thought. "You making plans for me I don't know about?" Manny said.

Caleb shook his head. "I know how you and Lucy feel about each other. What are you waiting for?"

"It's not an easy thing to marry a pregnant widow, Caleb."

"How would you know? You haven't even tried to find out yet. The bishop might go easy on you."

"I doubt the bishop would be so reasonable, the crotchety old goat." Manny knew he shouldn't have said it out loud or even thought it, for that matter, but it was true, and everyone knew it. The bishop was strict in his ways and would most surely not give them favor in this situation.

"*Jah*, but he's going to have to deal with a similar situation with one of his own. That might humble him a bit." Caleb's brows rose as he looked Manny in the eyes. "If you didn't hear about his oldest daughter, I'm telling you now. If anyone should give you pardon, it would be him."

It wasn't like Caleb to gossip, so Manny knew he was trying to help him prepare for the conversations that he would have, not just with the bishop but also with others in the community as well. Manny paused. He didn't want to know such things, but this time it was a secret he actually did need to know about.

There was gossip here and there, but he never paid much mind to it. He was too busy being alone and—Emma had made him realize—feeling sorry for himself. She was one of the main reasons he'd gathered the courage to approach Lucy. "Why didn't I know about any of this?"

"You don't get out much." Caleb smiled proudly, and Manny was happy for him. He'd be a great dad. "So are you gonna fill me in on this pregnancy stuff?"

"You make me sound like an expert, and I'm far from that." Manny thought back to when he'd first seen Lucy and didn't even know she was with child. She still wasn't as big as most of the women he'd seen. Toward the end, they shut themselves up and hibernated until the delivery day came. Most had midwives, but some with concerns were using some doc who had started showing up around the communities nearby.

"I'm just trying to figure out what to do and say. It's starting to seem like I don't do anything right." Caleb's brows drew together. "Come to think of it, maybe I don't."

Manny grinned, which just seemed to irritate Caleb even more. Manny slapped him on the back to get him out of his daze. "I've got something to do, and I'm about to get it done."

Caleb snapped out of it with a shake of his head. "I'll say a prayer for ya."

"I think I'll need more than one." Manny walked over to the post where Sweet Pea waited patiently. She was getting too old for many outings, but he wanted her with him for this excursion. He waved to Caleb as he tapped the reins on Sweet Pea's hide and let the *clip-clop* of her hooves calm his nerves. He tried to distract himself by looking at the weather. He said a simple prayer for wisdom and courage, but his mind kept wandering, thinking about how he should phrase what he was about to say.

When he got to Frieda's place, he saw Lucy on the porch swing. Her head was down as she read or prayed. Maybe she was tired. She had to be more than ready for the baby to come. He couldn't imagine how she must be feeling about now. He didn't have the vaguest idea how to accompany her through this pregnancy, but he would sure give it a try if she'd let him.

He climbed out of the buggy and took his time tethering Sweet Pea to the hitching post. Everything he had practiced in his head seeped away until he had nothing but bits and pieces of sentences he wanted to say. He stood in place staring at the top of Lucy's *kapp*. She must have been really distracted, because she hadn't even looked up to see who had come driving down the lane. He took his time walking up the stairs, hoping the sound of his boots would grab her attention. It was then he noticed her shoulders shaking and her hands cupping her face. He knew from being around Emma and her sisters that wasn't a good sign. She was either laughing or crying, and he was hoping for the first of the two.

"Lucy?" He stopped, hoping she'd look at him with a smile, but he didn't think she even knew he was there. "Luce, are you all right?"

Her head moved from side to side, and she covered her mouth. Her back straightened, and she lifted her head. When she dropped her hands from her face, he saw the blotchy cheeks and bloodshot eyes.

"What is it, Lucy?" A storm of ideas came to mind as he watched her rub her face and use her apron to wipe her nose. Her shoulders shook when she took in a breath, so he gave her another minute that seemed much longer. He shifted his feet. "Will you please tell me what's wrong?"

"I'm sorry, Manny. I'm not good company right now." She still hadn't looked him in the eyes, and he started to really worry. Whatever was bothering her was more than just the difficulties of being pregnant. He'd been around her enough to know that this was way over the top.

"Just tell me, Lucy. I can't stand to see you like this." He was about to plead again when she turned his way.

"My *mamm*." Lucy shook her head. "She's going to Tennessee, but she's back to her old self again, so I'm glad to see her go."

Manny jerked his head back. He and Lucy had come a long way since he'd gotten to know her, and he'd seen great strides after the explosion. He couldn't imagine what Verna was up to now. It wasn't right to put Lucy in a situation that had her all upset like this. "What is it now?"

"She's playing matchmaker again." Lucy shook her head. "She just has to stick her nose in everything."

Manny analyzed the situation from both sides. Besides the fact he didn't want another suitor on the scene, he could also see Verna's intentions. She was a caretaker, used to setting everything right and getting things in order. The hardest thing for someone like her was to leave something undone. Little did Verna know he already had the answer, if all went as planned.

"I might have a solution to this, Lucy. But first I have to tell you that what your *mamm* is doing is just tying up loose ends so she will know you're in good hands."

Lucy looked straight at him. Her tired eyes and red nose warned him not to push too hard. This was something she'd dealt with all her life, and now with everything going on with her body, it would be enough to really set her off. "What is it, Manny? What's your advice, right along with the rest of them?"

Manny ignored the sarcasm. That wasn't the real Lucy talking. He still wasn't sure enough of himself to think she'd accept his offer, but at this point what did either of them have to lose? "I have an offer."

Lucy scoffed. "What? What is it, Manny? Just tell me and get it over with." Her weary eyes watered. He couldn't stand to see any more tears. But clearly she didn't seem to believe what he had to say was worth much.

He looked down at his boots and at her face again. His black boots were the more appealing option. "Lucy, if you'd be so inclined..." He swallowed, glanced at her, and then looked down again. Her blotchy cheeks lightened a little, and she'd almost stopped shaking.

"Just say it, Manny." Her voice sounded more like herself, but still with a sad tone to it.

He let out a long breath and straightened up, looking into her blue eyes. "Lucy, will you marry me?"

Lucy's face went white. Her breathing quickened.

Manny sat beside her and took her hand. "I should have asked you a long time ago, after Sam died. But I didn't want to be disrespectful. Besides, I thought you'd turn me down, and if you had, we might not be able to remain friends. And having you means the world to me. So I let the time go, and now here we are with you ready to give birth."

She smiled, a little embarrassed. "Manny?"

"*Jah*, I'm here." He watched her eyes meet his. "I'm sorry. I made things worse. I knew you weren't well and did it anyway."

"Did what, Manny?" She pushed herself up and turned toward him. "Ask me again."

He didn't know if she was relieved or in shock. But he'd do what she wanted. He needed to hear it again himself. He took one hand as the other one was shaking, holding her up. She was so weak, he worried he'd set her off again. But this was what they both needed to hear.

"Lucy, will you be my wife? I should have asked you a long time ago after Sam died. But I was scared you'd turn me down, and if you had, we might not be friends. And having you as a friend means the world to me."

"*Jah*...if you are willing to raise two babies with me."

Manny froze and stared at her. "Two?" He grinned.

She smiled meekly. It was probably the biggest effort she'd made since he arrived, but he was sure glad to see it. He needed to know she wanted him as much as he wanted her.

Chapter Twenty-Three

*V*erna picked up the iron from the potbellied stove and dropped it down onto a blue dress. She pushed so hard, her knuckles turned white. Lucy knew that not even the tiniest wrinkle would remain in the little blue dress.

Lucy had mixed emotions. She was relieved to be able to tell her *mamm* that Manny had proposed, but she was worried what her *mamm* would say and do. *Mamm* was upset with her for refusing to meet the man who *Mamm* said just wanted to stop by for a cup of coffee. Lucy hadn't set foot in the kitchen until he was gone, and now she had to tell *Mamm* her news. She just hoped she would let go of her disappointment long enough appreciate what Lucy had to tell her.

The smell of steam rising off the material filled her nostrils as she made herself a cup of coffee. "*Mamm*, don't be upset with me."

Mamm pushed down harder on the iron and glanced up at her. "It's autumn. Everyone who is getting married has their companion. I spent a good deal of time talking with him about his farm that's a good distance away. I guess I'm not surprised you hadn't met him." She shook her head. "I know it's different for you, but it comes a little harder in your condition."

"*Ach, Mamm.* They probably just want the farm. There's few places as big that offer so much land for planting." She sat down at the kitchen table, watching *Mamm* tackle the poor dress yet another time.

"Well, it's not like you're the only widow with child. It just makes life easier to have a man around. I would know after the last couple of years being nursemaid to your *daed*." She hadn't lifted her head, which Lucy appreciated. *Mamm*'s gaze could penetrate right through her, leaving her to feel as if she knew everything about her just by staring at her.

"How is he, *Mamm*?" She asked each and every week, but the answer was the same. She was glad it didn't change, although perhaps her *mamm* was keeping information from her. Maybe she was waiting until after the babies were born, which would be soon. Lucy almost wanted to hasten the delivery, in hopes *Daed* would know they had come.

Mamm stared long and hard at Lucy. "He's better than you. You look tired. Maybe you're in need of a nap."

"I haven't been up that long. I feel lazy with all of you taking care of me." When she stopped and thought about it, she didn't need a single thing to get by except the love and care of those around her. She had spent so long alone with Sam, cooking, cleaning, and tending to him, that she hadn't gotten the precious time and care that she had now become accustomed to here.

"Don't push yourself. Your body's working extra hard about now. Those babies are taking everything you've got left in you." Unlike a few minutes ago her *mamm* was gently ironing a small black dress. Lucy wondered where the blue one had gone and what kind of shape it was in.

It was a good time to tell her. With the focus being on the babies, *Mamm* seemed to mellow a bit.

"*Mamm*, you don't have to worry about my raising these babies alone." She paused to see *Mamm*'s eyes lift to hers as she set the iron up.

"Well, of course not. You have your *mammi* and the girls. And me. Once things settle down, I'll be back. It'll be sooner than you think. And then there's Manny." She turned to Lucy waiting for her reply.

"*Jah*, Manny." She couldn't keep the mist from her eyes just saying his name.

"What's got you so upset?" *Mamm* stood straight and tall with a puzzled look on her face.

"I'm not upset." She shut her eyes and a tear dropped. "I am very blessed to have so many around me to go through this with me, especially Manny." She let out a breath of air as her *mamm*'s eyes grew wide. She backtracked. Maybe it wasn't the right time to tell her. For some reason, at this moment it didn't seem real. What she was leery about, she didn't know, but it made her pause.

Mamm put a hand to her chest. "*Jah*, praise *Gott* for that. I can leave here knowing you're in good hands." She whispered in such a soft tone Lucy's didn't think it could possibly be coming from her *mamm*'s mouth.

Lucy was glad to hear the words for more than one reason. *Mamm* approved of Manny, although who wouldn't? Lucy also knew that if her *mamm* knew she was in good hands, *Mamm* could go home to tend to her *daed*.

"I thought you'd approve of him." Lucy's voice was stronger than she felt. She was confident her *mamm* would accept Manny, but she could never be sure what her *mamm* might say. Manny had wanted to be here when she told her *mamm*, but he hadn't seen every side of *Mamm* yet, and Lucy didn't want their future to start out on a bad note.

Mamm let out a sigh. "I've gotten to know him over the past couple of weeks. He's a nice man. Hopefully he'll make sure you and the little ones are taken care of. More so than Sam ever would have."

"*Mamm!*" As much as her *mamm* stuck to the rules, she seemed to feel obliged to share her opinion even after a person was deceased. When Lucy stopped to think about it, she knew her *mamm* might be right, that Sam wouldn't have been truly prepared to care for a wife and two babies. The thought took her breath away, and she said a word of thanksgiving for putting Manny into her life.

"How blessed these two little ones will be with you and so many others." Her face contorted, and she suddenly seemed to be caught up in her thoughts. "*Ach*, how I wish I could be here to see them." Her face relaxed as if with a new thought. "And I'm still praying for a redhead."

"You can't pray for such things," Lucy said, more quickly than she meant to. Maybe the trivial was still worthy of a short prayer once in a while. After all, *Gott* had a hand in the tiniest of things, even the birds in the trees.

"Prayers are a gift we have to communicate with the Lord. Unlike during the four hundred years of silence the Bible tells us of, we are able to commune with Him every second of the day, if we so choose." *Mamm*'s strength came from her strong faith—the one thing about her *mamm* Lucy wished she had. But along with that came an air of legalism that Lucy resented. Lucy felt she didn't need to answer to anyone but God. Even the deacons in their community had to earn her respect through their relationship with the Lord before she felt she could trust and obey them.

Lucy chuckled. It wasn't in her Amish upbringing to go against the deacons or bishop, but when it came to her and Manny getting married, she might stand for what she deemed necessary.

"You don't agree?" *Mamm* asked, frowning.

"*Jah*, I believe you've taught me more than one lesson within the last couple of minutes." It was a thought that started running around her head, sparking more thoughts and then still more.

Mamm grinned and held up the two little dresses she'd made and ironed. "What do you think of these?"

"What if I have a boy?" Lucy giggled. "Do you want him to wear one or are you going to be sensible and make some fine pants just in case?"

"Hmm, I suppose for good measure, but I can't say you'll be needing them." *Mamm* took another approving look at the darling dresses and sat down to fish out more fabric.

"Do you need me for anything here?" Lucy was already grabbing a light jacket when her *mamm* looked up at her with her bifocals at the tip of her nose.

"Where are you going?" She looked ages older with the glasses she wore only when she had a needle in her hand.

"To see Rosy. I won't be long" She took one step out the door then poked her head back in. "*Danke, Mamm.*"

Mamm shrugged, either indifferent about what Lucy was thanking her for or merely distracted. With that, Lucy set her sights on finding Rosy. She was the only one of the three women she hadn't talked with yet about how things were.

The walk to the barn behind *Mammi*'s *haus* was short,

but Lucy was tired after just a few steps. She felt better when she was walking or moving around, but she lost her energy quickly, and her mind was pinging with thought. Of the three women she so admired, Rosy was the most like Lucy. She wanted to ask Rosy why she had never married.

The ladies were finishing up their quilting and rearranging the barn back to order. Lucy found it too difficult to sit and quilt. Her legs cramped, and the chairs seemed harder, so she preferred to watch or work in the *haus*. She studied the half-finished quilt they were working on and found the autumn colors calming.

"These colors are as beautiful as the leaves on the trees outside. When will it be done?" she asked.

Mammi was bent over, picking up scraps and putting them in a bag. Every single piece was saved, nothing thrown away. "*Ach*, Lucy. I know how you like these fall colors."

"How are you, Luce?" Rosy put a gentle hand on her belly. "I usually get a kick out of one of them. Maybe both, for that matter."

"Still can't believe I'm having two." Lucy knew she would have help from Manny, but the others didn't, and now, for some reason, she wanted to wait. Her conversation with her *mamm* was encouraging, but she felt some hesitation. It was as if something wasn't complete or finished yet, though what it was, she couldn't say. Sometimes she feared that she wasn't truly meant to be a *mamm*. But then how did anyone know until it became real?

"How did you know there are two?" an elderly Amish woman asked with a frown. "Only twins I know about is after they come out."

"A doctor checked on me, Martha." The less information the better. Some—especially the older Amish—didn't find anyone but a midwife acceptable for such a private event.

Bertha grunted, and a couple others looked over, listening to the conversation. "Why in the world would you have an outsider looking you over?" She moved closer, and some stared.

"I didn't ask him to come." Lucy didn't want to tell them who set up the visit, but she couldn't lie either.

"So Fannie did." The way the older woman said Fannie's name brought up the heat in Lucy's cheeks.

"It doesn't matter who. It was a kind gesture. Even though I didn't know he was coming..." She marshaled her courage, glad Fannie wasn't there to hear this, but also because Fannie wouldn't even let the conversation go as long as it had. "I'm glad he did."

Some of them shook their heads, and one put a hand to her heart. Others were indifferent. But it seemed this woman wasn't going to let up. Lucy stood tall, and Rosy took her by the hand. "I believe we did good work here today. Let's enjoy our evening." With that, they picked up Rosy's bag and started for the barn door, but Lucy stopped her.

"Is there somewhere we can talk?"

Rosy stopped and looked in her eyes. "She tends to complain about a lot of things, Luce. Don't get upset about her."

"It's not that. I know what she's like, and I understand her concern. Things keep changing, and most her age don't like it." Lucy looked over her shoulder to make sure they wouldn't be heard. "It might not be my business to ask, but I was wondering why you never married." She waited a moment to see how Rosy responded.

Rosy pursed her lips and looked down at her boots. "I don't mind telling you, but why do you ask?" She put her hands behind her back and kept her eyes downward.

"It seems to me that women who don't have a chance to find something for themselves end up wishing they did."

She shook her head. "*Nee*, I didn't marry because I was so shy, I'd never even look a man in the eye, let alone go courting. I thought for years I'd missed out on what every good, sensible woman wanted—to be married."

"But you don't feel that way now?"

"*Nee*, not so much. There are times I do, like now, seeing you with babies coming and knowing Manny will be there for you."

Lucy paused. "That's what I'm wondering about. I hope it doesn't become a burden for him. They aren't his children to bear the burden for."

They were both quiet for a long moment. "There's only one way to find out."

"What's that?"

"Ask him."

Chapter Twenty-Four

*M*anny's palms began to sweat. He'd not had much reason to have a serious talk with Bishop Atlee since Glenda passed away, and that seemed like a long time ago now. The bishop was unpredictable and always seemed irritated, but there was no backing out now. He could only hope the bishop was in a favorable mood.

When he did have a sudden loss of courage, all Manny had to do was start thinking of Verna, and he was back on track. She wanted to go to the bishop, but Manny had stood up to her for the first time. Lucy had been as surprised as Verna was. Maybe he was ready now, taking the lead with Lucy and the baby.

He stopped and grinned, realizing he'd thought *baby* instead of *babies*. He was still getting over the fact there would be two, but after waiting and wanting a baby for so long with Glenda and all the heartache that had caused, he couldn't complain. He would be very blessed to have two little ones. But would that thought last? He didn't exactly expect to have a complete family before getting married again, and such a short time after Glenda's death.

As he drove down the dirt path to the bishop's, a fleeting thought made him pause. Anxiety poked at him as he thought about the responsibility before him, but it was more than that. He felt the same concern coming from Lucy. He knew she was probably going through a flurry of emotions due to her pregnancy and the many changes that had happened over the last few months.

When he finally arrived at the bishop's house, he took in a long breath and knocked on the door. When the bishop opened it, he immediately put a finger to his lips and shushed Manny.

"The wife is asleep—headaches. She gets migraines, especially this time of day." He pulled at his long salt-and-pepper beard and although he gestured for Manny to come in, Manny felt like an intruder. The bishop seemed to lack the typical Amish hospitality, but Manny was prepared for it after their previous encounters.

"What's on your mind, son?" the bishop asked as he walked one step ahead of Manny. The *haus* was dark, with old wood floors and a banister leading through the dimness to a large upstairs, as Manny had been told. The counters were brown Formica, and the furniture was tan. The large windows were covered with heavy, dark cloth. Manny figured that was due to the wife's headaches.

They walked into the office, which smelled of mothballs combined with a musty scent. The bishop motioned for Manny to have a seat in front of his desk.

As soon as both men were seated, Manny told the bishop, "I thought I should share my situation with you, as you will need to be involved. It's just a formality, and I don't want to take up too much of your time."

"Spit it out, son." The bishop laid his sun-blotched hands on the desk before him. Manny noticed his drooping eyelids and the overlapping wrinkles on his face and down to his neck. He didn't know how old the man was, but he had an idea he was younger than he looked.

Manny took another long breath. The bishop wanted it out there, so he delivered. "I've asked Lucy to marry me."

The bishop frowned and stared. "Go on."

Manny wasn't surprised that the bishop wanted to hear more and was expecting him to tell him what was protocol.

"What do you suggest?" Manny waited a moment, and then realized he wasn't going to get a response, so he spoke again. "What is appropriate?"

Bishop moved from side to side as if uncomfortable in his own britches as well as his chair. "That you wait."

Taken aback, Manny didn't want to be deterred but knew the Amish ways, and going against the bishop wasn't one of them, even in this case. "Lucy and I don't want to take any steps that you don't approve of." Manny didn't know what else to say to a man who didn't seem to care as to what he and Lucy should do or what Manny's opinion was. Manny was doing what was expected of him, but felt he was bothering the man.

"Take some time; it's a big decision."

One side of his cheeks lifted ever so slightly. Manny wasn't sure if it was a twitch or an attempt to smile.

"But if it were me, I would be discreet."

"We'd like to marry before the babies come. We thought it only right for them to be born with the Keim name to them." That was the one thing both he and Lucy had agreed was the most important. But as soon as Manny made this comment, the bishop lifted his brows.

"You plan to have your widowed fiancée standing at the altar blatantly with child?"

He grunted, or maybe it was a growl. Either way, Manny tried to be respectful.

"*Nee*, it would be a private ceremony." Having family

there was important to Lucy, but it was more important to marry before the babies were born. They wanted to do it as possible in accord with the bishop's demands, whatever they were.

The bishop nodded and seemed to relax, resting his hands palms down on the desk, which had pin marks and divots covering its surface. "Have you gone to Minister Eben yet?"

"I thought it best to talk to you first."

The bishop nodded. "You will need to do as if you are courting."

Manny sat up straight in his chair at the thought of how difficult it would be not to spend time alone with her. It wasn't like they were the young courting couples, especially in their situation.

"It will be difficult to help Lucy in her condition, don't you agree?" Manny wasn't sure of anything, considering their situation and wondered whether the bishop was ill, or just not in a cooperative mood. Something definitely seemed amiss. "Are you well, Bishop?"

The bishop raised his head a little higher and stared him in the eyes. It seemed the man didn't blink, but that would be impossible. Maybe Manny was avoiding his gaze and missed him blinking. "I am fatigued. Life has taken its toll, as it has with my wife. But my disposition has always been the same. I am a strict man who abides by rules—my own as bishop and those of the Bible."

Manny nodded. "I understand." He was about to say more, but the bishop started in again.

"For my sake, if nothing more, use good sense as you move forward with your young family." His breath was labored, and Manny wondered whether it was his lungs that were ailing. The bishop hadn't given a long sermon for quite a while, now that he thought of it. The minister usually gave the sermon, but the bishop had been more vocal in the past.

"Thank you for talking with me. I'll pray for you and your wife's health."

"And I will pray for your stamina." He chuckled, but his voice cracked and turned into a cough.

When Manny had first come into the *haus*, he had felt uncomfortable, but now, knowing the bishop's strife, he took it all in stride. As he walked to his buggy, he knew he'd done the right thing, even if it wasn't what he'd expected.

He didn't have much reason to know the bishop. Manny kept to himself most of the time. Even on church days, he'd stay for the meal but scoot out and back to his place at the first chance he got. It was that way even before Glenda passed away. She liked to talk some, so he'd get comfortable in the buggy while he waited. Lucy was much the same way, which made him think he must like being with those drawn to simple company.

As he drove down the road, the wild plums drew his eye. The red color was similar to ripe grapes bursting with sweet flavor. He thought he'd take advantage of the opportunity, so he brought his horse to a slow stop. He didn't have anything but a corn sack to put the plums in, but he figured if he brought back enough to wet his whistle, Lucy would come back with him and pick some more.

As he plucked as many as he could get his hands on, he could taste the plum tingling on his tongue. They had to be picked at just the right time—before they were overripe with no taste, and not too early when they were sour.

As he picked the fruit, he thought of how Lucy seemed to be deep in thought lately. It must be tough to be so close to the due date. Maybe the fresh plums would cheer her up a little. There was nothing he liked more than getting a smile out of her.

When he'd filled the bag about halfway and his hands were purple, he decided that was as much as he or Lucy would be able to handle. He carried the bag to his buggy and wiped his hands on his trousers. He felt like a kid again, popping one of the smaller plums into his mouth and letting the sweet juices entice his taste buds. As he walked over to the driver's side of the buggy, he ate a couple more. By the time he got to Nellie's place, he let out a belch and knew he'd had one too many, if not three or four.

He fetched the sack and walked to the door. When no one answered, he opened the door slightly and called out, but there was no response, so he walked in and laid the plums down on the counter.

"Lucy." He waited, but nothing stirred except for the hot water kettle that began to boil. He was about to leave when Lucy walked into the room.

She startled when she saw him.

"How did it go?" A lock of her red hair hung down her forehead, and she quickly pushed it up under her *kapp*.

He didn't recognize her tone or the straight face that was usually a bright smile. She must be worried about the bishop. "I brought you some wild plums." He gestured to the counter.

"*Danke*. I'll make some more plum jam. We were getting low." She grabbed an apron and pulled it down over her head and straightened her *kapp*.

"The bishop gave his blessing, so to speak."

"That doesn't sound very hopeful."

He didn't want to worry her, so he tried another way to coax her back into her usual ray of sunshine. He decided less was more. She seemed to be getting more anxious about things— them and the babies. "It will work out in the end. The bishop and his wife were both not feeling well; that's probably all it was."

"*Ach*, I'm glad, but still worried."

Manny knew she would worry more if he didn't tell her about the bishop's wishes and decided to just tell her. "He wants us to court until the babies come."

Lucy laid a hand on her chest and stared at Manny. "I have rarely seen such a thing."

"Don't trouble yourself over it. He wasn't himself, and I'm hoping it will pass."

"Is there anything else I should know?"

He could see the concern in her eyes and considered the best way to handle the situation. "We'll deal with it when the time comes."

She frowned but followed his lead to the work at hand.

He took a long look around the room and then back at Lucy, who was intently working on something on the table. "What do you have there?" He walked over and read the words on the wooden sign she'd made: .

Manny pursed his bottom lip and looked at her. "What inspired you to do this?"

"I'm going to set up a roadside stand. Plums will get them interested, don't you think?" She looked at him and got close enough for him to brush her side and take her hand like he usually did.

"What gave you this idea?" He was careful with his

questions, wishing he knew more about plum jam. He was pretty sure he'd already heard from Verna and maybe others too about her newfound investment.

"Truth be told, I can't stay in this *haus* even one more day." She put a hand on her back and stretched.

He thought he understood. She needed to get out and do something. But he wished it wasn't something that involved her standing for too long. "Do you need some help setting up?" It was the last thing he wanted to do, but he had to give her this; the time was too close, and the twins couldn't come into the world soon enough.

She looked a little surprised but nodded her approval. "I need some sort of covering and a chair."

He went to the pantry and pulled out a folding chair and table he knew was there, because he'd used them a time or two. "As far as a cover, how about the table umbrella?"

"*Jah*, that should work." She paused for a moment and smiled.

He was so glad to see it, he didn't care what she said next. "Is that everything?"

"*Jah*, *danke* for not scolding me or trying to change my mind." She looked away and started loading up fruits and vegetables into small wicker baskets. Then she handed him an armful of quilts.

They walked to the end of the road to an area where tourists often gathered, and decided where to set up the stand. They had been sitting for only a second or two before tourists started to slowly stop by the stand and compliment her quilts. It was just enough to make Lucy smile.

ᴄᴀ Chapter Twenty-Five ᴀᴅ

*A*re you sure you want to sell that quilt?" Manny ran his hand over the rainbow-colored quilt that a customer was haggling over with Lucy.

"*Jah*, Manny, I can always make another one." Lucy was just glad to get out and be around people. She couldn't stay in the *haus* like a cooped-up chicken for another minute, but she had nowhere to go and nothing to do that would keep her occupied without overexerting her. She also thought about the money Sam's farm would supply for her—blood money. She wanted her own income, even if it was trivial compared to what she would have once everything was settled. She didn't expect Manny to understand that and didn't want to bother him with it.

"Sorry, it's just one of my favorites." He smiled politely to the tourist, an older woman who seemed set on the quilt and held a wad of money out to Lucy.

"*Danke*." Lucy thanked the lady and started packing up the stand. It would be dark soon, and her feet were starting to swell. Lucy thought about Manny sitting contentedly beside her. He was everything Sam wasn't, doting on her and taking care of her every need. Maybe it was the hormones raging in her, or maybe she was gaining the confidence she'd been lacking.

After hearing *Mammi*'s story of her husband dying young and leaving her alone, and Nellie's story about starting her own quilting business and how she never married due to the restrictions the bishop had put upon her, Lucy had begun to worry the same thing could happen to her, and a surge of concern had filled her. But the one she resonated with most was Rosy.

Lucy didn't want to be like her, but she was, lacking self-esteem, not speaking her mind, taking mistreatment for years at Sam's whim—much like Rosy thinking she might have married if only she'd been bold enough to pursue a relationship. After evaluating their lives and situations, Lucy decided she would take from each of their strengths and live a life she would be happy with.

"Lucy." Manny was staring intently at her, concern and possibly confusion flashing in his eyes. "What were you thinking right then?"

"Nothing important. I need to quit thinking so much." She packed up what was left on the table, and Manny took down the umbrella and folded down the table and chair.

"I would sure like to know what's on your mind." His voice had an edge to it, and she suddenly felt like she needed some time to breathe, and the harder she tried to get it, the more she felt suffocated.

They walked back to the house and upon arriving put everything away. Nellie came in the room, smiled, and turned around to give them some privacy. After she left, Lucy saw the look on Manny's face. That was enough to make her realize how she herself couldn't seem to stop worrying.

Manny watched Nellie walk out and stared at Lucy. "What is it, Luce?"

His pleading eyes and serious face made her sad.

Why do I feel so blue? It's not fair to anyone around me.

"I am worried about everything, as if there is a huge

weight on me. What if I'm not a *gut mamm* or you're not a *gut daed*?" No one was in earshot, but even if they were, Lucy didn't care; it had been all she could do to keep her mouth shut with him at the stand.

Manny frowned, unable to answer. "What makes you think it will be so hard?" He took her hand and looked her in the eyes. "You're going to be a *gut mamm*, and I'll be an even better *daed*." He grinned, and she smiled.

"How do you always know how to cheer me up?"

"I'm just that kind of guy." He took her other hand as well. "I suppose I should give you some time to rest."

"You don't have to be by my side all the time. I know you have chores to do. And we do have the bishop's request to think about." She sighed, her strength giving way. "It's not like you won't know when the babies come."

"Are you saying you want me to actually get some work done?" He scoffed, but his eyes told her he was confused. "I'm not sure how much to follow the bishop's requests, but I don't plan to stay completely away from you."

She balled her fists and tightened her lips. "*Jah*, I know." It wasn't the dysfunctional response that was deep inside her from the time spent with Sam. She'd accepted his derogatory comments and condescending words, but she was now learning how to change that.

Manny shook his head. "You and the babies have become as important to me as my own family." He caught her gaze, but then she looked at her boots. "Thank you for trusting me and accepting me caring for you."

She mumbled to herself, not daring to look in his eyes and let him see the gratitude she felt for him. "I'm glad you did."

The tears started to rise when she thought of him, but

she quickly brushed them away so Manny wouldn't see. She didn't want to seem vulnerable and dependent on him. She knew she didn't ever want to be that way again.

"It's not a choice. I know you care for me in the same way I do for you." His voice wavered. He stuck his thumbs in his suspenders and stared at her as if he'd lost his words.

"Your feelings could change." Her insecurities came tumbling out, building a wall brick by brick. She rubbed her belly, thinking of her future, and closed her eyes, wishing Manny wasn't there with her at that moment to see this side of her she didn't understand.

"No, they won't change." Manny planted his feet and crossed his arms over his chest. "I'm not Sam, Lucy. I won't ever leave you or mistreat you. And I would never, ever hurt you."

She looked away, ashamed. Manny had known her feelings even without her telling him. But her life hadn't been exactly how he thought. "He never touched me, but he beat me with his words." After looking into Manny's eyes, she knew he was up against more than he should be. That was it. She didn't want to show him the other side of her. She'd lived with it for far too long to expect those insecurities to just go away. Maybe this was all too soon; maybe she wasn't ready to be married. But how selfish would that be, to have two children with no husband when there was a man like Manny who loved them even before they were born?

"You look tired, Lucy. Burning the candle at both ends is hard on me, so I can't imagine the toll it's taking on you while carrying two babes. Why do you keep going and doing? What's driving you?"

She sat down hard on a bench her *daed* had made, and

that made her sad for a moment. Then she started thinking about what he would say to her if he were there. She knew what he'd tell her, but she didn't want to hear it from her *daed*, even though she knew he would be right.

"I guess I thought that during this time with Sam gone, that I was adjusted to his death and ready to start over." She glanced over at Manny. He had his arms crossed and looked at her unwaveringly, being the usual helpful, kind man she knew him to be.

She dared herself to look at him when she spoke—he deserved that—and when she did, his blue eye twinkled against the sun but his brown eye seemed to morph into the darkness that was creeping in around them. "I know I need to start something new to get out of the old. The ghosts from that time with Sam have taken their toll on me."

His brow unfolded, and he nodded a little, letting out a sigh. "If it's time you need, so be it."

"*Nee*, that's not what I meant. It just might take longer than I thought. Please be patient." She stood and gave him a kiss on the cheek.

With that, he pivoted, headed out the door, and started down the path leading away from her. Part of her felt relief, but she also wanted to run down the road and bring him back. She didn't understand herself, so how could she expect Manny to?

She didn't dare try to talk with him until whatever was ailing her was taken care of and she was in a decent mood. She wondered whether the two little ones could be causing all this trouble and whether it had changed her permanently.

She stepped outside to watch Manny continue to walk

until he was out of sight, all the while wishing she could better control her thoughts and actions. Knowing she couldn't on her own, Lucy sat down on the porch swing and bowed her head in prayer. She hadn't talked to *Gott* much lately—something she used to do faithfully. "*Gott*, what's happening to me? Help me find the way," she whispered, and opened her eyes to see her *mamm* looking down at her.

"Have you forgotten I'm leaving tomorrow?" Her *mamm* looked honestly disappointed that she had forgotten, but Lucy felt even worse.

What is wrong with me?

She couldn't blame all of this on her situation. Who better to ask than *Gott*? Now she could only wait and listen to His call.

"I'm sorry, *Mamm*. I've got a lot on my mind. But that's no excuse." She sighed. "I wish I could go." She looked down at the ball of a belly that seemed to grow bigger each day and realized how scared she was. But she brushed away the fear as quickly as it came.

"Well, you must come and see us. Very soon, once you and the babies are up for the ride. These buses would be a good way for all of you to travel. The drive isn't bad at all." Verna smiled like the cat that swallowed the canary.

"Why are you smiling?" Lucy was in no mood for games. Her *mamm* obviously had news to tell, so she waited with patience she didn't have.

"A mother wants to see her children happy in marriage. It's not hard to see how much Manny cares for you. I'm happy that you two have plans." Her *mamm's* voice was unusually soft, and she paused long enough that Lucy knew she was expecting more information.

"*Jah*, it's not been said openly, but it's been heading that way." That was all she could say at the moment. After all, this was about her and Manny. She prayed for strength, wishing she'd done so more often, and decided to change the subject with a question. "Will the men be cutting up hay bundles soon?"

Her *mamm* sighed and nodded. "I guess you have the right to keep your plans secret. But since I'm leaving tomorrow, I'd like to know what to expect. And you know your mother well enough to be prepared for me to give my opinion, take it or leave it. I'll always have something to say about you and now these two, hopefully all four of you, if you can hold on to the most wonderful young man in the community."

"*Mamm*, as soon as I know, I'll tell you. Until then, let me work things out, and I promise to tell you when the time is right." The instant she stopped talking, she realized she sounded much like her mother and gasped quietly. Since when did she tell her *mamm* what she needed instead of her *mamm* telling her?

Verna gave her a sideways glance. "I know what you're feeling right now, and believe me, it will pass. Don't make any decisions just yet. Get things steady in your heart, mind, and soul, and things will go better for you."

Lucy felt like crying, so different from the anger and frustration she'd felt for days, but she believed her *mamm* was right. Time would help and give her the right answers when she needed them most.

"*Ach, Mamm*, what will I do without you?" Lucy tipped her head to one side.

"Well, it will be hard, but you'll be in good hands." They both chuckled, and Lucy looked over to the last quilt they had been working on. "There's a lot of living in that quilt." *Mamm* glanced over to where Lucy was looking. "Should we finish it before I leave?"

Lucy didn't know how they possibly could, but she agreed. She walked over and grabbed some large colored patches and sat down. The chair creaked and wobbled. The thimble was made of wood instead of metal, and she broke a needle when she tried to stick it in the pin holder.

Her *mamm* clucked her tongue. "A broken needle is bad luck."

Lucy sighed. If things didn't start getting better, she didn't know what she would do.

The next morning, Lucy found herself a little sad. She and her *mamm* had come full circle since she had first arrived to visit. Saying good-bye would be much harder than she would have thought when *Mamm* first came.

Lucy decided it was time to get up, but doing so became more difficult with each day. She rolled to one side and then the other and slid down onto the wood floor. As she got dressed, she heard a buggy driving up. She peered out the window to see the same young man who had brought *Mamm* walking up to the *haus*. She hustled to finish getting ready and took careful steps down the stairs.

"*Mamm*, are you leaving already?" Lucy's breathing was heavy as she tried to speak, and her emotions were flaring up again. She didn't expect it with her *mamm*.

"*Jah*, I guess so." She pointed to her bags. "Both of those are mine." She gave the young man a small smile as he grabbed them both and headed out the door.

"I'm going to miss you, *Mamm*." Lucy's throat constricted,

and she tried to swallow. The trials had brought them together in a way only God could create.

Mamm moved forward and put her cheek next to Lucy's, and then looked her in the eyes. "Don't let him go, Lucy. He's a good man." She put a hand on Lucy's belly and smiled. "I wish I could be here." She pursed her lips and walked to the buggy without looking back—so typical of her—but as the buggy pulled away, Lucy saw *Mamm* wipe away a tear.

Chapter Twenty-Six

Manny stood in the barn separating milk. The cream forced its way to the top and ran into the spigot. He cranked the handle, making the bell ding, a noise that didn't usually bother him in the least, but today it pierced his eardrums. Whatever was going through his head was a mystery to him.

He'd done every possible thing he could think of to court Lucy without courting her, due to her situation. After his talk with Bishop Atlee, he'd felt confused about following the plans he'd made, but now he just missed her. When he saw Lucy at church, she seemed to be having the same thoughts. He tried to think things through to have an excuse to spend more time together, but though they'd agreed on courting the way the teenagers did, it didn't help much. He hoped that with Verna gone, she'd be more relaxed and lean on him a bit more. But she had the "girls" and her sister for support.

Manny held his head up to the sun, closed his eyes, and let the air flow out of his lungs. This was God's country, a place where the Amish settled centuries ago—good, solid soil, rich with minerals for crops, a perfect place to raise a family. He and Glenda had never gotten that far. They lost their child during childbirth, and months later she was gone too.

He dropped his head in thought and kicked a clod of dirt, watching it fall apart in front of him. He hadn't given himself permission to think about it. He grieved the loss of his unborn child. The doctor couldn't know for sure what the final issue was with the baby, but it didn't matter at that point.

And Glenda was gone too.

There wasn't any way he could keep himself from thinking about the same thing happening with Lucy, especially with two on the way. He knew that was why he was overprotective but didn't know how to stop the worry that had rooted deep inside him. And he couldn't tell Lucy why he acted the way he did; that would just make her worry right along with him.

"Morning." Caleb's voice brought him back, forcing him to push away the negative thoughts. "You doing all right?"

Manny held up a hand. "*Nee*, nothing I want to talk about right now." That probably wouldn't keep Caleb from pestering him because he'd been so quick to decline the conversation.

He forced a smile, and they pumped hands. Caleb held on a second longer, staring at him. Manny hated it when Caleb looked at him like that. "Whose farm are we going to first?"

"The Troyers', and then yours." Caleb grinned at Manny's surprise. "It was decided due to the fact you're gonna have your hands full. *Jah*, there are others who are with child, but not two like you will have."

The gravel crunched under their boots as they walked and Manny digested the news. His hay was in need of baling, and the grass he'd cut at the end of spring was dried out and ready, but his head was elsewhere.

"That's good news, although I won't have a table of food laid out come lunchtime." This was one of the many times he missed having a wife by his side to do what normal couples did, especially on a day like today. Hospitality was important and expected, but he couldn't provide what he didn't have.

Caleb put a hand on his shoulder. "Everyone understands."

Manny decided not to worry about it and settled in to enjoy the ride to the Troyers'. Once they got there, they set right in to gather the hay into small bales for easy handling. The square bale was the easiest for stacking. Some of the dried grass that was missed was gathered by a couple of young men on horseback mower.

Manny looked up to see what time of day it was. Not time for lunch, but the women were bringing their goods and starting to set up the tables. He glanced at Caleb, who was keeping an eye out to see that the blade was on line so no grass was lost and all could be used for feed.

"So I'm getting off easy?" Manny asked. "That's good, because I also didn't clean up the *haus* before I left." He walked alongside Caleb's flatbed.

"*Jah*, I told 'em I didn't want to see the inside of your place. 'It's more like a bachelor's pad' is what I said." Caleb grinned and made a turn for the barn.

"Most Amish probably don't even know what that is." Manny kept his place in decent shape, but it was Emma who made it shine, he thought, as he watched her walking toward him. Closer still was Lucy.

"Good morning, Sunshine." He knew maybe he shouldn't have been so bold, but that was how she made him feel.

She smiled slowly and kept walking. "I hear we'll all be at your place next." Her breath was labored, causing him concern, but she didn't seem worried. Her cheeks were rosy, and her smile showed contentment—both things good to see. But she still didn't seem herself. If only the babes would come quickly, perhaps things would be as they once were.

Emma joined them. "Early lunch this afternoon, due to you." She grinned and pecked him on the cheek. "And *you*"—she pointed at Lucy—"will be sitting a lot and helping only a little if I have anything to say about it."

"There's no denying it at this point. I'm not good for much these days." Lucy stuck out her bottom lip, showing her displeasure. "But I'm not complaining. I'm just glad the weather cooled a little. The hot flashes have been ex*haus*ting this summer."

"It's the same as last summer, but you weren't carrying around two little ones then." Emma pulled her away, and Lucy gave Manny a slight grin. And that was all he needed, at least for the moment.

He was on his way to the barn to help Caleb with the work horses but kept his eye on Lucy. He didn't want her to strain herself helping with the lunch spread. Homemade root beer was kept cold in large tin buckets. The tables were loaded with doughnuts, canned meat, cheese, bread, and vegetables. As the men grew closer, Minister Eben said the prayer, and the food was passed around.

Lucy gave Manny quick glances as they ate. He wondered what was on her mind, hoping it was something favorable. He wanted nothing more than to share their walks and talks that had become so frequent. Fannie touched her arm. They talked for a moment and then went about clearing tables and starting the cleanup. Manny rode up next to her in Caleb's buggy as she walked by.

"Need a lift?" He felt sort of English the way he said it,

and when she nodded, he stopped on a dime and helped her up and into the buggy. "What were you doing walking?" he teased, though he was serious.

"Waiting for you to give me a ride." She leaned back in the seat and sighed. "I can't walk but a few steps these days, and my feet swell something awful."

"Then I'll be your chauffeur for the time being." Not wanting to give her a chance to say no, he quickly changed the subject. "Did you make whoopee pie?" He'd seen her carrying one, so he took a guess.

"How did you know?" She faced him and narrowed her eyes, suspicious of his question.

"Yours is honestly the best I've had."

"You men know how to get a woman to cook for you." She lifted one side of her mouth with a small smile, knowing it was one of the few dishes she made well. Manny noticed her scar was lighter than ever and wondered why. Maybe it was internal as well as physical. Whatever the change, it was one of many that he had gone through with her. The only thing that hadn't changed was how he felt about her, and that wouldn't stop, no matter what she looked like or how she acted.

"What are you thinking about?" She'd been watching him, and he was taken off guard. He kept his eyes on the road even though he didn't need to because they were in a procession of buggies, hay mowers, and flatbeds.

"I was just wondering what you were thinking," Manny told her.

"I'm thinking I'm ready to have these babies. I don't expect you to understand, and I might not be the best person to be around right now, but it's all I can do to not either break down crying or laugh hysterically." She sighed. "I also didn't want my *mamm* to go."

"Your *daed* needs her now. And I'm here to help, along with all the girls. I might understand better than you think." He hadn't talked about Glenda since she died, and he didn't want to talk about her now, but it might help Lucy understand that he could be more supportive than she was letting him be.

Her brows furrowed. "What do you mean?"

"You know of my wife, Glenda." Saying her name made him relive more than he wanted to, but he wanted to make this personal for Lucy's sake.

Lucy hesitated, maybe because she was surprised. "*Jah*, although I don't think I ever met her."

"She got sick not long after you came. Glenda didn't have an easy pregnancy." He was gentle with his words, choosing them carefully so as not to alarm Lucy but also let her know what he went through with Glenda to show her that he knew how hard it could be. Hard but also very good. "And we're praying for your health, and for big, healthy babies. With *Gott* in it, we've done all we can. Now we just wait and keep praying."

He slowly turned to her, looking at her expression to see if there was any comfort in what he'd said. Tears flowed down her cheeks as she looked forward, not trying to stop them.

"Did I upset you?" He put his hand on hers and slowed to give her a moment. They were almost to his place.

"*Nee. Danke*, Manny." She wiped her tears with a hanky and then leaned over. The gentle kiss she placed on his cheek made him blush from his toes to the top of his head.

Just as they arrived and he had helped Lucy out of the

buggy, a blood-curdling scream came from the meadow. Manny jumped and followed the cry to where two men were standing by Peter looking at Caleb.

One of Caleb's hands cradled the other, which was covered with blood.

"What is it?" Manny expected to see a foot caught in the blades, but a different sight met his eyes. Caleb's finger was gone. Manny pulled out a handkerchief and wrapped it over what was left of the finger. It did no good; there was too much blood.

Manny scanned the area and found what was left of the finger. He wrapped it in another handkerchief and then he and four other men helped Caleb onto a flatbed covered with hay, and then rode off the field. When they pulled up on the dirt path, a buggy waited for them. Luke, who had the fastest horse around, told them to bring Caleb over to his buggy.

Before they could take off for town, Jake, the owner of the mower, rushed over. "Let me take a look." He plopped the finger into a can with kerosene. Then Jake started to treat Caleb's injured hand. "This might sting a little."

Caleb braced himself.

Manny looked for Emma and saw her standing with a group of Caleb's relatives who were consoling her.

"How did that happen?" Fannie took Lucy's hand as she came over with some other women who had stopped preparing snacks and drinks to observe the accident.

"It's the blades on that mower." Jake offered the explanation once he made sure Caleb's family wasn't around.

"But how? I could see a foot getting cut, but this was his hand." Fannie glanced over at Lucy and frowned.

"He must have been grabbing for something. A big rock

or a sturdy branch can stop the blades from spinning." He shook his head.

"He'll be all right if he goes to that same doctor Lucy had," Fannie chimed in. "Someone should get him here." Fannie turned away and was soon walking toward her buggy.

"Luke's going to take him to Pomerene." Manny caught up with her, which wasn't easy with her long legs keeping in stride. "Did you see his finger?"

"A glimpse, the tissue is gone, down to the bone." Her composure was so professional it took him by surprise.

"Do you think it can be saved?"

"It looks pretty bad, but I'm sure the doctors at Pomerene understand the importance of a man's hand to be able to work his farm."

"Don't you think so, Lucy?" Fannie stopped short when she didn't see Lucy and scanned the area.

"Where is she?

Manny stood and looked around. "No sign of her."

They split up, but still nothing, until he saw her sitting in his buggy. He walked over to her. "What are you doing in here? Are you sick?"

She shook her head. "*Nee.*" She wiped sweat from her forehead. "I think the babies are coming."

Chapter Twenty-Seven

Lucy groaned in pain. She'd never known such misery. The only positive she could think of was that the babies would be healthy; she'd prayed so long for a babe that *Gott* simply had to grant her petition. She opened her eyes and then shut them again, wincing through the sharp pricks that ran down her belly. Her body contracted and released before repeating. Her strength ebbed away.

A cold cloth made her sigh, but within seconds it was warm as biscuits from the oven. The room seemed as hot as a kitchen after cooking lunch, but she was in a bedroom and a bed—whose, she didn't know.

"Squeeze my hand." A man's voice forced her to open her eyes. At one time she would have protested, but all she cared about was birthing healthy babies.

"Manny...is he here?" Her voice was weak and just above a whisper.

"He's in the kitchen. Would you like him to come in?" The hand moved away, and Lucy worried he was fetching Manny.

"*Jah*, but he shouldn't."

"It's fine if you'd like him here."

Ahh, yes. This was the city doctor. "It's not proper." Her eyes fluttered, and she wished she could sleep.

"Whatever you're comfortable with. It does create a bond, which is why I suggest it. Give it some thought."

He walked away, and panic gripped her. *What if he didn't come back?*

Why, she didn't know, but her concern did lift with the arrival of a secular doctor to deliver her child. It would be one thing for a husband to be there for the birth, but another for Manny to observe, because they weren't married. Remorse took over, and she cursed herself for her waiting to marry. She had waited too long, letting her fears control her, and look where she was now, a widow with no *daed* for her babies.

She couldn't think straight as to why she'd become so scared of remarriage. After living with Sam, she'd been terrified more times than not. Losing that stronghold was good, now that it finally happened.

"Did I fall asleep?" Unheard of. Her water had broken, and that was the last she remembered. Then fuzzy images came to her, and she remembered sleeping and the pain dissipating.

Fannie touched her shoulder. "A small cat nap when the babes let up." Her face glowed. "You're finally gonna have those babies."

"Stubborn ones. Must take after their Aunt Fannie." A prickle zipped around her stomach. "Guess I shouldn't talk that way; they must be partial to you." Just seeing Fannie's face gave her courage, but still she wished it was Manny by her side.

Tears pricked Lucy's eyes. She wiped them away and kept her eyes closed.

"The pain getting worse?" *Mammi* asked, but she sounded much like Lucy's *mamm,* and more remorse stifled her. Only a few more days, and her *mamm* could have been here for this. Why was it all such a mess, so unlike what it should be?

Lucy shook her head. "I wish I was a married mother of these two; they deserve that, not to suffer because of my mistakes."

Frieda's heels clacked across the room, loud enough Lucy knew she meant business. "Don't you fret, Luce." The door opened and closed.

"What have I done? Should have kept my mouth shut." Lucy huffed out a breath and rubbed her tight belly. Just as the contraction melted away, she heard the door again. Manny's face appeared, and he smiled as he slowly took her hand.

"I'm glad you asked that I come in, but I'm not just here to hold your hand. The minister is outside. I've asked him to marry us. With your permission, of course." His grin faded slightly as he waited for her response.

Lucy covered her face with her hands and sobbed. Tears of joy and fear, comfort and love streamed down her cheeks as she became aware of her desperate affection for this man who had been so patient with her and would surely be so with their two children.

"It's okay if you aren't ready. I can wait. But those two little ones aren't gonna wait, so I thought I'd give you the opportun—"

She moved her hand away and touched his cheek. "*Jah*, I'm ready. I have been, but was just too stubborn…scared or something, I'm not sure." She patted his cheek. "I'm sorry, Manny."

"I know. It's all right. Everything's just as it should be right here, right now. I can't ask for more."

His smile could have lit up the room, which just made her cry even more.

He put a hand on her head, stroking her hair. "Are you ready for the minister?"

She nodded, not daring to try and talk with all the emotions going inside her. She didn't deserve this, him, or everyone who had helped her through the difficult time she'd had with Sam and now her two little ones.

The door opened once more, and Minister Eben walked over and stood between them. He gave Lucy a small smile. "You're having a busy day, now, aren't you?"

When she laughed, her belly contracted again. She put a hand on her tummy and breathed out, hoping there was time. "*Jah*, I sure am. Hope I can make it through this." She wanted him to hurry, which made her a little bit sad, but the babies might come any minute. The pressure increased, and her body told her to push.

The minister opened his Bible. "Well then, let's get to it." He cleared his throat, spoke out of both the Old and New Testaments, and said the wedding prayer. The small number of people speaking was good. Lucy couldn't speak during some of it because of the pain. Hymns were sung without the *Ausbund*. It was plain and simple as most, only much shorter because of the situation.

"Are we finished, Eben?" The doctor spoke to him as if he knew him, and the minister gave him a nod to continue with Lucy's needs.

"Do you know him, Doctor?" Lucy's curiosity had gotten the best of her, but she also wanted to know. What was it about this man that seemed a bit mysterious?

"Yes. Let's time your contractions." He went about

getting his instruments without a moment for her to say a word to Manny. "Hand me the stethoscope, Fannie."

Fannie opened her mouth and frowned.

"Of course you will." Frieda said as she stared Fannie down. Thank goodness the two of them were together. There was no one else who could tell Fannie what to do, except for this doctor who seemed to have picked her out of the group.

Fannie tilted her head and took deliberate steps to the dresser where his bag was.

"Lay these out for me on that table next to Lucy." He handed Fannie a box full of rubber gloves, light blankets, and a bar of soap.

"Excuse me, Doctor." Manny moved in closer and kissed Lucy's cheek. "Now, are you going to let me stay in here?"

The doctor interrupted. "You're not going to have a choice. Stand back."

Fannie took her hand as Lucy's back arched and she groaned. It was all she could do not to scream. Immense pain forced her to go with what her body was telling her, and she pushed...hard.

"*Gut*, Lucy." Fannie squeezed her hand harder.

The next thing she heard was fussing from Frieda, but she kept her distance, which Lucy appreciated. She wanted Manny to be the first to hold them. She had carried them for nine long months. Now it was his time to bond with them.

"Good. Now one more." The doctor concentrated on the last little one with intensity. Lucy felt a twinge of concern, creating even more of an effort to push. She worked through the pain and looked first in Manny's eyes. There were both sadness and gladness in his face as Frieda and

Rosy took the babies to clean and dry them off. One cry was loud, almost screeching. The other sound was weak and intermittent, causing alarm to seep into her mind.

"You did it, little sister." Fannie soothed her forehead with a cold cloth. She had a calming way about her that Lucy felt she needed right now, and it was exactly what she wanted.

When the doctor came over to her, he looked her straight in the eyes. "Your babies are alive and well. Although your youngest is *nay-nay*, crippled. But both of their vitals are good."

Hearing the doctor's words brought a mix of emotions. For him to use a Pennsylvania Dutch slang word told her it was something she needed to understand. But she wouldn't let herself go there. She had two babies. One would just need more care, and she could do that, especially with all the love that would be around him...or her. "Are they boys or girls?"

"That's the response I was hoping for." The doctor almost smiled. "Your strong son will be a great help to your little daughter."

Lucy thought she saw a flicker of sadness in his eye, but he didn't seem the type.

"We will work to make her stronger to the best of her abilities." Fannie chimed in with words that sounded more like a nurse's response than a sister's, but was just what Lucy wanted to hear right now.

Mammi held up the fat-bellied boy. "He came, and he came from muck and mire crying."

"What do you mean?" Lucy felt left out. Manny held the tiny girl, beaming from ear to ear. *Mammi* wasn't walking fast enough for her. She motioned with her hands for him to hurry. *Mammi* carefully lowered the little guy into Lucy's arms. She took in all the senses. His brown eyes blinked away a tear, and Lucy wiped it away with her finger.

"He's just beautiful." She couldn't stop staring at him, enjoying the moment.

Fannie was talking to Manny as she cleaned up the girl. She tenderly handed her back to Manny. He walked over holding the tiny girl and sat down beside Lucy with a nod toward the little boy. "I was thinking we might want to name him after your *daed*."

Lucy didn't even try to stop the tears from falling again. Manny's gesture was so like him and her *daed*. "I'd like that. His name is Timmy. Is that okay?"

"That's just fine. And this little one?" He couldn't take his eyes off the infant. He stroked her face. Her head was quite small and she had distinctive facial features.

"Do you have a name in mind?" She leaned forward to see the little one's thin legs. She almost started to cry, and then looked up at Manny, who hadn't taken his eyes off the tiny one. At that moment Lucy knew God had given them this child to raise because he knew they would have the love she needed from them.

"My *mamm's* name was Rhoda." He moved the baby's hair off her forehead.

"Didn't she pass away from cancer?" It came back to her now as they were talking about it, and she had a sudden feeling of remorse for him losing his *mamm* before she could see her grandbabies.

He nodded and let Rhoda touch his fingers with hers, so small next to his. "*Jah*, a while ago." He nodded toward little Timmy. "Are you going to give someone else a turn to snuggle with him?"

"I've hardly had a chance to get a good look at Timmy, with him getting passed around." She looked down and studied his little face. She moved the strands of hair from her face to get a better look.

She took in his features and held one hand to her lips. Although he was a newborn, he looked older than his few minutes of life and much too familiar. He had the features of her deceased husband, Sam.

Chapter Twenty-Eight

*M*anny watched Lucy scoop up Rhoda and hold the babe to her chest. The rocking chair creaked as he slowly rocked Timmy. The little guy wasn't much bigger than his sister, but was stronger. Rhoda's wailing kept them both up at night. With Verna gone, he didn't know what they would have done if not for Lucy's *mammi*. Frieda cooked and cleaned along with Rosy and Nellie. Fannie helped too, but did more of the scheduling, food preparation, and finances. He wasn't sure whether he liked it, but he wasn't going to complain. He'd tolerated Verna. Fannie couldn't be much different.

"What are you thinking about?" Lucy was staring at him. She might even have said something, but he was heavy in thought. He hadn't bargained for all these women around every minute of the day in a house he didn't live in…until now.

"Still getting used to all this." He didn't want to say more. There was no reason to give her one more thing to think about. They would be on their own soon enough, and he'd probably be begging for them to stop by and help.

"If you need some time, one of the girls will take him." Her eyes flickered toward Timmy and then away. It concerned him that she hadn't held him other than to nurse him since she'd given birth a couple days ago. Granted, Rhoda was the one who needed the most care, and that was probably all there was to it. Even though he wasn't their real *daed*, he felt like he was.

"*Nee*, I've done the morning chores and don't need to go back to my place until the afternoon to get the milking done. Emma dropped by with an update on Caleb. The finger isn't as good as new, but the doctor says he'll be able to use it just fine."

"Oh, I'm so glad." Lucy hugged little Rhoda even closer to her chest.

Even though he was only gone for an hour or so, Manny actually appreciated the time alone. But he was always glad to come back to Lucy and the babies. He studied Lucy's face and wondered whether she'd had a minute to take a breath outside or be alone. He doubted it but thought she should. "Why don't you take a step outside? It's crisp out there, but it might do you some good."

Lucy tilted her head and stared at him. "This has to be hard for you, getting married and fathering two babies in one day. You must have a million thoughts going through your head."

"Only a hundred. My mind isn't in full gear yet." Manny tried to grin, but he found even that took too much effort. He didn't want to admit it, but he'd never been so tired. He had baled hay, threshed wheat, chopped tobacco, and more, but none of those chores caused the ex*haus*tion he was feeling at that moment. When he studied her face, Manny knew she needed him to reaffirm that he had made the right choice. So did he.

"This is where I'm supposed to be, with the people I'm to be with. There's no looking back or second thoughts. We both made a choice, and I'm glad we made the one that we did."

Lucy lifted her hand over her face and wiped away a tear. It was then he knew he'd said the right thing, finally. She'd been so upside down and around in circles with him the last couple of weeks, he wasn't sure what to think. But now he could see the emotions flowing, relieving her of all the worry and stress she'd surely been under, from Sam to the babies and her *mamm* and *daed*.

Manny gathered Timmy closer to his chest and walked to her. He sat on the footstool at her feet and then looked down at her. "You sure are attached to her."

"*Jah*, such an innocent little thing. Starting out with challenges the minute you come into this world just doesn't seem fair." She still had her eyes on Rhoda.

"Nothing's fair in life. You've said that now a number of times yourself. The Lord giveth and the Lord taketh away." But something was different this time. Maybe it was because it affected the little one now, not just Lucy with all she'd dealt with. Having a babe to bear the burden with would make things different.

"I wish I could take it all away from her, lessen the load she'll have as she grows older." Lucy stroked the baby's cheek and smiled slightly.

"We all have something. Some people's load is just less visible is all." He didn't know whether she was hearing a word he said and felt inept. He'd heard of moms having baby blues and all. Maybe this was something like that. He'd ask the doc when he came to visit today. Soon, he hoped.

"You go on and do what you need to. We'll be fine here." She seemed to mean it, so he stood up to give the baby to Fannie as soon as she walked in the door. The doctor came in behind her.

"Morning, Doc, good to see you." Manny couldn't mean it more. He honestly didn't know what he was in for. He loved his new bride, and he'd learn the ways of being a *daed*, but at the moment he felt completely out of his comfort level. The doctor wasn't a talkative man, but maybe Manny could get some words of advice before he left.

"Morning, Manny." He grinned as if he knew Manny's concern, and then made his way to Lucy. "May I?" He reached for Timmy and held him like a sack of grain, tucked into his arm. He checked him over and then handed him to Rosy, who beamed from ear to ear. Lucy hadn't been generous in giving anyone much time with the babies, especially with Rhoda.

"How is she eating?" he asked. Doctor Daniel's frown told Manny he was concerned. He was a man of no emotion. Extra words or facial expression alarmed Manny.

"What is it, Doc?"

When Doctor Daniel turned to Manny and looked him in the eye, he knew it was something important. He almost wished he hadn't said anything, but they needed to know. Good, bad, or otherwise, they all had to be aware of what lay ahead.

Doctor Daniel crossed his arms over his chest and looked down at the worn wood floor. "Your daughter may have a genetic disorder." He put up a hand when Lucy gasped and put a hand over her mouth. "We just need to keep a close watch to see how she progresses."

"What kind of problems?" Fannie spoke up from behind him, which he seemed to have strategically arranged. He didn't turn around but kept his focus on Lucy and Manny.

"Narrow rib cage and lungs may cause breathing and heart abnormalities—"

"How common, and how does it affect the heart and lungs?" Fannie took a step to his side.

"About half of these cases have those abnormalities. As far as the heart issue, the medical jargon is atrial septal defect, if you'd like to look it up." He looked over his shoulder and narrowed his eyes. "Any further questions will be directed to me by the parents."

Fannie opened her mouth to speak but then shut it and squeezed her hands together. Manny was torn as to how much he wanted to hear, but the doctor would know better than any of them. He wouldn't want to go up against Fannie, on just about anything for that matter. Her blue eyes were seared into Doctor Daniel's at the moment, so he thought it was a good time to keep things on track.

"Why her?" Lucy seemed to be taking the news well.

"It's genetic. Intermarriages." His curt responses didn't bother Manny. The less he knew now, the better. There was only so much he could handle at the moment.

"But Manny isn't their biological *daed*." Lucy said it like that might help the situation, that he would come to save her once again from something bad happening in her life.

Doctor Daniel nodded, turned his gaze to Manny, and then continued. "It's rare, but coming to our attention more due to the fact it is limited to the Amish and especially those in Lancaster."

"Maybe this is enough information for one day," Manny said to Doctor Daniel, but kept his gaze on Lucy.

"I agree, but with one last note." He looked around at each of them as he spoke. "Some cases are so mild that symptoms are not readily apparent if at all. This is a rare medical condition. Keep that in mind." He looked back at

Fannie and then reached for his bag. "I'll be calling again soon unless you need me sooner. Take care of yourselves."

Right before he walked out the door, he stopped. "Fannie, will you step outside?" He said it more than asked and went out on the front porch.

Lucy watched her go and held Rhoda even tighter.

What was to become of their little one, so weak and mild? As far as love and attention, the women who lived in this *haus* would give her more than ever. That was one thing Manny was sure of. He watched as Lucy clung to Rhoda, her hands gripping the homespun blanket her *mamm* had made, until her hands went white. She was holding on too tightly and needed a break, or it would consume her. He wanted to do the same—protect Rhoda and never let her out of his sight—but right now, they needed that for themselves, just as the doctor said.

He took slow steps to Lucy and sat next to her on the footstool again. "Let's take a walk."

She frowned and moved Rhoda down a couple inches from her chest." I don't think we should; the babies aren't ready." She patted the baby's cheek.

When he touched her arm, she slowly looked over at him with eyes glazed. "We shouldn't leave them...not yet."

Manny took her hand and tucked his finger under her chin to get her to look at him. "You need to get out of the *haus*, even for a few minutes. Take in some fresh air, and we'll come right back."

She nodded. He called for Nellie, who hadn't held Rhoda even once since she was brought into this world. It was time for Lucy to trust others and give herself time away from them, even if it was just for a moment.

Lucy's hand lingered on the babe's cheek before she

relinquished her to Nellie's embrace. "*Danke*, Nellie. The folded diapers are in the second drawer, and—"

Nellie put a hand on Lucy's. "She'll be fine, and so will you. Take a stroll and enjoy your husband for a while. We'll all be here when you get back." She grinned.

"Let's go." Manny took Lucy by the hand to keep her on task, and she only looked back once. When she took a step outside, she closed her eyes and took in a long breath.

"The sun feels good."

Her pale face seemed even lighter outdoors. This would be good for her. For an Amish woman to be stuck in a *haus* for as long as she had would surely give her the baby blues. He did not intend to let that happen.

She took slow steps to Manny's buggy and leaned against it.

"Do you feel up for a ride?" He didn't want to push her but also liked seeing her outside the four walls she'd been in for days.

Lucy peeked into the buggy. Manny had a nice upgraded buggy, with cushions and velvet covers. Leather dashboards and a good many windows made for a comfortable ride. "Maybe a short one."

Manny couldn't help but smile as he helped her climb into the buggy and get comfortable. He got in the other side and studied her. She was smiling and looking forward, ready to go. "You'll tell me where to go and when you're ready to head back, *jah*?"

"*Jah*, I will. I'd like to go to Sam's place." She kept looking forward, sure of herself. Now he was the one who wasn't comfortable. He'd honestly thought she'd be okay to be out. He'd seen other women up and running the household within a couple days, but their situation was different.

"Are you sure?" Sam's wasn't that far, but he wanted to make sure she could go that far, and he wasn't crazy about being on Sam's place.

She looked over at him with a smile. "We won't stay long. I just need to see it one last time."

The elders had decided to clear any leftover debris, open the place up, and help Lucy sell the farm, but they weren't in a hurry due to the high cost. Maybe that was why she wanted to go there—to see that things got wrapped up.

At the end of the long lane to what was left of the barn, Manny tethered the buggy and went over to help Lucy out. She took a few steps to where the barn had once stood and picked up a large piece of wood. It caught on her finger, and she jumped back as if stung by a bee. She sat on a large tree stump and looked down at the parched ground beneath her feet.

His curiosity got the best of him. "Why did you change your mind to come here?" He just had to know.

"There are only bad memories here, but this is where I felt I needed to be right now."

"Whatever for?" He couldn't take it in, but decided to just let her do what she needed to.

"This was my hiding place. I hid from everything and everyone here, not just Sam." She gestured to the barn and the piece of wood she held.

"You can't hide from *Gott*," he offered, to remind her she was never alone, even back then.

She gave him a slow smile and nodded.

"So what brought you here today?"

She closed her eyes to the heavens as the clouds hid under the sun. "The comfort that comes from knowing that I don't live here, and neither will my children."

~ Chapter Twenty-Nine ~

Lucy looked out the kitchen window to see Abner hobbling down the lane. He slowed as he got closer to *Mammi's* front door, took a breath, and bent over.

"Rosy, will you get the door?" She held Rhoda as she cleaned up the kitchen, glad to be able to help again. The girls had made every meal and done all the cleaning until just yesterday, making Lucy feel useless. She knew they didn't mind, but it helped keep her preoccupied about what might happen to her baby girl. Doctor Kauffman made regular visits, but Lucy didn't always understand what he was saying. If it weren't for Fannie asking him question after question, Lucy would only know half of what she did.

Abner knocked once and opened the door with a *bang*. "I've got news from back home, Lucy." He took in a breath.

"Who is it? Is everyone all right?" Lucy handed the baby to Rosy and put on a shawl. Her mind twinged each time her shoe hit the wood floor.

"It's her *daed*, isn't it?" Rosy held Rhoda close and stayed near Timmy in a basket on the kitchen table.

"*Jah*, afraid so." His hearing wasn't so good, so everyone in the room usually heard what he had to say.

Lucy headed out the door. She kept walking, not waiting for the answer just yet. She knew what the call was about. Thoughts flew through her head that she didn't want to face. It wasn't as if she hadn't thought about him every day and known this time would come; it was just that having it actually happen was more than she could bear. Part of her wanted to run fast and far away from hearing the truth. It would be so much easier to deny that this was happening...and what of her *mamm*? She was such a strong woman, but not with this. *Daed* was her solid ground, laughter, and sunshine, the only one who accepted her the way she was. "Oh..." Lucy groaned. How would her *mamm* ever cope?

Lucy had aimlessly followed Abner to the community phone. The minister lived a good mile away, but she hadn't said a word except to confirm she wanted to use the phone.

Abner dialed the number she gave him, the only one she knew. When he turned to hand her the phone, his eyes were moist and his smile was dismal, confirming her thoughts.

Lucy's hand shook as she grasped the phone. She let out a long breath and sucked another in. "*Hallo*?" Her voice was not her own, raspy and faint. Only silence on the other end. The eerie silence seemed forever before she heard the sound of sobs.

"*Mamm*? Is that you?"

"Lucy, it's so good to hear your voice."

The crack in *Mamm*'s voice brought the tears. Lucy recalled how she had dreaded her visit for nothing.

"*Jah*, you too, *Mamm*." Lucy wanted to ask, but couldn't. So she waited, listening to her *mamm* try to pull herself together so she could talk.

"Well, I was just fine until I heard you." She cleared her throat. "When did it happen?"

"Just a couple of days after I got back. You should know

that your *daed* died smiling, literally. He was telling your sisters a joke, believe it or not."

Lucy couldn't help but smile, picturing it in her mind. Her sisters surrounding him and *Mamm* trying to keep a straight face but failing. "That doesn't surprise me. Which one?" She remembered how he repeated the same jokes but tweaked them just enough to make them smile again.

"About the potatoes."

Lucy grinned. "Why did the farmer use a steamroller to plough his field?"

"Oh, that's silly." *Mamm*'s voice was a little stronger with each word she said, and to hear her repeat one of *Daed*'s jokes would make Lucy smile.

"Don't you remember?" It was quiet for a moment, just long enough to make *Mamm* respond.

"To make mashed potatoes." And then she started to cry again, a good cry that made Lucy bawl too. But it was a cleansing weeping, which drew them closer together than they ever had been. Those precious couple of months together couldn't have come at a better time.

They talked about the wake and friends who had come from near and far to pay their respects, and then Lucy spoke with two of her sisters and promised she and Fannie would call them again when they could. Lucy wondered how long she had been on the phone, knowing it was costing money with every minute they spoke.

As soon as the phone was on the cradle, Abner peeked around the barn door. "I'm sorry, Lucy. I know how close you were to him."

"*Jah*, he was a *gut* man." She pulled her shawl closer and prepared herself for the cold that was starting to come each morning and evening once the sun was down.

Abner stuck his hands under his arms. "I'll walk you home."

Lucy wouldn't usually want to bother him, but today she accepted his offer. Silence filled the air. What was there to say when something like this happened?

Manny was waiting for her and stood when she got back to *Mammi*'s. When she nodded, he lowered his head. She felt a void, wishing Manny could have known her *daed*. But she praised God she had Manny to fill the hole in her heart.

"Thanks, Abner." Manny took Lucy's hand, and they turned to go into the *haus*. She looked down at their hands twined together. Manny had asked her to move to his *haus* a number of times, wanting to make it a home for their family, but she was overwhelmed with Rhoda's needs. It was at that moment she realized how selfish she had been, letting fear control their relationship, robbing them of time alone to become a family.

"How was your *mamm*?" His voice brought her back to reality.

"She was better than I expected. We had a good talk."

Manny pursed his lips. "I have to admit I'm a little surprised. But things did get better between you two. What did she say?"

Lucy didn't want to talk of sadness, death, or how far away her family was right then, so she grinned and turned toward Manny. "Potatoes."

He chuckled. "I guess I'm missing something."

"*Jah*, my *daed*. I wish you would have met him."

"Me too, but if he's anything like you, I guess I already have, in a way."

"You heard Fannie say that, didn't you?"

"I suppose I did. But she's usually right about those kinds of things."

"Don't tell her that. I'll never hear the end of it."

He stopped, turned her toward him, and wiped a tear from her cheek. Then he held her close and waited until she stopped shivering.

"You're a *gut* man, Manny. I'm glad *Gott* gave you to me."

"I'd say the same thing, but I think I'll show you, instead." He took her by the waist and held her close, kissing her long and hard on the lips. Then he let go, took her hand, and started walking again. He grinned when she let out a breath, and she decided she liked it.

"Manny Keim, I didn't know you had it in you," she said after she caught her breath. He was always so private and slow to show affection, this had taken her off guard.

"I'm sorry I've kept us in *Mammi's haus* all this time. I know you want to spend more time at your farm. I've kept you from that, and it's time I let go and let us be a family, just the four of us."

Manny's head shot up, and he nodded. "I'm glad to hear you say that."

"Well, we can pack up and go tonight if you want to. I've made you wait long enough, and I'm sorry for that."

She truly was, but was more concerned about the trouble she had with Timmy. She hadn't dared to say it, but he needed a lot of care, and she felt badly that she didn't have the energy to care for him as she wished. *Mamm* had told her she was a fussy child, but it went away once she was a bit older.

She appreciated the fact that he was his own little person, not Sam but Timmy, innocent of anything similar to Sam. She'd prayed her heart out asking *Gott* to put her mind in the right place so she could love her son and daughter, but the feeling of having two children all at once tested her confidence, and she was plagued with guilt.

As she stared at Timmy in his crib, his wide newborn fastened on hers. The more she gazed at him, the more she could see the hint of a dimple on his chin and more hair than Rhoda had.

"Lucy, where were you?" Manny had stopped on the porch, waiting for her attention.

"I...guess I'm tired. Can we wait until tomorrow to settle in at your *haus*? I just don't have the energy right now." It was a big job to move and to make his home hers. She was just happy to be with a man who she believed truly loved her. Each and every time she looked at her son and daughter, she felt blessed to have Manny as her husband but worried his *haus* might not feel like hers.

When they returned, Nellie handed Rhoda to Lucy. When she looked over at Manny, she knew she had to say something to him. It had become so obvious, he had to know something was amiss. So she decided to tell him a bit of how she felt.

"Does it feel strange to you that we'll be living in the *haus* you and your wife had together?" She glanced down at the babe she held and turned away.

"*Nee*, we're a family now. It doesn't matter where we live as long as we're together. I'm more worried about Rhoda than anything else."

Lucy paused but finally responded. "I worry about her too."

"Maybe it's okay for now that you spent more time with her, but your boy needs you too. Fannie and the girls are good to love on him, but he needs his *mamm*."

She nodded toward Rosy as she walked away from the basket on the table and watched Timmy's eyes catch hers. "Timmy just looks so much like Sam. It's been hard." A comfortable feeling took over as his eyes met hers. His brown eyes, large and focused on hers, caused her to go to him. She had too many images in her mind of times Sam would simply stare at her for something she had done that he disapproved of, she was so glad Manny was his *daed* now. Maybe she was overreacting, but Lucy didn't know how to make it right, to clear her mind of Sam and create a new view of how to care for her children.

A warm hand grasped her wrist, and Manny held her close. "You have to stop yourself from letting the evil one take you places in your mind that aren't safe. Pray it away, and eventually you will see Timmy in a different light." He pulled her away. "The doctor will let us know if he needs anything from us."

Lucy shook her head, wishing she had never said anything, and waited for it to all go away. "I'll try. I want it to be different."

Manny picked up Timmy and cradled him in his arms. "I don't know what went on between you and Sam—I can only imagine—but this is your chance to start over with me, Rhoda, and Timmy." Little Timmy grasped Manny's callused finger and kicked his feet.

Mammi walked into the kitchen. "Oops, didn't mean to interrupt some family time."

"We were just talking about packing the babies up and moving to Manny's. Do you feel all right if we do that, *Mammi*?" She'd been so good to take them in that Lucy didn't want to upset her in any way, but after what Manny had said, she knew she had to face what was yet to come and in her own home with Manny.

"Well, it's about time." *Mammi* took Timmy and cradled him close to her. "You need to grow as a family." But the tears that filled her eyes said something different indeed. "You can go as long as you promise to come visit often."

"You know we will," Manny responded to give Lucy a minute to compose herself.

"I'll be expecting you at our *haus*." Lucy couldn't say more, knowing she would be living in a home she didn't know would feel like hers only if the girls came to visit.

There wasn't a dry face in the *haus* as Rosy, Nellie, and Frieda all came around and helped them pack up and then worked together and promised they would make a scrumptious meal. Fannie wouldn't be coming with them, so she said her good-byes for the moment.

Lucy worried that all of them could live in harmony in the strange new place they would now call home.

～ Chapter Thirty ～

anny looked over his shoulder again. Milking seemed to last forever. He was more concerned about Lucy than the milk that served as part of their livelihood. She'd come out with Rhoda and stood on the porch three times now to try and keep her from crying. If it happened again, he'd leave his chore, at least for a minute or two.

Little Rhoda's wails were weak and pitiful. Her voice wasn't as strong as Timmy's or any baby that he'd heard cry. It was as if her lungs were deflated, barely pumping in the oxygen she needed. He'd asked Lucy if she thought they should take her to the doctor early, before her regular visit, but Lucy said she could hold out until the week was over. He wasn't sure if that was wise at this point. At least one of the girls had made the effort to visit each day, usually more, but today no one had come over, and this was a day they needed the help.

A Holstein kicked the ground and mooed, bringing Manny's attention away from the *haus* and back to the job at hand. He removed the cups from the cow's udder and cleaned them, then put away the machine until he would repeat the process that evening. He opened the stalls and guided the cows out of the barn one by one, with a few pushing their way through. He had started to muck the stalls when he heard sobbing.

It was too loud to be either of the babies. He dropped

the pitchfork and came running. "Lucy!" Manny ran faster than he knew he could, when he saw her shaking body and the tears falling against Rhoda's blanket.

He slowed when he got closer, and eased in beside her, sitting on the porch step. He put his arm around her and waited for her to calm down.

He asked her what was wrong, whether the children were all right, and every other question he could think of. She nodded her responses.

He was out of words. The more he tried to guess if she was happy or sad, the harder it was. First with Sam and all she'd gone through with him, and then the pregnancy. He'd known what he was getting into with two little ones to tend to right after marriage, but all it took was one look, and he was smitten with both of them—no second thoughts or regrets.

She had come such a long way since he first met her, coming down the lane, worried about a coyote and telling him so. He'd appreciated her unexpected bold comment defending the animal that had been tearing into his livestock. He grinned.

"What made you smile?" She turned to him with a smile.

"I was just thinking about how we met." He turned to look at her, with her freckled nose and blue eyes. "Do you remember?"

She smiled. "How could I forget?"

"You were out walking down the road, heading home, and I was looking for the varmint that was eating my chickens." He liked the thought of her scolding him for hunting, and him mystified with this petite little redhead, alone and with child.

She turned toward him and drew her brows together in

confusion. It was better than the puckered forehead she seemed to have most of the time now. There were just certain things you didn't expect in life, and Lucy had had plenty of that in her lifetime. So had Manny.

"I still don't like guns and never will." She paused. "Neither will Timmy, if I have anything to say about it."

He'd changed her orneriness to her bright side, and now that he'd done it, he wasn't sure which one was easier to deal with. But he could see the fight going out of her. She was getting some of her energy back and must be feeling it too, by the look of her. He wished he could sweep her up and take her to bed. That was probably all Lucy needed. She'd feel better in the morning if she got some decent sleep. Manny hated to admit it, but he was really missing Frieda and Fannie about now.

Manny took Rhoda from her when Timmy he started to fuss, and nodded toward the *haus*. "Go fetch him. I've got Rhoda."

He watched her thinking about it as she tried to push herself off the steps and looked from him to the baby. Manny hadn't realized how tiny Rhoda really was or how soft her cries were. One of her tiny squeals was nothing compared to Timmy's, which might be one reason why Lucy didn't worry about him as much.

"I wish Rhoda would eat more. Does that worry you?"

Her question caught him off guard. He'd been thinking along the same line, only about her lack of sleep more than her lack of appetite. He moved back a bit and then looked over at little Timmy. "I know he's stronger and a minute or two older than Rhoda, but Timmy needs his *mamm* too." He took her by the arms and stared into her eyes, waiting for a response he wanted to hear.

"I'm trying, Manny. These little ones are a lot of work, but I wouldn't have it any other way." She squeezed her hands together until they turned white.

"I don't know what that's like, but what I do know is you're going to be a great *mamm* to him once you trust *Gott* to get you there. He doesn't do anything without a reason. Find out what that is, and maybe you'll be able to be the *mamm* you want to be."

She turned to look at him. "I do want that, Manny." She picked at some grass coming up around the cracks in the porch, now brown and withered from the change in the temperature. "I didn't think it would be this hard."

He almost started to talk again with wisdom that was redundant, words he had repeated too many times already, but finally realized that as much as he wanted to make everything all right, he couldn't. It was up to her now with Timmy and Rhoda. Even though he felt those babies were as much his as hers, she was the one who'd carried them and now fed them each and every morning. She looked at her son, an innocent little angel who grew on Manny more and more each day.

"I can't imagine what Timmy might be like as he gets older." Manny grinned. "He'll probably be a mama's boy." He loved the smile that slowly grew on her face as her spirits lifted. That was one thing he'd learned to do right with her—get her to smile.

He thought he'd ask her the question he'd been holding aside until the time was right. "Dr. Kauffman thought it would be a good idea to take Rhoda into the hospital, just so he could get a better look at her. It might tell us why she cries so much." He thought he knew, just from the information he'd read and talking to another family in the community who had a similar situation to contend with. The more he thought about the different families in the area, the more he realized how common it was. Yet it wasn't something so out of the ordinary that any of them would make a fuss over the special needs of the affected children. But now that it was happening to Manny, he was noticing much more than he'd ever thought he would.

"I'm sure it's nothing the doctor can help us with. She just needs time to gain her strength."

"Well, that's just it. The doc said she won't change a lot, that they have to have help the rest of their lives. Like the Benders and the Grabers and the other kids around who need a little more help." The more he explained it to her, the more real it seemed that their little girl would have special needs. He thanked *Gott* they lived around others who would help them and love their child unconditionally and without blame.

She nodded. "I'm scared, Manny." She took his hand in hers and squeezed.

He wasn't sure what to say to that, since he was feeling the same way. Then he remembered the minister talking about fear and how it's all Satan's and not *Gott* at all.

"The first thing you do after being scared is the most important thing you'll do. That's what makes you do what's good or bad." He was scared too but knew his place as a father and husband was to grow his family up and teach them to honor the Lord, and that's what he intended to do. "Fear makes you isolate yourself and make wrong decisions that get you stuck."

"*Jah*, it does."

She seemed relieved to hear what he was saying, so he

continued. "Whatever the enemy makes bad, *Gott* turns to good."

She lifted her tired blue eyes. "Where's the good, Manny?"

He didn't know the answer but thought about what he'd been praying and where he'd found comfort. "*Gott*'s there, waiting for us to be in His presence. He comes; sometimes we just miss Him."

"*I've* missed Him, not you. I've been too busy for *Gott* lately, and I'm feeling it right now." She took in a long breath and slowly let it out. "You're a good man, Manny Keim."

He almost had a minute to appreciate her compliment before both babies started to cry. They stood and walked side by side as they made their way into the *haus*.

They found their rocking chairs and rocked the babies and then spoke soft words to each other until everyone was resting comfortably. "Wouldn't it be nice if it was always like this?" He asked but didn't expect an answer. It was obvious that it wouldn't be. The babies would grow up, but he didn't want to take this time for granted.

"Manny." She rocked quietly except for a slight creaking from her rocker. "Maybe we should listen to the doctor and take her in for a checkup."

"It might put our minds to rest and answer some questions." Or it would make things worse, which was why Lucy was scared. He understood that. Everything he'd just told her was what he told himself. It would be nice if they could stay strong together. "I can call and ask the doc."

He said it with hope. He had never been a big proponent of doctors and hospitals until recently. These two little people who had come along in their lives had changed him about a lot of things. One of the biggest revelations was how small he was without a family and how much he loved these little ones he called his own.

"Manny, I never thought I'd like having a doctor, especially for my children..." Her voice trailed off. Whether she didn't know what to say or the emotions took over, he wasn't sure. "You've been through this before. I hate to bring it up, but—"

He held up a hand. "It's all right to talk about Glenda and what she went through. Although I don't like to relive it, you might feel better about taking Rhoda to a hospital."

"You don't have to explain. I just want to know we've tried everything before we go there."

Rosy was the one they turned to for remedies, so this would be outside Lucy's element and maybe her loyalties, as well. He had seen Glenda decline all too quickly, and only after going to the hospitals had they been allowed another month together before she passed away.

"Are you comfortable with Dr. Kauffman taking care of us at the clinic?" That was the biggest question, and Manny knew where he stood. Although he'd been skeptical at first with the doctor's brash manner, his confident way with Rhoda assured Manny that this man knew what he was doing. "I know I am."

"*Jah*, he does make me feel that he knows the ways of medicine, and his direct approach is something I'm used to." She shrugged. "With *Mamm*."

Manny hadn't thought of it, but Lucy's *mamm* did carry herself in much the same manner. He was glad all over again knowing Verna was safe and sound at her home. "*Jah*, you probably feel comfortable." He smiled, but she didn't, and he hoped he hadn't upset her. "If you're not ready, I understand."

"*Nee*, I am. I just got to thinking about my *mamm*."

"*Gut* thoughts?"

"*Jah*, I learned to love despite my *mamm*'s ways, and it ended in such a positive way." She bent her head down to Timmy's as he slept in her lap.

Manny wondered whether she was thinking those same thoughts for Timmy that she did for her *mamm*, to love the reality of their relationship, mother and son.

"Where do we start?"

Manny's mind rushed with thoughts of what he wanted to share with Lucy. He'd hoped and prayed she would come around and give the doctor a chance so they could get Rhoda more help.

Manny stood and placed Rhoda in a bouncy seat. "I want to show you something." Before she could ask any questions, he went into another room and grabbed a stack of papers from the desk. He took quick steps back to his rocker and sat down.

"What are you so excited about?" She glanced down at the brochures and frowned. "You were assuming I'd say *jah*." Her expression made him think she was surprised. Maybe he'd done too much at once, but he couldn't help it. He'd waited for the right time and felt this was it. If he failed, at least he had tried.

He nodded. "The doctor told me the last time he came that we should be thinking about it. I told you that much. Just not about this information." He handed her the first page.

She took it and started to read. "A clinic for special

children with genetic disorders. I'd hate for the community to have to pay for this."

"It's nonprofit. Keep reading." And she did, while Manny prayed as he watched their two children sleeping.

↬ Chapter Thirty-One ↫

W hat do you mean you're going to see a doctor?" *Mammi* stood with her hands on her hips. "Is it the babies?"

Fannie answered *Mammi*'s question before Lucy had a chance to. "It's little Rhoda, isn't it?"

"*Jah*, we are going to see what Doc Kauffman has to say. She's not gaining any weight, and you know how she fusses and cries. We can't seem to satisfy her." Lucy was talking to *Mammi* but looked at Rhoda. She couldn't get enough of this little one who both ex*haus*ted her and gave her such joy. Lucy had never felt more needed and filled with purpose. But with that came the agony of watching her little girl struggle.

"You should pack, in case they keep you there," Fannie suggested as she studied Lucy and then Rhoda. "He might want you to stay overnight."

Lucy rubbed the scar on her cheek and thought deeply about what it would be like to take her away from their *haus* and stay at the hospital. Fannie didn't seem fearful of such things. Every time Doc Kauffman was around she stood looking over his shoulder to study his ways. He didn't seem to mind, the way he did when others started breathing down his neck.

"I don't know if I'm comfortable with that, being away from all of you and our own home." Lucy glanced at Manny, who stood next to her.

"No sense worrying about it right now. I can always come back and get what we need, if I need to."

The lines around his eyes showed worry and lack of sleep. She said a soft prayer for strength and went to pack for the drive.

Manny followed behind her and paused when she laid out some clothes. "Lucy, I thought we should come back home after the visit." There was a change in Manny's tone. She glanced up to see him staring at her.

"Fannie said we should get ready, just in case." She went into the babies' bedroom and folded the twins' clothes, wondering how much to bring.

"I think it would be better to keep our family together at our *haus,* if possible."

The edge in his voice was new to her. He was a soft-spoken man who didn't provoke easily, but now she could see his frustration. But she was irritated too, so she let go of his resistance to staying at the hospital. "What if they want us to and we're not prepared?"

"Why go to all this trouble if we turn around and come home?" His voice quieted. "Let's take things as they come and not fret over things that don't need to be done."

She stopped her packing and stood in front of him. "Don't fret. We don't want to make this more stressful than it already is." She rubbed her forehead and closed her eyes. She hated to see him worry.

He nodded but didn't do what she expected when he kissed her forehead, turned on a heel, and walked away. Watching him go only made her more uncertain about whether she should finish what she'd started. She went to the closet to find a bag and suitcase. The distraction helped, but as she folded nighties for Rhoda, her mind drifted back to the last time she'd felt so unsure of her place in the world—shortly before birthing her babies. She'd felt safe, especially with Manny, and here she was worrying again. She could blame it on hormones as Fannie said, but this time was different, and Lucy sensed she was just letting the evil one take over her beautiful little family. But the knowledge did little to make her pause in her busywork. Hands in motion seemed to be the only thing keeping her together.

Lucy thought of just packing for herself and Rhoda to give Manny a rest, but that wasn't possible with Timmy needing to be nursed. The familiar guilt came over her for thinking of any way that would separate their family, but she pushed it away.

Lord, give me strength.

Would it always be so difficult for little Rhoda? She had heard other women talking about such things, so maybe what ailed her wasn't as much to worry about as she thought. A rap at the door pulled her back as she realized her eyes were full of tears.

"I brought you my bag if you need another." Fannie didn't even pause long enough to know something was wrong and began to gather Timmy's clothes. "I'll go with you. Manny will need to keep up the farm. He and I can switch off so you will always have someone with you."

"*Nee,* Manny will take us so we can go as a family." Lucy had her back to Fannie, unable to keep her emotions in check. Her bouncing back and forth between worrying and crying was out of control, and she needed to keep the turmoil in check.

She felt a warm hand on her shoulder and took in a

breath. Fannie turned Lucy around to face her. "What is it, Lucy?"

"I don't know. Fear of the unknown, I suppose."

"It's just the baby blues, Luce."

Fannie barely got the words out before Lucy lost her composure. "It's not just that, Fannie. It's just not knowing exactly what's wrong with my baby." She wiped her face and lowered her voice. The last thing she wanted was someone else hearing her distress and coming to check on her.

"What do you mean? We understand, Luce. You've been through a lot, we all know that." Fannie closed her eyes and squinted. "I could open a can of worms here by mentioning Sam, but there's no point. It will get better." She said it so matter-of-factly that Lucy almost believed it. But no one could possibly know how she felt. She'd seen what other women had gone through during and after having their babies, and it wasn't like this, not to this extent.

"Manny is a good man. He'll take care of you and your babies." Her eyes formed into slits. "And you will let him, even if I have to make you."

This was the one thing that made Lucy wary of her sister. Once she got involved in something, she took control and made things go her way, which was usually good, but Lucy hadn't dealt with her for years now and wasn't sure she liked it as much as she used to. She had been forced to grow and mature into someone who could stand up for herself. Unfortunately that opportunity had come only after Sam was gone, leaving her to fend for herself until Manny came along. It wasn't fair to him, the way things happened, but that was how it was for both of them, like it or not.

"What are you thinking about?" Fannie hadn't stopped eying her, watching Lucy wade through her thoughts.

"Looking back, there have been a lot of changes. I've changed. I just don't know if it's for the better." She thought of Sam and how beat down she was when Manny came along. Maybe she'd rushed into things with Manny. But how could she have resisted him with his gracious and nurturing ways toward her and now with the babies? What would she have done if he wasn't there for her? The girls would have been there, but it wasn't the same as having a father around. Even though he wasn't their *daed*, it felt like he was.

"There's bitterness flowing through you, rightly so, after what's gone on. But don't let Manny take the brunt of that." Fannie's forehead creased as Lucy took her time to respond.

She resented what her sister was saying, even if she was right. She stood and placed some tiny socks on the bed. "I know you're just trying to help, but I think enough has been said." Her voice was even, but not her mood. She'd always admired her sister's straightforward demeanor, but a lot had happened over the years, and she had her own mind about her. She wasn't the meek scapegoat she'd once been.

"He's a good man. You're fortunate to have him. Maybe someday I'll be as fortunate." Fannie said it nonchalantly but sincerely.

Lucy didn't need to be told she wasn't appreciating Manny as she should and grunted with thought.

"What was that for?" Fannie's brow furrowed.

"You're one to talk. You're tickled pink every time the doc comes by, but you ignore him." Lucy grinned, and then stopped Fannie before she could deny it. "And don't say anything differently. It's written all over your face." Lucy watched as her sister stonewalled and distracted herself with folding clothes from a basket by the bed. "You're not denying it."

"Is there anything else you want to take?" Fannie placed her hands on her hips and turned each way to examine the room. "If you need anything more, one of us will be there in a moment's notice."

"*Jah*, I don't doubt that. It's the unknown I'm worried about. Not knowing is what keeps me up at night."

"Literally. That's one good thing about being in a hospital and having nurses help us share the load. You might actually get some sleep."

"I can't remember the last time I slept through the night." Lucy'd had no idea how demanding it would be to nurse two babies. When Manny had offered to help, she'd only laughed and asked whether he could grow breasts, and then they'd both laughed deliriously. Remembering made her smile.

"Okay, let's go." Fannie helped her out with the suitcase and sat down next to *Mammi*. "She's all ready to go."

"Are you ready for this?" *Mammi*'s eyes were soft as they took Lucy in, and Lucy almost felt guilty leaving her. They had become attached to the two little ones, and Lucy knew she was going through withdrawal already.

"*Jah*, for my baby."

Fannie frowned. "You mean babies."

"Timmy isn't the one I'm worried about. He's a strong boy." She looked over at her baby girl. "But we don't know what's wrong with Rhoda." She stopped short and took in a jagged breath.

Rosy had been leaning against the doorjamb. "She'll be all right, Luce. Even if there is something that needs care, she will still be okay."

Leave it to Rosy to say the most touching words. She was a delicate soul, and Lucy wondered whether, if she had been bolder with young men all those years ago, if her life would have been different. Lucy nodded and held back tears that were trying to build up. "*Danke*, Rosy. You're good to have faith in our little one."

Nellie held Timmy, who was sound asleep in her lap. Lucy wished Rhoda could rest like he did, but she seemed out of sorts much of the time. Lucy had learned early on as a mother how painful it was not to be able to soothe your child.

Manny came in, rubbing his hands together. "It's a bit cold out there." His eyes met Lucy's. But when she smiled at him, he turned away and went over to Nellie and then stroked Timmy's cheek.

Nellie lifted Timmy up to Manny. "You want to hold him? I wouldn't want to take a father's son from him."

"I wish I could sleep like he does." Manny got situated and sat back on the couch as Nellie handed Timmy to him.

Lucy made her way over and sat down next to him, remembering the little joke she'd made about nursing and smiled. She was ex*haus*ted, so she didn't talk but just appreciated the moment—the two of them together, both resting.

She prayed he'd never leave her, and that their babies would grow strong and healthy. And for Manny, because if not for him, she might be raising these babies alone.

❧ Chapter Thirty-Two ❧

*M*anny paid the English driver and went to the trunk to gather the bags. He'd rather have driven his own buggy but wasn't sure his family would have been as comfortable. He doubted Rhoda's cries were from pain, but he wanted her to be as content as possible.

As he set the bags on the sidewalk, Manny studied the building. The clinic was nestled in the heart of Lancaster County, between two Amish farms in Strasburg. From the information he'd read, they had the most comprehensive and affordable care for children like Rhoda. And he prayed to *Gott* they truly did.

"Let me help with those." The *Englischer* offered a hand, and Manny readily accepted. He would need to humble himself into receiving help from others through this and leave his pride back home where he could yell and scream and call *Gott* out as to why him, and even more, why Rhoda.

"Sir?" The *Englischer* was watching him as he thought about what was before them. "Go on in. I'll get these." The young man did as he promised and went ahead of them to the glass doors. "The admission desk is to your left." He tilted his head, unable to lift a hand to direct them.

"*Danke.*" Manny followed the young man's direction and took Lucy's arm as they walked to the waiting room. "Wait here."

Lucy was busy adjusting her bag and setting Timmy's

baby seat on a chair. *"Jah"* was the only response she gave him, but that was enough.

"Keim is the name. Rhoda…she's my daughter." He stuttered, uncommon for him, but under the circumstances, it was probably normal at this point in time. To be taking the final step to admit her into a facility that they hoped could help the baby they couldn't care for made him feel utterly useless, beyond making his family as comfortable as possible and letting the doctors do their work.

The young woman at the desk was talking, so he focused his attention on the words he wasn't taking in. He glanced back at Lucy and his babies and held up a hand. "Can you please repeat what you've said?"

The secretary smiled. "It's just what I have to say to new patients. Don't worry. Just take your family to the room to your left, and someone will be there shortly." She handed him a pamphlet. "This will come in handy. Read through it when you can."

He was starving for the information but apprehensive. Would it give him horrible scenarios that would haunt him or overly encourage him into thinking that after a weekend here his little girl would be cured?

With each step he took toward Lucy, he became more frightened. In their home he could take care of their basic needs—food, shelter, and safety, without the worry. And if for some reason he couldn't, the community was there for them.

"Come this way." He placed his palm on Lucy's back, causing her to jump. "It will be all right. They seem like *gut* people."

"I hope so." She put the pink blanket over Rhoda as if hiding her would calm her cries. They were intermittent at the moment. Maybe the babe knew her surroundings had changed or felt the pulse of stress between her and her *mamm*, her *daed*, and the new environment.

Manny held Timmy's baby seat as they walked to the designated room, set down their belongings, and waited.

Within a few minutes, an older gentleman stepped in. Manny recognized him from the pamphlet he'd been given. This man was one of the founders of the facility and was taking the time to meet them as soon as they came in the door. His wore a gray suit jacket and red bow tie. Manny knew he was a respected man here and gave him a nod.

"You must be the Keim family, from the community that had that nasty fire, if I recall."

"*Jah*, that would be us." Manny responded, appreciating that the man remembered the tragedy they'd been through.

"You're a strong bunch, good things said of you and of helping one another through such events." He scratched his chin and peered down at Timmy and then set his eyes on Rhoda. "This must be the special one." He smiled. "*Gott* bless you, little one."

Manny heard Lucy's breath catch, and she held a hand to her mouth. "That's our little Rhoda."

"*Jah*, I know her name. Namesake?"

"*Jah*, on my *mamm*'s side," Manny explained.

"You'll be well taken care of here. You can hold me to that." He extended a hand and pumped Manny's and then Lucy's.

As he walked out of the room, Manny felt some of his anxiety go as well and sat down next to Timmy's baby seat. The little guy's face turned crimson, a good sign he was going to belt out the news that he was hungry. "I think this might be a *gut* place for us."

"*Jah*, I hope so. I've never prayed for something as much as I have now." She held Rhoda close. "*Gott* wouldn't take her from us now, would He?"

"We're gonna be fine. These are *gut* people, and Rhoda will get better. Have faith, Luce. Have faith." Manny was telling told himself as much as he was tell Lucy because he was scared to death.

A rap at the door brought them back from their thoughts as a short redhead walked through the door. "I'm Miriam, a registered nurse here. I'm going to take Rhoda's vitals and then show you to the room you'll be calling home for a while."

After she had finished and made her notes, she said, "I can take you to her room." She led them along the white-floored corridors to settle them in again.

"I don't like this shuffling around," Lucy whispered to Manny, trying to keep up with the nurse.

"*Nee*, it will be over soon enough." Manny couldn't think any differently. If he did, it would ruin him, and that couldn't happen.

"This is where you will stay while working with the doctor. Often the care of a physician on a daily basis helps to reveal new opportunities for treatments."

"How long does it usually take? We can't afford to be here for long." Lucy was swaying from side to side to keep Rhoda content.

"The doctor can give you more information about that once he makes an assessment of your situation, and he can answer any other questions you have. Make yourself at home, and the doctor will be in shortly." She smiled brightly and left.

Lucy turned to face Manny. "Everyone is sure friendly in this place. I wonder how much we're paying for that."

"This is no time to worry about money. The community will help us out if we need them to."

She sighed. "I'm worried about everything; that's just one tiny piece of it. I know you're as worried as I am, but you just don't show it."

He took a seat and gently rocked Timmy in his seat, hoping he wouldn't fuss and want to be held. Manny was just too tired. "This all reminds me of when Glenda was sick. It's a helpless feeling, and all you can do is wait and hope they pull through."

They were both silent for a moment. "But she didn't, and that has to make you more scared than I am, even though that doesn't seem possible."

"Still, it isn't as bleak as all that with Rhoda. I just pray *Gott* gives her strength to live a decent life."

"*Ach*, she will. We'll make sure of that." She chucked little Rhoda under the chin and smiled sadly with pinched brows and trembling lips.

Manny felt the need to get busy and organized to take his mind off what was to come. He and Lucy unpacked and took note of where everything was that they needed and what they should have to get situated. Then came a knock at the door. Manny glanced at Lucy and opened it.

"*Hallo*, Keim family. It's good to see you here." Doctor Kauffman almost smiled, as if in relief they were there. "Let's get started."

Instead of going to his office, they sat around a table together. The doctor asked questions but mainly listened, not offering any information until they had expressed what they had been through and why they had come.

They were out of ideas and knowledge about how to raise a child with a congenital disease. It was nice to talk in Pennsylvania Dutch, as they understood who they were when they spoke their mother tongue with one another.

"If you take away anything from this conversation, I want you to know these diseases are not unique to Plain populations. We receive many diverse families from different backgrounds."

"One last thing, Doc. We didn't go over expenses." Manny hated to ask; it wasn't talked about, just given when there was a need from where he came.

"We're nonprofit." That was all he said and all he needed to, Manny guessed, but it was also just the doctor's way, blunt and to the point. Manny could see that money was the least of his reasons for being there.

He let out a sigh of relief, as did Lucy. "*Danke*, again."

He stood to go and started for the door, stopped as if to ask a question, and then held up a hand and slowly started to shut the door.

"Fannie will be coming tomorrow." Lucy threw that out of nowhere. If Manny hadn't heard it from Lucy, he wouldn't have been sure about what he heard.

Doc Kauffman continued matter-of-factly, as if he hadn't heard Lucy. "Get some sleep. We have a busy day tomorrow."

As soon as the doctor shut the door, Manny and Lucy looked at each other.

"Are you playing matchmaker?" Manny asked Lucy with a grin.

Lucy actually smiled, and Manny decided it was a perfect time for there to be a diversion with all the grief they were going through.

✑ Chapter Thirty-Three ✑

*I*t doesn't get more peaceful than the farm." Lucy looked out the hospital room window at the spinning weather vane and white house with black trim next to the clinic. The days seemed to go on and on with no end. Genetic markers that matched up were difficult to detect, and some of the medical conditions were so rare that doctors didn't even have a name for them yet. Without a name, there was no cure.

"Are you homesick?" Manny came up behind her, and Lucy shuddered at his touch. She couldn't let herself relax, hadn't been able for far too long now. How long? Since the day she set foot on Sam's farm.

She heard Manny let out a breath. He was just as worn out as she was, staying the course as a husband and as a *daed* to the twins.

"When is there going to be an end to this?" Manny sat on the edge of the double bed and twined his fingers together. His blue eye was unusually dull, penetrating into hers. She didn't know how to answer his question and, in the midst of everything else going on, didn't have the patience to deal with it.

"This *is* us, parents of a child who has special needs. We're doing what parents do in this situation." Her words were strong, but not her voice. She felt the tears well up but willed them away. She didn't have the energy to spend on a conversation right now.

Manny looked down at the floor. He was so still, she wondered whether he'd heard a word she said. He probably didn't want to. It wasn't the answer he was looking for.

"We need answers." Manny kept his eyes on the floor, not moving, staring at his boots, which didn't seem to fit where they were. White hallways and rooms much like a hotel with adequate meals, but nothing like what he was used to back in the community. She thought about how he must be wishing he was outdoors in the fresh air. Even doing chores was better than staying cooped up all day with doctors and nurses who were telling them the next step or procedure they recommended.

"What else can we expect?" But as soon as her words came out, she knew exactly what he meant. Lucy lifted a palm to her head and closed her eyes. On cue Rhoda began to fuss. Then came the cry. It was different than other babies' cries, different than Timmy's. Lucy could tell after having lived with it for weeks on end, and she knew Rhoda was like the others here.

"It's just like the doctor said. Cohen syndrome." The crippling disease was a genetic disorder, a handicapping condition.

"Is this *Gott*'s *wille*?" He shook his head.

"That's what the bishop will say and many in the community." The doctor had prepared them for this, but Lucy had ignored his words, denying it would happen to her or to Rhoda. But in the back of her mind, she analyzed the conditions that the doctor had explained, knowing it fit her baby to the letter.

Manny finally looked up to meet her eyes. "You don't believe it is?"

"*Nee*, I don't." She held his stare. "Will I be shunned for not believing the church ways?" She held her baby more tightly to her, placing her tiny cheek next to hers.

"You might be, Lucy." He seemed irritated, but she didn't care at the moment. She hadn't had to deal with this way of the Amish until now. It was easy to say to others what they wanted to hear when she believed what she was saying. But now that it was her own daughter, her mind was changed.

"Does that make me a hypocrite?"

Manny dropped his head. "I'm not in the frame of mind to discuss it. We'll deal with the bishop when need be."

A knock on the door got Rhoda crying again, and Lucy wanted to join her. She felt she was the worst person on the earth at that moment. An awful wife, worn-out *mamm*...and now going against the church. She could do no right.

Manny stood and walked to the door slowly, as if his legs were bags of corn. As soon as the door opened, the doc walked into the room. "Morning," Manny said, gesturing to a chair. "Have a seat." But the doc shook his head and glanced over at Lucy holding Rhoda.

"I'm going to be honest with you and tell you something you already know. There is no cure for your daughter now, but I am hopeful there will be one at some future time."

"What does that mean for Rhoda?" Manny's tone was without emotion, straightforward and to the point. The fatigue had gotten to all of them.

"Rhoda will have a host of physical problems. She has a condition that causes retardation. But what I want to share with you is the quality of life she *can* have."

"How can you begin to tell us there is any quality at all?" Manny's nostrils flared, and his face reddened.

"You will make it so. There is no telling how Rhoda will progress. One family with three girls varies from a twenty-four-year-old who functions at a nine-month-old level to a five-year-old performing well enough to join the children at her Amish community school." Doc paused. "You are her *daed*, a darn good one taking in these three." He gestured to Lucy and the babies.

Then he turned to her. "And I hope you appreciate this man as much as you should."

Lucy knew what she had in Manny and had tried every way to get over her bad side. But it had taken this man standing next to Lucy to call her out on it.

Manny stood abruptly. "I need some space." He turned and grabbed Timmy's baby seat, the bottle of breast milk from the refrigerator, and his bag.

"Where are you going?" Lucy could hardly get the words out before he shut the door behind him. When the door clicked, she turned to the doctor. "I can't believe he just left like that." But then again, she could. She was feeling the same way he was.

"You just lost the most important piece of this whole situation." Doc let out the air in his lungs and then stood. "There is hope."

Without Manny she couldn't do this—not alone. But then she couldn't blame him; this had worn their relationship thin. It was just a matter of time before he'd had enough. She was tired too. When would things go back to the way they were?

"Your sister is here."

Her eyes began to water. "Fannie? Is here?" Lucy tried to stand, but didn't have the energy. The next she knew, the doctor was gone, and Fannie was by her side, holding her hand and rocking Rhoda.

"You are a mess." She shook her head, a familiar gesture that was one of Fannie's condescending ways of warning her that she was about to be whipped into shape.

"What am I going to do?"

"One thing at a time."

"Manny—"

"*Nee*, you have to get yourself together first. And let him simmer down. If I were him, I'd run the other way and never come back." Fannie's frown and pause meant Lucy was to answer, but Lucy didn't want to hear the words as to how things had gone.

"You had a lot going for you and your family."

"I know, I know. *Mammi* said it was the hormones, and Rosy gave me herbs—"

Fannie shook her head. "Excuses. You had the perfect fit, and if you don't make some changes, you'll blow it all away."

Lucy she was ready for Fannie's chastising to end. "I'll fix it. Just give me some time to figure things out."

"You don't have time. I heard Doc Kauffman telling a nurse you'd probably be released tomorrow, or, I suppose, whenever you and Manny can sit down together long enough to get through what the doctor needs to tell you before you're discharged."

"You mean that's it? There's nothing more they can do?"

"They can help you raise your baby girl in the best way possible. There is no magic herb from Rosy, and you can't blame the change on everything that's eating at you. You have two beautiful children and an incredible man who would walk on water to make you happy." She lifted her brows. "Take it and make it right."

Lucy wiped away the tears and looked over at her confidant, friend, and sister. "I'm glad you're here. What took you so long?"

Fannie looked at the door and then back to Lucy. "I came one other time and wasn't comfortable..."

"Why, what do you mean?" Lucy couldn't imagine her sister being intimidated with just about anything.

Then it came to her. "The doctor."

Fannie crossed her arms over her chest.

"That's it. You're fond of him."

Fannie shook her head. "That's a silly notion."

Lucy finally had a good reason to smile, and it made her feel a hundred times better. "You know how fortunate we are to be with someone we truly have feelings for instead of just taking in a man we don't even like?"

Fannie blinked and bent over to pick up Rhoda. "I brought my things to stay the night, but it seems plans have changed."

"*Jah*, I think the doctor was discharging us, but didn't finish with Manny taking off like he did." It pained her heart when she said his name and remembered his face as he left. "I wish he was here."

"*Jah*, but he has to come back for more milk."

Bottle feeding wasn't common but in their case necessary to care for two babies, another difference that Lucy didn't like, but in this case she was glad about it.

She smiled. "*Jah*, I guess he does."

Chapter Thirty-Four

When Manny left the clinic, he had gone to his friend Harvey Graber's *haus*. It had been a good visit with his old friend, and now he was ready to go back. Manny loved his little family and would make sure they were going to get through the obstacles before them. He loved each and every one of them. Hearing the news about Rhoda had been hard to take, but deep down he resolved to make the best of the situation and help his daughter become everything she could be.

He wished he could contact Lucy; they didn't have phones, but he sure wished he did right at this moment. She was familiar with Harvey and his family who lived in the area, but he knew she probably had her hands full with Rhoda. They might even be getting ready to leave, after what the doc said. The thought of their being discharged prompted him to go back to the clinic.

Manny sat beside Harvey in his buggy, thankful they had taken him and Timmy into their *haus*. Everyone was kind enough not to ask too many questions, but Manny felt that Harvey deserved an explanation. "*Danke* for picking me up and taking us back. Mighty nice of you."

Harvey forced a smile and nodded once. "I'm glad to, but I am concerned about you and the family. You all right?" His plump, cheery face made him look even friendlier than he was.

Manny's excuse of needing some air away from the

clinic was obviously not persuasive—not that he wanted to make it so—but he didn't want to share any more than needed. "Things have been difficult lately, ups and downs." He turned to look at him. "Sorry for the sad story, but you did ask." He grinned in an effort to make light of it.

"We had some troubles early on too. It'll get better. Doesn't sound like you've had time to settle in or had a honeymoon." He winked.

The minute Timmy started to fuss, Manny reached for the bottle he'd warmed. He only had one left, which was also why he was going back.

But then again, he could understand how Lucy must have felt those years with Sam. He was a wicked man, a term Manny didn't like to use, but the longer he was with Lucy, the more he knew about the goings-on between them—things he found unthinkable. He'd tried not to pry into her thoughts while she was absorbing Sam's sudden death and then the birth of her babies…their babies…a responsibility that he'd grown to love and which seemed to bring them together.

As they pulled up to the clinic, Manny noticed a group of young boys playing at the park nearby. It was a place for families and their children to spend time outdoors together while staying at the clinic. He had taken Timmy there a couple of times when Rhoda was wailing so much Timmy couldn't take his nap.

"*Danke*, my friend." Manny pumped Harvey's hand, and Harvey messed Timmy's brown hair.

"Stop by on your way home and say *hallo*."

"We will."

As soon as Manny turned around, he heard laughter and a woman's voice between a couple of young men.

He picked up his pace and found Lucy pushing her way to the clinic. She would take one step and then turn another direction to avoid them. They chuckled and said a few things he couldn't hear well enough to understand, or they may have been English slang words he didn't recognize. These were the times he wished he knew a bit more about the English so he could understand their ways.

The next thing he saw was Lucy's *kapp*. Her face was pale and her body rigid. Manny ran as fast as he could with little Tim bouncing against his side. He wished for her to run. Manny didn't know why she stayed put until he caught a glimpse of Rhoda's baby seat behind Lucy. He picked up speed and didn't stop until he was face-to-face with her.

"Are you all right?" His quick breaths broke up his words as he looked at Lucy and then Rhoda. "What happened?"

"Nothing really." She hadn't met his eyes, just stood and held a hand to her scar and stared at the young men who were walking away.

Manny knew there was more to it but wanted to get his family out of danger before diving into the situation. Taking her by the arm, he walked toward the room where they had been staying and got everyone settled.

The minute he tucked Timmy in, he turned to Lucy.

She moved close and wrapped her arms around him. "I'm sorry, Manny. That was tough news to hear from the doctor. But you missed hearing about the positive side of things."

"Shh." He held up his hand and touched her lips with his finger. He inclined his head and touched his forehead against hers. "Now, tell me what happened."

But she couldn't, not right away. She let a tear fall. "Sam

used to tell me my scar was ugly, just like those boys did just now."

A burning sensation spread within him, and he clenched his jaw. "They're ignorant young men, Lucy. Don't give them a second thought," he said, although he was thinking something completely different. It was probably best he hadn't been there earlier or he might have gone against the vow of no resistance. When it came to his family, he would do whatever it took to keep them safe.

Her weary eyes peered into his. "You're a *gut* man, Manny." Her lower lip trembled. "From the minute you left, I wished you were here. I knew you needed some time to think, but I missed you."

He touched her lips and then her scar. "Christ wore His scars, His sacrifice to us. Wear yours boldly." He watched her eyes widen at the name of Christ and nestled in against his chest. "Our being together is *Gott's wille*; only the love of *Gott* can keep us together. I believe that's what He wants for us and our family."

"I love you so much, Manny. I really do." She shook her head, avoiding his stare. "And the way you've taken in the babies..."

"I wish I could have heard that earlier." He grinned, and she half-smiled in response. He had a good feeling neither of them would be eager to be away from the other again. She had tested her will, as he had his own.

He guided her to the bed and sat next to her. "It's been hard for you to let go of Sam's mistreatment. But if you would stop putting yourself down, you'd see yourself the way I do, the way our Savior does."

He felt her breath against his neck, slowing down to a gradual rhythm. As he looked around the room, at the babies in their seats and Lucy by his side, he knew he was in the place *Gott* wanted him to be. It wouldn't be easy. *Gott* never promised that. What He did expect from a godly man was to care for his family, no matter what might come. And these two little people were as much his as they were Lucy's.

A knock at the door drew him out of his thoughts. "Hi, Doc. Rhoda is sound asleep, for a change." Manny shut the door behind him and leaned against the doorjamb, feeling the fatigue set in.

Doc nodded. "I'm actually here to see Lucy."

Manny stood straight and furrowed his brow. "What about?"

"I heard there was an altercation and her scar was mentioned."

"Word travels fast." Manny wasn't surprised, as it was a public scene, but was impressed at the doctor's quick response.

"Fannie came looking for Lucy, and when she saw what was transpiring, she came to me." Doc turned his attention to Lucy. "I might be out of line here, but I know of a doctor who can take care of that scar for you if that's what you want. I'm not suggesting this for any reason other than wanting to give you the option."

"Is there any risk?" Manny stood straight. Everything he'd said to Lucy, he meant. His eyes went straight to hers, waiting for her response. She kept her eyes on the doctor and then glanced at Manny, just long enough for him to see in her what he predicted.

"An honest doctor should never rule it out, but with a case like this, no, it would be plastic surgery, not internal, so less of a chance for any problems."

"I fell when I was a child and my cheek hit on my *daed*'s hoe. The doc was away so *Mamm* put some salve on it. It took a long time to heal, and when it did it left this scar. It's been there so long now, I barely remember what I looked like without it." She paused as if in thought.

Doc held a hand up to her cheek and examined the piece of pinkish skin that Manny'd come to know as what defined her and the burdens she had borne. "I can't make a guess." He leaned back and looked into Lucy's eyes. "What would you like to do?"

Lucy stared for what seemed much longer than it probably was, turned to the doctor, and finally answered. "*Nee,* but *danke.*"

Manny let out a breath and smiled. When their eyes met, he knew she was at peace with her decision, and he was elated. He let out a small grunt to hide a laugh when he thought about how strongly he'd felt about the tiny part of Lucy that had become so relevant to their journey together.

ᵔᵔ Epilogue ᵔᵔ

The grounds around the clinic were packed with people, booths, food, drinks, and more. A large tent took up most of the green grass on one side of the clinic that was crammed full of Amish who came from all over the northern area to support the auction.

"I think I'll take a go at the corn-hole." Fannie's eyes narrowed as she tried to make out the sign next to the covered area near the picnic tables.

"Do you always squint when you look far away?" The doctor asked as he walked up behind Fannie. She turned around quickly as a warm pink spread onto her cheeks.

Lucy grinned to see her sister so affected.

Fannie smoothed out her dress and adjusted her *kapp* before she answered. "*Jah*, I suppose I do. But I didn't ask for an examination, *danke* very much."

The doctor grunted and gave a small smile. "Just making an observation." He turned his attention to Manny and the twins. Lucy felt sure she saw his eyes water just a bit. "They look healthy."

Lucy nodded, knowing that was as close to a sentimental comment as she would hear from him, but understood perfectly. He was tough on the outside, but all soft on the inside. "Timmy is as healthy as a horse, and Rhoda can sit on her own now. After a year of therapy, time, and money, she is making her way, thanks to the people here and this auction." It was still hard for Lucy to believe how much progress Rhoda had made in the year since they'd first visited the clinic.

"That's remarkable progress. I have clients who are as old as twenty-four who still can't sit up and probably won't." He looked over the grassy knoll thoughtfully. "My hope is that premarital testing would be considered. It's a powerful tool if the Amish would use it."

Lucy understood his thoughts, and she partly agreed with him, but she knew the ways of her people, and it wouldn't happen anytime soon, if ever. "That's our lifestyle; we trust *Gott* to take care of us." She paused, thinking about his last name. "But then, you know that already."

He lifted his head and pursed his lips. "I respect the Amish heritage. I don't wish to change that. But I also see that half of the headstones in Amish cemeteries are for children." An awkward silence settled between them, but not a negative one. Both parties wanted the same thing and didn't know exactly how to make it happen.

"You're a good man, Doctor Daniel Kauffman."

The doctor shook his head.

Manny pumped the doctor's hand as he handed off Timmy to Lucy. "*Jah*, but I have to admit that I wasn't sure when I first met you."

"I get that a lot." He grinned as his eyes moved to where Fannie had wandered to collect her bean bags.

"I have some hands to shake and people to thank."

He turned to walk away. Lucy had watched him stop more times than she could count.

"*Danke* for everything, Doc." Manny said loud enough for him to hear. Doc held up a hand in acknowledgement.

A bake sale offered whoopee pies, pretzels, chow-chow, beef jerky, sausage, bologna by the slice, and beverages.

The live auction was at the far side of the grounds, which was big enough to offer horses for sale along with quilts, furniture, crafts, vegetables, and flowers. There was also a silent auction of handmade items. Local vendors helped out, and large donations came in for the clinic.

Manny sat on a blanket with Rhoda. He had worked long and hard with her to strengthen her to at least enough to sit without tipping over. It was an accomplishment Lucy hadn't believed would happen, then one day Manny was sitting on the floor with Rhoda, cross-legged, with his arms circling her. When her eyes had lifted up to his without her losing her balance, they'd said prayers of thanksgiving.

"*Ahem.*" Bishop Atlee cleared his throat.

"Afternoon, Bishop." Manny stood and pumped his hand.

"She's coming along." He tilted his head slightly, watching Rhoda roll from one side to the other on the blue blanket.

"*Jah*, thanks to this clinic." Lucy handed Timmy a bite of oatmeal cookie and walked over to them as she wiped her hands with her skirt.

The bishop kept his eyes fixed on Rhoda. "The limits of the *Ordnung* have been stretched. It's time to discuss the rules that are acceptable in your situation."

"I'm sure you don't mean today." Manny's brows drew together, and his hands rested on his hips.

"*Nee*, but soon. We've put it off long enough. It is our way and we must follow."

"I believe we are cooperating with *Gott*'s *wille* by caring for our children in the way we are called to do."

"And there is also that matter of a marriage that took place." The bishop turned to go without another word. He had given them time with both issues, more than usual, and they would be expected to explain their actions accordingly. Most Amish were still leery of places like the clinic, and the bishop was no exception.

Lucy could have let herself get riled up about this but chose to let it go. "It's too *wunderbar-gut* of a day to let anything ruin it for us."

Manny shook his head as if to dismiss the conversation.

He had showed Lucy what love in action truly looked like, by being the best husband and *daed* there could possibly be. Sam's view of her had made her feel unlovable, but she had learned the humility of seeing herself for who she was and allowing *Gott* to love her where she was in her growth.

When Manny took her hand in his, she knew there would be more storms. She also knew that after what they had been through, nothing could keep them apart.

GLOSSARY

ach — oh
daed — father
danke — thank you
dawdi — grandfather
dawdihauses — addition to the house for grandparents
die eltern — parents
Englischer — non-Amish person
Gott — God
gut — good
hallo — hello
haus — house
jah — yes
kapp — hat
mamm — mother
mammi — grandmother
nee — no
Ordnung — a set of rules
wille — will
wunderbar — wonderful

∾ *Chapter One* ∾

*F*annie will never get married," Verna muttered as she stirred the pot of boiling soup. The steam floated upward, swirling to the ceiling and spreading throughout the kitchen. The scent of onion and other spices wafted through the back door as Frieda walked in carrying a basket full of eggs.

"Let the girl alone for Pete's sake," Frieda said as she waddled over to the kitchen table. "She'll settle down in good time."

Verna turned sideways, frowned, then waited for Frieda to acknowledge her. "Well, good morning." She put a fist on her hip and leaned against the cabinet. "You're awful sure of Fannie. She's as tough as beef jerky on a winter day. I'd like to see the man who takes her hand."

Frieda grunted as she watched Verna's forehead tighten. "You will, I have no doubt. After all, my son married you, didn't he?"

Fannie took each step on the stairway with meaning as she went down to the kitchen expecting fireworks to fly after that comment. Why wouldn't her *mamm* and *mammi* consider that she might be able to hear them? She shouldn't be surprised. Even if they did realize she might overhear, they wouldn't hold their thoughts.

"Is this going to be a good morning?" Frieda asked, casting a sideways glance at Verna.

"What's going on in here?" Fannie asked as she rounded the corner to the kitchen. Her *mamm* and *mammi* both gave her long looks before they started working again.

"I was just telling your *mammi* that you are strong-headed. Don't try to say anything different. It wouldn't be bad if you were the man of the *haus*, but you're not."

"Fannie, never you mind. You're just like your *mamm*." Frieda pushed up her nose when she took a big whiff of the bubbling soup. "Too many onions."

Fannie grinned, knowing what would come next: a very lengthy conversation on how much onion is enough and what was too little.

"Clears your chest," *Mamm* said as she gave the pot another stir.

Gazing out the large kitchen window, Fannie wondered what else was out there in the world. She put her weight forward and rested a hand under her chin. She knew there was more than she could imagine, and she had a pretty good imagination. Thoughts of leaving the community wafted into her mind then slowly dissipated.

Before she and *Mamm* moved from their community to be near her sister Lucy, Fannie was to court with James Miller. He was older than her and about as stiff-necked as she was, which is why she knew no commitment would have ever been made. She was just too independent to have a man in her life—at least for now.

"What are you daydreaming about? Manny and Lucy will be here soon." Frieda was a bossy woman, but Fannie had to admit she kept things in order.

"Yah, I'll see how much milk there is compared to

yesterday. We need some nice green grass to keep producing milk for market." Fannie couldn't help but notice that the cows hadn't been producing as much milk. But she seemed to be the only one concerned.

On her way back from the milk barn, Fannie noticed a trail of dust behind an old truck. And as soon as she was sure of who it was her stomach stirred a little. She pushed her shoulders back and headed toward the *haus* to wash her face. She got to the mudroom just before Doc stepped inside.

"Morning, Fannie." Doc pulled off his boots and put them next to hers. "After you." He motioned to her and kept a close distance as they walked into the white kitchen that was now filled with the smell of bacon as *Mamm*'s soup simmered on the stove.

Doc seemed to lack his usual sharp manner, which made Fannie put up her guard. "What brings you here?"

It was a common question. When Dr. Daniel Kauffman came to the community, it usually meant that someone needed extra care and the community needed to be notified so they could chip in whatever they could to pay for the expense.

He ignored her question and greeted Verna and Frieda, who were busy cooking up a delicious breakfast. They would give him little choice about having a bite, but Fannie knew he would eat only a light meal. A heavy meal meant a tired doctor, and he was always on call, if only in his mind.

"Just coffee and toast, Frieda. I have a delivery coming to the hospital soon. My time is short." He took a sip of the coffee and then another. "Wish they had this at the hospital."

"I'll never tell you what the secret is or you won't come back." She handed him some homemade bread with strawberry jam and two slices of bacon on the side. He didn't refuse it, but he ate only the toast.

"I'm here to see Fannie." He wiped his mouth and dropped the napkin on the table.

Fannie was startled to hear the sound of her name coming from him, as he rarely used it.

"About what?"

Verna frowned, giving Fannie a warning stare.

"Due to the increase of clients, I'm as needed here as I am at the hospital. I've decided to split my time between the two."

"What do I have to do with that?" Fannie figured that whatever he wanted with her probably wasn't something she wanted to hear about or do.

"Fannie, you're in demand." Verna said with a big grin. "Isn't that so, Doc?"

Doc put up a hand. "I'm sure Fannie will be able to help with whatever is needed."

With the way they were both deciding her life for her, Fannie decided to give them her opinion. She couldn't imagine working with Doc Kauffman. They were just too much alike. The strange thing was that he had to know that too.

"Will you step outside with me?" Fannie said with a tone that was so much like her *mamm*.

The *click-clack* of her boots caught his attention, but he stopped to say good-bye to Frieda and Verna then took his time getting to his truck where Fannie waited.

"Yes, Fannie, what is it?"

When she turned around, he was still a good length

away and seemed to have a put-upon look on his face. "Just what do you take me for, putting me on the spot like that?"

As he drew closer, she could no longer read any expression on his face, which was the norm. But she wanted some answers. "I'm not here for your bidding."

"This is your community, not mine. If you want your people to get the medical assistance they need, you'll help and make this happen."

"You dismissed yourself of us too easily. Do you think this will bring you acceptance after shunning us and our ways, those you made a vow to keep when you were baptized?"

He scoffed and climbed into his truck. "You might want to talk to the elders before you start making assumptions. They asked me."

The motor coughed as he drove away, leaving a cloud of dust behind him. She covered her face, wiping it with her apron.

"Ahh!" She let the word trail off as she regained her stability.

As she walked to the barn she wondered why this and why with her? Was he that desperate or was there another reason for him to involve her? Whatever was going on she needed to find out, and not from him.

"Why did he leave so quickly?" Verna stood by the milk barn, her voice interrupting the swishing sounds of the handheld milking machine.

"Need some help?" Her *mamm*'s offer was casual enough, but Fannie figured there was something brewing, and it didn't involve milking cows. She knew her *mamm*'s goal in life was for her daughters to become brides, and she was the only one left.

"*Nee*, you forget. I do most of the milking."

"*Ach*," Mamm smiled. "So what do you think of Doc's offer?"

"That he's manipulative and controlling. He gave me no option."

Mamm was unusually quiet for a moment. "No option for what?"

"Being his assistant."

Mamm looked at her daughter and frowned. "I would think it was a compliment. Choosing you shows how much he thinks of you."

Fannie snorted. "I doubt that. And I don't want to be 'picked' by anyone."

"Well, I don't know why you're being stubborn about it, especially when you've been saving to buy that Appaloosa you've become so fond of."

Whenever her *mamm* suggested something, Fannie figured she meant the opposite, so she paused, trying to decide what was the right thing to do. She hadn't thought about the horse, but the extra money would help her get him sooner.

"I didn't think you favored my working to save money to buy Ap."

Mamm's head snapped up. "You've named him? *Ach*, no." *Mamm* knew once Fannie gave an animal a name, it was a keeper. "You're going to have to expect some questions if you have an Appaloosa running around the community."

"It's been done. Remember the Fishers' horse?"

"*Jah*, but that was a different situation. She was new to our ways. You are not." She lifted a brow, her way of saying she was sure she was right.

"It's for me to decide." As soon as Fannie said it, she

realized she shouldn't have. Her *mamm*'s eyes lifted, her warning to be wary.

Fannie knew then that she'd work with Doc, if for no other reason than to buy her horse. She looked at the sun making its way up into the sky and wondered what she was getting herself into.

Be Empowered

Be Encouraged

Be Inspired

Be Spirit Led

FREE NEWSLETTERS

Empowering Women for Life in the Spirit

SPIRITLED WOMAN
Amazing stories, testimonies, and articles on marriage, family, prayer, and more.

POWER UP! FOR WOMEN
Receive encouraging teachings that will empower you for a Spirit-filled life.

CHARISMA MAGAZINE
Get top-trending articles, Christian teachings, entertainment reviews, videos, and more.

CHARISMA NEWS DAILY
Get the latest breaking news from an evangelical perspective. Sent Monday-Friday.

SIGN UP AT: nl.charismamag.com

CHARISMA MEDIA

P0780